Other Books by
V.E. Cesena
R.R. Waters

Prince Eric Alexander
The First Event: Survival
(Series)

John C in Kyoto
(Series)

Daughter of GOD – The Conception
(Series)

Author Website
www.vecesena.com
www.rrwaters.com

Purchase books Links at
www.vecesena.com/links
www.rrwaters.com/links

Prince Eric Alexander
The First Event: Survival

By

V.E. CESENA

Book I - Prince Eric Alexander Series

This book was developed with the help of many dear friends and family. I would like to thank the following, without their help this novel would never have been published: Elizabeth Cesena, Amanda Colin and Janelle Moore.

Edited by Amberly Finarelli, Amanda Colin
Cover Design by Michael Oliva
Cover Art/Painting by Olibori Babaoye
Photograph cover art Kevin Richtik

ISBN: 978-1-949186-08-6 (Hard Cover Edition)
ISBN: 978-1-949186-07-9 (Paperback Edition)
ISBN: 978-1-949186-06-2 (E Book Edition)

10 9 8 7 6 5 4 3 2 1 First Edition, May 2021

To Elizabeth and Victor, my amazing children. You both bring a happiness that I can never put into words. This is for you and your unbounded futures.

von Battenburg of the Moon Empire

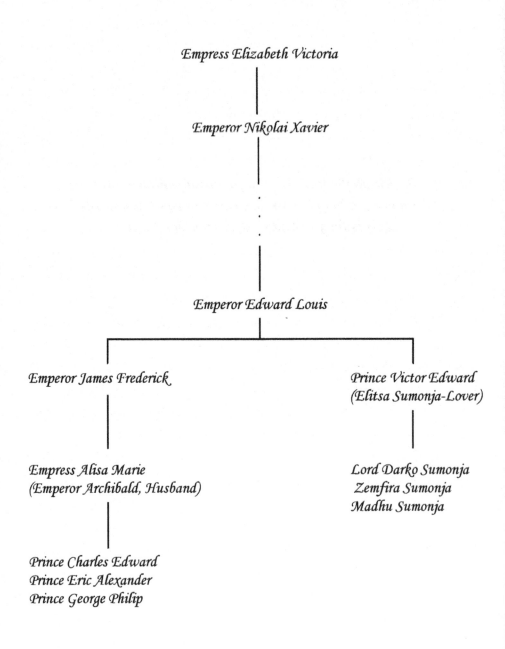

Empress Elizabeth Victoria

Emperor Nikolai Xavier

Emperor Edward Louis

Emperor James Frederick

Prince Victor Edward
(Elitsa Sumonja-Lover)

Empress Alisa Marie
(Emperor Archibald, Husband)

Lord Darko Sumonja
Zemfira Sumonja
Madhu Sumonja

Prince Charles Edward
Prince Eric Alexander
Prince George Philip

PROLOG

I am Sami Khan.

Homer, Herodotus, Voltaire, and Ganshof were great historians. They wrote about your history. They told you of how things were. I tell you what will be.

I tell you of your future.

It is said, light is the carrier of information. I look from a billion miles and follow the light to earth. I see through time to you and further. I see Earth when the dinosaurs rule. I see the Egyptians build the great pyramids. I see the first steps on the Moon.

After your time, I see the great space explorers and pioneers. I see the start of the Moon Empire as it expands into space across the galaxy.

As I look back through the light to your time, I must tell you of what will come. Whether it's hopeful or not is up to you to decide. I can only tell you the facts.

The history of mankind is like the winds: violent in its nature, serene in its beauty, and brutal in its full force. Earth's history speaks of the essence of humans from Cain's destruction of Abel, the wars of the world, and the invasion of the Viduians. And later, the rebellion and resurrection of Earth's people at the beginning of the Moon Empire.

Earth's return to greatness was led by the courageous and resourceful Empress Elizabeth Victoria von Battenburg. Like Joan of Arc, she led a ragtag army of men and women born on Earth and the Moon in a winner-take-all battle against the outer worlds.

Their victory created the Moon Empire and the dynasty of the von Battenburgs.

"*So what?*" you say. "*Why should you care?*"

Because there is still time for you to change the future. To change the civilization you are creating. But if you do, he will never come—the prince born to the Moon Empire who will change the lives of over a trillion people. Thousands of planets in the galaxy will never know of his greatness.

"*Who?*" you ask. "*Who will have a name so feared and loved on hundreds of planets it is against the law to say it?*"

I hear his name on the solar winds that now push my ship across the galaxy. The sails fill with the strong current as we speed across a solar system to fulfill his commands. But these winds are mere wisps of current compared to the power he possesses. Like a hurricane, typhoon, and tornado he leads the Moon Empire army on conquest.

But I'm telling you the end. It is the beginning you want to hear. How a great man came to be. A prince from birth, born to the royalty of the Moon Empire. Stolen from his family when he was a child.

He told me his turbulent life all began one day when he was a boy of ten. This is where I start my story. Learn about your future, about an illustrious empire and the unforgettable events of Prince Eric Alexander von Battenburg.

one

He sat alone, legs stretched out, beside a four-hundred-year-old English oak table in the western castle hall. With his back against the wall of white Italian marble tile, Eric stared at the famous painting across the hall. He felt the power of the battle—the Prince on his powerful horse and the fear in his enemies' eyes. Eric treasured every detail and pride overwhelmed him.

Angrily, he shifted his legs, allowing more freedom from his ceremonial uniform. It attacked him like an octopus with hundreds of arms which constantly squeezed every part of his body. Eric wanted to tear off the tight clothes. His mind drifted back to the meeting with his mother two hours before.

"Mother, I hate this uniform. It's too tight."

"Today's ceremony is very important. The outer planets are swearing their loyalty to your father and me. We all must look our best."

"It makes me look fat." Eric pushed out his stomach to make himself look fatter.

"Just a little baby fat." His mother smiled, pushing in his stomach and smoothing the white uniform.

"I'm almost eleven years old," Eric declared, lips tight, his face turning red.

He regretted his words as the smile disappeared from his mother's beautiful face.

She pulled him into a tight hug. "You're growing too fast. I want you to stay my little Prince."

"Mother," Eric said as he wiggled, trying to break free. "Someone might see." Finally free, he pushed her hands away. "I'm growing up."

Not fast *enough*, Eric's mind shouted as he looked up at the painting. *I want to be a man now.* He wanted to be tall and strong like the man in the painting, leading his army into battle. *But I'm not a man. I'm only a small boy.* Eric's shoulders slumped as if the weight of the whole empire pushed them down. He was a small boy for whom nothing ever seemed to go right, only wrong. *I'm the black sheep of the family. No one likes me.*

His father, the Emperor, shouted at him constantly, asking, why, why wasn't he more like his older brother Charles?

The harder I try the worse it becomes. Eric knew he could never please his father; it was an impossible task.

His thoughts returned to the painting. On both sides of the golden frame, the crystal chandeliers bathed the battlefield portrait of Prince Victor Edward von Battenburg in a warm glow. His tall, lean body bent forward on the gray charger as his sword—waving above like a flag—wreaked havoc on the Moon Empire's foes. Victor fought like a demon. His ferocious attack drove and scattered the enemies over the battlefield. They looked up with wide eyes at Prince Victor, fearful of his quick sword and their grim future.

Eric relaxed as he eyes focused on Victor. Eric didn't know why, but something about Victor comforted him.

I have the same royal blood flowing through me as you, Victor. Like you, I will fight the enemies of the Moon Empire. I will conquer the galaxy.

Grabbing the leg of the antique table, he pulled himself up. With determination, he marched across the marble floor to the center of the great hall.

two

Eric came to attention and saluted the painting with a make-believe sword. He felt his chest heave as he pictured himself beside Victor.

I'm here, Victor, at your side," Eric said. "I will defend the Moon Empire and destroy all her enemies. With my sword, I will defeat the evil armies who swore to rebel against the von Battenburgs." He touched his imaginary sword to his head as he declared, "I will fight with you and protect my family with my life."

Eric jumped into a fighting stance. His eyes moved around the hundreds of pretend foes suddenly attacking him. He lunged, then ducked and darted around as the soldiers increased their attack. In his mind, thousands of giant warriors swore to defeat him. *I will never give up, never surrender.*

He gripped his great longsword, and thrusting, slashing, dashing, he moved perfectly, a master swordsman. The enemy stood in shock, surprised by his amazing blade skills. Eric dived onto the floor to dodge a sword aimed at his head. He rolled away, then sprang up and again fought like a madman in the heat of battle. With a final thrust, he defeated the last soldier of the enemy's army.

Eric lifted his sword up to the battlefield portrait and declared, "I am Prince Eric Alexander von Battenburg, the destroyer." His shout echoed throughout the great hall.

In his mind, thousands of cheers erupted from his loyal troops for his bravery, courage, and skill as a fighter. But it was Victor who made him feel the best when he said, "I thought we were going to lose. You were wonderful; I couldn't have done it without you."

Eric bowed. "I will always be here for you." He thrust his pretend sword in the air again and heard cheers and praise in his mind. Eric joined in the shouts ring through the hall like a church bell on a calm summer day.

Then, in Eric's mind, came the royal parade as he returned to the Moon castle victorious. The hero-prince riding on a great black stallion that pranced down the lane. Thousands of people lined the streets, hoping to see the prince's return. All the boys wore looks of envy, wishing they could be a mighty fighter and guardian of the empire like Eric.

At the entrance to the Moon castle was his family. Eric walked down the center of the red carpet, up the steps, to the top of the platform. He stopped in front of his father. The look of pride on his father's face made Eric stand taller. Then, his father, the Emperor, turned and looked at his eldest son and asked, "Charles, why can't you be more like Eric?"

Eric smiled at his brother's uncomfortable look.

His father pointed behind Eric. "Your admirers want you." Eric turned to the thousands in the courtyard and raised his hands to the cheers as he shouted back, "I am Eric Alexander the Destroyer. I am Eric Alexander the Destroyer."

three

No one heard Eric's shouts of victory in this distant western hall of the castle where people rarely inhabited. Only when a dignitary or aristocrat wanted to see the portrait of the great Prince Victor von Battenburg did visitors come here. Touching the famous painting of the destroyer, in this distant hall, brought excitement to this type of visitor, but still, it was a rare occurrence.

The youngest son of Emperor Edward Louis von Battenburg IV, Prince Victor's exploits were legendary. To have won so many battles in his short lifetime now seemed inconceivable, yet when they placed Victor in his grave, his armies had won back several solar systems and its people.

For generations before Prince Victor's birth, the Moon Empire had been shrinking, dying. The empire built by Elizabeth and her children was a fraction of its former self. Like the Roman Empire, it would soon only exist in history books.

No longer did the recent Emperors care about running of the Moon Empire and its people. Their sole interest was enjoying the luxuries the position brought. The Emperor chose his administrators not for their talent, but for their noble birth. The administrators spent their time attending constant royal festivals and parties—singing, dancing, and drinking brought more rewards then resolving urgent problems of the empire. As a result, the empire shrank, contracted, and lost outer worlds and solar systems every year.

Emperor James von Battenburg was Eric's grandfather and Victor's older brother. Like his father and grandfather, James enjoyed the benefits of his position, and his fame centered on his grand and extravagant parties.

Eric pondered the contrast between memories of his grandfather and the visual of Victor in the giant portrait above him. His grandfather had pale skin, thinning gray hair, and a drink always in his hand. It was impossible to believe they were brothers.

Since birth, Prince Victor had been different from his father and brother; not only in actions and deeds, but in looks, too. Like Elizabeth, his features represented a strong diversity of Earth's ancestry: the light-olive skin of countries surrounding the Mediterranean Sea; the thick, raven-black hair from the Far East; the tall stature from the Americas; and the emotion-filled gray-blue eyes from Northern Europe.

Eric now looked down at his own hands. How different he was from Charles. His older brother was perfect. At sixteen years old, he was already tall and handsome like their father, and with his mother's blond hair and fair skin, he captured everyone's attention. Even at five, Eric's younger brother Prince George Philip resembled the rest of the von Battenburgs with his fair skin and blond hair.

Eric took after his great-uncle Prince Victor. He had the same thick black hair, light-olive skin, and deep, gray-blue eyes. But America was missing from him. He wasn't tall and broad-shouldered, like Victor, but short and round instead.

Why am I so different? Why do I look like an outcast in my own family?

Charles constantly reminded him of the difference and of being the unwanted black sheep of the family. He regularly made Eric painfully aware of his place below him. Prince Charles Edward von Battenburg would be the Emperor when their father died.

"You will be my court jester," Charles promised as he pushed Eric's face into the floor. "At every party, you will perform like a clown to entertain me and the royal court."

Eric's plump cheeks turned red at the thought. *I will be no one's jester.*

Eric froze in terror as a gong sounded.

four

Eric gasped, his eyes widening in fear as a gong sounded in the distant hall. Its sound sent a chill down Eric's spine. "No!" he screamed aloud, but his mind shouted, *Father will be so angry.*

The gongs were signaling everyone to come to the throne room. *The ceremony! It's so important to my family.* Each year, the noblemen and ladies who led the outer worlds came to the Moon castle to kneel in the great throne room and swear their loyalty to the Emperor and Empress. In return, the Moon Empire would swear to protect them. Each year, fewer and fewer came to the Moon castle to kneel before his parents.

He couldn't be late to this important ceremony. Eric felt his heart beat faster and his breathing came in quick gulps. His body trembled at the thought of his father's anger. *Maybe if I'm not too late it won't be so bad.*

Eric thought of his older brother as he heard another *bong*— how Charles would nod in agreement as his father declared how Eric had let down the family.

"You are a Prince of the Moon Empire," his father would shout, his face red with anger. "Why must you always act like an unruly child, causing so many problems?"

His father would then look at George, Eric's younger brother. "Follow in the footsteps of Charles, not Eric's blundering, clumsy ways."

Eric knew Charles would later remind him over and over how he had disappointed everyone. Especially his parents. "Not only do you look different, but your actions show you really must be

16

a commoner." This was a common refrain of Charles'—that Eric couldn't possibly be a von Battenburg. "Some horrible servant switched you for my real brother when you were babies. You have no royal blood in your short, pudgy body," Charles would swear.

His mother would be kind, taking the time to listen as to why he was late. When Eric insisted it was an accident, her bright smile would show she believed him and his promise not to do it again.

Bong. The gong echoed throughout the castle, reminding Eric again of the ceremony. He turned toward the hall's entrance closest to the throne room and started running as fast as he could.

five

Damn this *uniform,* he cursed. His tight uniform and his slippery black dress shoes made for slow progress. With each passing minute, his anxiety increased as he ran recklessly through the long halls and banquet rooms. Several times he fell, and once he slid into a large antique flowerpot full of roses that exploded when they collided. Quickly, Eric rolled out of the dirt and flowers, got up, and continued running to the great throne room.

Why is the castle so big? Eric ran as hard and fast as his little legs would take him, but still, the main part of the castle was far away.

Coming upon the servant quarters and work areas, Eric hesitated. "You are forbidden," his father had warned him several times.

This is an emergency. Eric pushed hard on the door to the kitchen and ran through. The heat from all the kitchen fires was like a desert, but he didn't care. *I have to get to the throne room.*

He saw Molly, his mother's handmaiden. Her eyes widened and her hands flew to her face in horror at the sight of Eric. Then, he heard a gasp from behind her as another servant saw him.

They all know what's going to happen to me.

He dodged around a mountain of potatoes and through an open door. Too late, he saw the gathering of waiters carrying large trays of food to the throne room. Eric hit them like a battering ram slamming against a castle gate. The waiters all went to the ground with Eric in the center. The food fell on them all like thick rain in a winter storm.

"Stupid boy!" one of the waiters screamed out. Then he looked up to see the boy in the once white royal uniform, now multicolored filled with food, drink and dirt stains. "Prince Eric, I...I..." but stopped with his apology and started to pick the food off Eric like the other waiters.

Eric pushed their hands away and fought to get up, but slipped on the splattered food, falling again. Several hands pulled him up.

He kept running. Other people he passed had the same horrified look as Molly, but he ignored them. Only one face filled his mind. It was red, with eyes narrowed and teeth clenched tight, and it belonged to his father.

six

Finally, Eric came to a long hall. Hand-carved gold molding accented the ceiling and walls. The floor was an intricate design of the solar system, with the sun in the center, surrounded by all the moons and planets representing the Moon Empire at its greatest.

This was the reception hall before the throne room. Portraits lined the hall of every Emperor and Empress who had ever sat on the throne. Elizabeth the Great, founder of the Moon Empire, came first. The last portraits in the hall were of the present rulers, Eric's parents.

Eric slowed and then stopped in front of the far wall. His breathing came in gasps as he leaned against the wall for support. Sweat ran down the side of his face and pasted his hair to his forehead in clumps. His tired arms hung down and his legs trembled.

He turned his head and looked down the long hall. Through the labored breathing, a smile appeared. *The doors are still open.* He wanted to jump for joy but didn't have the energy. *I've made it in time.*

Eric pushed himself off the wall and started walking toward the throne room entrance. Only a hundred feet away, a few guests were still going in. The anxiety left him. *When I get into the throne room, I can move along the walls until I get to the dais. Maybe Father won't notice. I'll be like a cat and quietly move into place.*

The smile left his face when he looked down at his ceremonial uniform. It wasn't the large wrinkles crisscrossing the entire uniform which made him cringe. The once-white uniform was now multi-colored, and looked like a painting George made with different colors going randomly in every direction. Then his sight fell upon a five-inch-wide brown streak that ran from his upper left shoulder across his chest and down to his right hip. A wide banner proclaiming him Prince of dirt.

I'm in so much trouble, Eric's mind screamed, the anxiety returning.

With both hands, he urgently tried to straighten his uniform and wipe the brown dirt away. But after several seconds he realized he had made it worse. Now, instead of a brown banner, Eric had a mess of swirling design that went everywhere. He moaned.

For a brief moment, Eric considered going back to his rooms. But it would take far too long. *If I don't show up for the loyalty ceremony, it'll be worse.* He moved to the center of the hall in the direction of the throne room.

Eric looked down the hall at the tall men guarding the throne room doors. In their crisp white, red, and blue uniforms, they stood stiffly at attention to the side of the entrance, their faces grim as their eyes stared forward.

Eric heard another *bong*. In an instant, his fear returned. The guards beside the large bronze doors slowly moved away as the last of the guests went into the throne room, and then they positioned themselves to close the doors.

"Stop!" Eric shouted, still fifty feet from the doors. *If they close the doors, I'll never get in.* "Stop!" Eric said again, starting to run. "I have to get in!"

The guards seemed deaf as they placed their hands on the entrance doors.

"Please," Eric said, but the guards started to push the doors inward. He began to wave his arms, trying desperately to stop the guards. Suddenly, two more guards appeared in front of Eric, blocking his way and causing him to stop abruptly.

"The ceremony is beginning," the guard on his left said.

"I must be in there," Eric pleaded. "I have to be standing with my family when the subject planets and moons promise loyalty and tribute."

"The Emperor gave direct orders. No one enters after the fifth gong."

"The doors are still open. There's still time," Eric said, anger building in him. He could see the doors half closed. Unless these two guards moved out of his way, he was doomed.

Both stared down at him rigidly, holding their position.

"I command you. Move out of my way," Eric said in his best deep voice.

After a few seconds, smiles appeared on both guards' faces, but they stood rigid as statues.

"No," said the guard on the right.

Teeth clenched, Eric moved to his right to walk around the guards. One guard shifted his position to counter.

Eric's hands balled up into fists, ready to fight. But then an idea filled his mind. Looking around the guards he said, "Father."

The two guards snapped to attention and stared forward.

Quickly, Eric darted around the guards. *It worked.* Through the half-closed doors, he could see into the throne room. He lifted his leg to start running but suddenly felt his uniform jacket tighten around him.

He looked over his shoulder at the smiling guard who held his jacket. Eric saw laughter in his eyes.

You will not stop me, his mind shouted. *I am Eric the Destroyer.* With all his might Eric swung his elbow back, catching the guard in his chest.

The guard let go of Eric's jacket.

As fast as his short legs would move, he hurdled himself in the direction of the closing doors.

"Stop him!" the guards behind him shouted to the guards at the door. At the throne room entrance, the guards stopped pushing the doors and shifted their positions to serve as a barrier between the prince and the room within.

I am Eric the Destroyer. In Eric's mind, the guards were the enemy soldiers in the battlefield portrait of Victor. Eric put his head down like a battering ram and put every ounce of his strength into hurdling forward.

"I am Eric the Invincible," Eric said through clenched teeth, keeping his legs driving. With his head down, he rammed one guard and his shoulder caught the other.

One guard flew back as he took the full force of Eric's head in his stomach. Desperately, he tried to stop the momentum from both their bodies, but he was off balance and moved backwards too fast.

The guard and Eric hit the last row of people in the throne room, launching them forward into the next row. Gasps, screams, and curses filled the air from the falling guests. It was like a game of dominos: men in crisp uniforms and women in elegant gowns were hit and then tumbled to the floor.

Eric quickly untangled himself from the legs, arms, and fallen bodies around him. Standing up, he stepped back and looked at half the guests tussling on the floor and the other half with looks of shock across their faces.

But his attention was pulled forward by a single word shouted by an angry voice he knew all too well. "Eric!"

seven

The Emperor's voice reverberated around the room, forcing Eric's eyes toward the throne. His father stared at him wide-eyed, his fair-colored skin a deep shade of red. Against his white uniform, he looked like a blazing sun. Emperor Archibald's body was so tight, Eric began to worry it might explode.

In contrast, his mother, the Empress Alisa Marie von Battenburg, leaned out of her throne. Her lovely face was lined with concern for her son.

It was through her body that the von Battenburgs' royal blood flowed. Eric's mother, the daughter of Emperor James von Battenburg, was an only child and destined for the throne. But it wasn't the throne which had brought scores of young men to court. Like Helen of Troy, her stunning beauty had brought numerous suitors fighting for her hand in marriage. When the time came to wed, she chose a dashing young man in an officer's uniform, Archibald Holstein, son of Archduke Holstein, ruler of Ceres.

Eric noticed movement and saw Charles peer around his parents, then quickly cover his mouth to stop himself from laughing.

The fallen guests were struggling to stand up. Eric tried to hide behind them from his father's furious eyes—eyes that told him of the storm to come. But the guests left a wide, empty corridor between him and his father.

Although there were hundreds of people in the room, a deafening silence fell and everyone stared at him, making him feel like an animal in a zoo. His head turned one way then the other. All the guests' expressions mirrored his father's anger. *Why me? Why is it always me in trouble?* Feeling as if he were going to a funeral, Eric's shoulders hunched over and he looked down.

Why do I have such bad luck? I must be cursed. Eric's embarrassment slowed his progression toward the throne platform, and he concentrated his gaze on the floor as if it were a masterpiece. Anything to avoid the glaring eyes of his father and guests.

Finally, standing in front of the throne, Eric could feel his father's anger. He dropped his head further. In the continuing silence, he moved to his place on the low platform behind the throne, standing between his little brother George and Charles and in front of the nobility and the Emperor's personal advisors.

Eric held his breath, his gaze still on the floor. It seemed like an eternity until his father must have given the signal because the ceremony started again.

It took a while before Eric mustered the courage to look up. He gazed at his father standing in front of his throne, making his opening speech to the assembly. In a loud, strong voice, the Emperor lectured about the history of the Moon Empire—from its beginning under the leadership of Elizabeth to the defeat of Jupiter's army, to the conquest of the outer worlds.

At the end, Eric heard the characteristically tepid applause. *It's always the same speech. Everything always the same.*

Like everyone else, Eric knew what came next. The herald called out the titles of those assembled. "Lord Emperor," he started, "May I present to you the King and Queen of Jupiter."

Eric heard their footsteps but didn't bother to look up at the couple walking forward. Since entering the room, Eric's mood had changed from fear and anxiety to concern, to now boredom. He yawned as Saturn's rulers were called forward. He knew everyone in the room must come before his parents. Eric rolled his eyes and sighed heavily. *It will take hours.*

eight

"The Lord and Lady of Makemake." Eric stiffened and looked up. He shifted to his left to get in a better position to see the rulers of the distant planet. Makemake was a dwarf planet past Neptune.

The planet's first inhabitants had not been families looking for a new beginning. Makemake was a pirate port, where the most daring captains resided: Khalid the Quiet, famous for sneaking up on his prey. Nadine the Enchantress, whose beauty left men ogling her, until her blade was deep within them. And finally, the boy, a youth of sixteen, Tal Cabot, who ravaged the space merchants from Venus to Neptune.

It was a wild planet where anything illegal could be bought, and where the only justice was to be found at the point of a sword or neutralizer shooter.

Then, a huge Quisite strike was found on the planet—the most precious metal in the solar system. The population tripled overnight, a mining rush that brought millions of miners to the planet. Suddenly, the dwarf planet became the most important property in the system.

Makemake had a turbulent history within the Moon Empire. It led the first outer-planet rebellion—the rebellion crushed by Emperor Nikolai Xavier, the grandson of Empress Elizabeth. Seventy years ago, it was involved in another breakaway rebellion. This one succeeded, and Makemake and another hundred planets claimed independence, no longer part of the Moon Empire.

A smile appeared on Eric's face. *Independent until Victor came. Their might meant nothing to Victor the Destroyer.* Eric loved going to the royal library to read about Victor's adventures and conquests. He remembered, though Makemake's army was led by the famous warlord Eizenberg the Invincible, Victor landed on the planet with an army half the size of Makemake's.

Eric clenched his teeth together to stop laughing. *Invincible, yeah, right. Maybe for second-rate generals. When Victor attacked, it was like a cat toying with a mouse.* First, he had employed guerrilla tactics—small fights that interfered with Eizenberg's supply lines. Victor's forces were everywhere at once.

In every encounter, Victor led his soldiers into battle. He was unstoppable. Finally, on a gloomy, overcast morning, the main armies met. Eizenberg sent his superior numbers against Victor. So massive was the charge that Victor turned and retreated.

Ha! Eric laughed internally. *Eizenberg was dumb to think he could scare Victor.* The brilliant maneuver forced Makemake's army to spread out and divide in half. Driving forward like a madman, Victor cut the enemy's army to shreds. In the heat of the great battle of Furiate, Victor captured the enemy's flag and vanquished Eizenberg in a personal dual.

Sadness suddenly filled Eric. *Why did he have to die?* At the very end of the battle, Victor refused to leave the battlefield to recharge his personal shield. Many soldiers claimed to have fired the neutralizer that killed Victor—anxious for the claim of finally destroying the destroyer.

Eric craned his neck, as far as he could. A tall, thin, elderly man and a short, plump, white-haired woman stepped forward. Eric scratched his head. The new rulers didn't look like fierce warriors from a turbulent planet—more like the type who would have trouble fighting off a puppy. *No way anyone like that could have defeated the great Victor.*

Like all the others rulers, the elderly man and plump woman walked to the throne and then stopped. Eric's father and mother stood up to greet the Baron and Baroness.

The subject rulers bowed and the baron said in a clear voice, "I, the Baron of Makemake, give my solemn vow to follow the commands of the Emperor and Empress and the laws of the Moon Empire."

Eric noticed the Baron's sloped forehead and beady eyes, and the baroness's darting looks and nervous twitches. *They're lying.*

"As subjects of the Moon Empire you will have my guidance and protection," the Emperor proclaimed.

The Baron of Makemake bowed. But the Baroness looked past the Emperor and Empress and stared at Eric. Eric leaned back, uncomfortable at the attention. Timidly, Eric brought up his right hand and gave a shallow wave. *Is the Baroness staring because I look like Victor? Victor wouldn't be so shy, but bold.* Eric stared back and gave a firm wave, bumping Charles standing beside him.

The Emperor and Empress noticed the look and followed the Baroness gaze. Eric saw the tension return to his father's face and quickly looked down. The Emperor cleared his throat to get the plump Baroness's attention. She promptly bowed.

Then, Eric beheld a most beautiful sight. For several long seconds, his eyes locked on his mother's face. Her smile warmed him. "Are you all right?" she mouthed quietly to Eric.

He nodded and returned the smile. Her eyes twinkled. Then, his father squeezed her arm, bringing her attention back to the ceremony.

Almost the instant his mother and father turned back to the ceremony, the curse struck again.

nine

Eric's small body jerked from a harsh blow—an elbow to his ribs. He stared at the sadistic smile on Charles's face. Before he recovered, a swift knee smashed into his leg. Eric bit his lip to stifle a cry.

This was the normal game they played. Stationed behind the thrones, Charles tortured Eric. He knew the consequence of making a scene during a royal ceremony. Only once did Eric react. The outcome delighted Charles, but of course was extremely difficult for Eric. His father disciplined Eric until Eric promised it would never happen again.

Eric's eyes pleaded with the moon's nobility and his father's advisors for help. *They won't help me, they never do, pretending not to see my agony,* he quickly realized. *They all know Charles is father's favorite and future Emperor. I'm the cursed middle child, the black sheep of the family.*

Another stab of pain seared his body as Charles stomped his boot hard on Eric's foot, and Eric covered his mouth, once again stifling a cry. Charles continued to grind his heel into Eric's foot, and Eric's eyes watered from the agony. He clamped his teeth together like a vise, hoping to absorb the pain.

Suddenly, the pain was gone. Eric dropped his hands and exhaled in relief. He'd survived Charles's torture once again.

He finally opened his eyes.

On Charles's face was the evil look Eric knew so well. It spoke of more pain to come. Eric watched as Charles raised his left boot heel a foot off the ground. Then, his brother sent it downward with all his strength and weight.

The outcome was a muted cry from Eric from both pain and frustration.

No more! A change came over Eric. The frustration, anger, and mistreatment by his older brother had push Eric to a new level. He was a volcano ready to explode. *I can't be like Victor if I'm weak. I will no longer be Charles's victim.*

An inner force took over his mind and body, causing it to react as if on its own. Eric sucked in a deep breath through clenched teeth. He turned his volcanic gray-blue eyes, burning bright in anger, upon his brother. Charles pulled back, but not quick enough.

He heard his father say to the ruler of Brocadstan, "As the Emperor of the Moon Empire, I swear I will defend you with all the power of the empire."

Eric swung his right fist with all his might and connected it with Charles's jaw. The power behind the blow sent Charles falling back into the Moon Empire's nobility. The majority fell while the rest fought to keep their balance, all looked like flailing fish out of water. Eric stood over them.

Eric felt movement beside him and turned to see George staring in wide-eyed horror at the result of Eric's actions. His younger brother's head snapped around to look at Eric and his eyes became even wider.

Eric's neck burned as he felt his father's hard stare. Still buzzing with his newfound courage, Eric turned to face his father as if nothing had happened. The Emperor's eyes narrowed in fury and then widened as Eric gave him a smile and casual wink. Eric started walking toward the door. Close to his father, but out of striking distance, Eric yawned. "I'm bored. I think I'll go take a nap."

Eric turned his back to his father, and his heart began to pound. He was in big trouble. He hesitated, suddenly feeling indecisive, and ventured a look in his mother's direction. Her sad look made his stomach tighten.

I made my decision. There's no turning back.

He walked down the center aisle, waving to the guests like an official at a parade. But halfway toward the door, he noticed many of them whispering to each other. He could overhear some of their comments.

"If the Emperor can't control his own son, how can he truly protect us?"

"The empire is all show. It will be gone before Charles takes the throne."

These words meant nothing to Eric. All eyes stared at him as if he'd gone mad. But when he went past the rulers of Makemake, they lowered their eyes and bowed.

Eric disregarded the rulers of Makemake and marched to the throne room doors. This time the guards did not bar him but opened the doors. Eric walked out of the room and into the reception hall as his father continued to shout his name.

At the far end of the hall, he was suddenly overcome by the need to look up. He stopped. To his right hung the portrait of Empress Elizabeth, founder of the Moon Empire.

To Eric, it seemed as if their eyes made contact. Then, for the first time, he noticed she was smiling.

ten

"**He's just** a boy," Eric's mother said.

"A boy?" Emperor Archibald spat out.

They were in the royal library, which was a large room off the family quarters. Every wall was lined with a custom-made bookcase, the shelves of which held the rarest books of the empire. At the four corners were little sitting areas for reading and private discussions.

They weren't alone. Eric, Charles, and the two guards who had tried to block Eric's entrance into the throne room were also present.

For the past hour, Eric's father had marched back and forth, bellowing Eric's many faults. His hair was in disarray, and his forehead was lined with overwrought wrinkles. Eric and Charles stood in the center under a large chandelier, while the guards stood rigidly at attention by the doors.

"He will learn how to conduct himself," the Empress promised. "He needs a little more time."

"It would be easier to teach a monkey to sing," the Emperor said. "Why is it always Eric?"

Eric had stopped listening almost from the beginning. It was the same as every other visit to the library. Over and over again he was reminded of his faults. How he didn't measure up. *It's madness, like a never-ending merry-go-round. No matter what I do, I'm always doing the wrong thing.*

Eric looked at the row of books across from him. Was the answer to his problems in the books? He looked right and left at the thousands of spines that surrounded him. *Thousands of years of history and knowledge in these books. Surely at least one must have a way to fix me.*

While his father paced facing the opposite direction of Eric, Eric stared hard, hoping to find the one book. There were tall, small, thin, and thick books filling the shelves. To the right were bookcases with glass doors that were kept locked. *The answer must be in the special ones locked up.* With his father's gaze still focused elsewhere, Eric turned to take in more books and his gaze fell on his brother.

Charles stood at attention, looking forward like a well-trained dog. *Why doesn't Father understand it's Charles who started it?* The longer he looked at Charles, the more heated he became. *He never gets in trouble.*

Eric watched his brother make sure his parents were deep in their argument before turning his face toward Eric and mouthing, "Loser."

"It's Charles' fault," Eric shouted, forcing his parents to whirl around and focus their attention on him.

"Me?" Charles looked shocked. "Father, I stood like a good soldier behind your throne. I understand how important the ceremony is to you, Mother, and the Empire."

Eric watched as his father's features softened as he looked with pride at Charles.

"He's lying," Eric yelled at his father. "Don't be stupid and fall for his tricks."

"Stupid, am I?" The anger quickly returned. "I've been stupid and an idiot for being so lenient with you. No more!" The Emperor gestured to the guards standing by the doors. "Come here."

Together the guards marched up and stood at attention.

"You will take Prince Eric to the castle dungeon."

A great cry of anguish filled the room. "No. You cannot. Why must you always be so cruel to Eric?"

Eric's father turned on his mother. "It's because of you I *must* do this. You continue to coddle Eric and make excuses for his unacceptable behavior. This will help him become a man."

"Eric's still a young boy."

"He acts like a boy, but he needs to be a man."

"You go too far," Eric's mother said, shaking her head.

Eric's father leaned over his mother, using his height against her. "Not far enough. Eric was late, rammed into a score of guests—didn't you see Baron Gilbert limping after the ceremony?" He shook his head as if trying to forget the memory. "Then, when everything was settled he struck his brother and sent the ceremony into disarray again, and was so cheeky with his smiles and waves as he left the room. To top it off, I ordered him back but he disregarded my commands."

Eric's mother turned her head away from the Emperor, trying to suppress a smile the memory brought.

"I will not tolerate his infantile actions." The Emperor threw up his hands in frustration. "Why can't he be more like Charles?"

Eric looked down at the library's marble floor, the words ringing in his head. '*Why can't he be more like Charles*?' Yes, why couldn't he? *Why can't I do things right?* He felt the black sheep of the family more than ever, never fitting in, always doing everything wrong.

"Charles is Charles. Eric is Eric. Do not judge one's action by the other," Eric's mother said.

"I have given my orders," the Emperor said.

The Empress stood up. "I will not allow it."

Eric gasped at his mother bold assertion.

"Not...not allow it?" Eric's father stood rigid, red-faced, his eyes beady. Consumed with rage he roared loud enough to be heard throughout the castle, "I rule."

Eric's head jerked up. He had never seen his father so angry. The Emperor took a threatening step toward his mother.

"Father!" Eric bellowed, pulling the Emperor's attention toward himself. "I will go to the dungeon."

"Eric. You mustn't go," his mother said, moving toward him.

"Please, Mother, I'm not afraid," Eric lied. Eric had never visited the dungeon, but his imagination told him all he needed to know. It was deep under the Moon castle, dark and forbidding. Only very bad men were taken there.

"No," Eric's mother said.

"You want to be with him so badly, perhaps you should go with him."

Eric's gray-blue eyes blazed at the Emperor's comment. All emotion seemed to drain from him as he looked defiantly at his father. "I don't need anyone to go with me to the dungeon."

Before Eric's mother could say anything, the Emperor once again addressed the guards, who were still standing at attention in front of him. "This is your fault. You were ordered to stop anyone from entering the throne room. If you can't stop a boy from getting into the throne room, how can you possibly protect the royal family?" Emperor Archibald straightened his uniform. "You will take Prince Eric to the dungeon master. Then you will report to the royal guard commander to be sent directly to the outer planets. We'll see if you do any better in battle."

The two guards saluted and marched to stand on either side of Eric.

Tears ran down his mother's face. Her sadness was too much for Eric. He turned and left the room, followed by the guards.

eleven

Eric walked through the dark lower levels of the castle, followed by the two guards. The change was like from day to night. Above were the important parts of the castle—the levels where he had always been, where the royal family lived and received guests. There, every room was specially decorated to meet the high royal standards.

Here, no colorful tapestries or paintings highlighted the walls, nor did any soft rugs cover the cold steel floors.

Eric pulled his uniform jacket tighter; the warmth seemed to have been left on the higher levels too.

Though his surroundings had changed drastically, Eric couldn't get the vision of his mother's grief out of his mind as he was taken from the library. *It is not Mother's fault. I don't want her to be sad.* His shoulders slumped and he lowered his head. *I don't want to cause her problems. I love her too much to see her heartbroken.*

Suddenly, Eric thought of Victor and the battlefield portrait. Victor had overcome so much. He was strong, brave, and determined, overcoming any difficulty in his way.

I will be like Victor. My father thinks to scare me by sending me to the dungeon. Eric pulled his shoulders up and walked taller. *I'll show him. I'll come back carefree, as if I'd been on a vacation. Then my mother will laugh instead of being sad.*

A spring came to Eric's step, and he shuffled his feet as if dancing. He started to whistle as he walked down the barren corridor to the elevator that would take him and the guards down to the dungeon.

Eric heard a low grunt, then a growl, as if animals were with him. He looked around but he saw only the two guards. The cruel look on their faces should have warned him.

I'm Eric the Conquer, Eric's mind shouted. No longer did Eric feel he was being punished, but part of a game and adventure. Eric ran all around in the dark halls. Charging, shifting, and twirling, he was fighting pretend enemies of the Moon Empire again.

The two guards stopped in front of the large elevator which would take them hundreds of feet below the castle. They watched as a red light began flashing. The grinding of a motor started and the yellow light flashed, telling them the elevator was on its way.

The wait time gave Eric several minutes more to destroy more of his imaginary enemies.

The light changed to green and a second later the two elevator doors slid apart. Eric raced into the empty elevators, followed by the two guards. The shorter one pushed the button to take them down to the level of the dungeon master's office. The elevator's doors slid closed, sealing them in.

Eric, still wild with energy, jumped when he heard another grunt and groan. He ventured a look at the guards.

"Dodge, what're we going to do?" the smaller one said in a voice edged with panic.

"I don't know, Hugo," Dodge said in despair.

"Do you remember John? The handsome bloke who was part of the royal guard."

"The one caught with the Duchess?"

"Yeah, him. He was a lover and a damn good fighter too. John didn't last a day fighting on the outer planets." Hugo took in several quick, uneasy breaths before finally saying, "We won't live a day. The empire is crumbling; we'll be sacrificed for nothing. I'm too young—"

"Quiet, I'm thinking," Dodge said. Then, a smile came to his face. "We won't go."

"Don't go…we'll be in big trouble," Hugo said.

"At least we won't be dead." Dodge looked down at Eric with a scowl on his face. "But first we'll have some payback. Take care of the one who took away our cushy job."

"Kill the prince?"

Eric took a step back when Dodge didn't answer.

"They'll hunt us like dogs if we kill the Prince. They'll never give up."

"We'll pay back this little brat and get time to escape."

"How?"

Eric watched as Dodge leaned toward Hugo and spoke into his ear. He took a step back as Hugo's eyes found him while Dodge continued to whisper to him. When Hugo's lips parted in a devious smile, Eric moved backwards until his back was against the elevator wall.

Both guards turned to face Eric. Dodge extended his finger and pushed a button. The elevator came to an abrupt stop between levels.

"What are you doing?" Eric asked.

"You caused us trouble," Hugo said, drifting to his right.

"I didn't do anything," Eric said. Dodge drifted to his left and moved forward. "What are you going to do?" He turned right, then left to look at the guards. They both looked down with the same anger as his father.

"You've destroyed us," Hugo said. "I'm not going to die because of the actions of a stupid boy."

"You shouldn't have let me in," Eric said, then regretted his comment as the two guards' faces became twisted, their eyes narrowing.

Dodge lunged for Eric, but Eric turned and darted forward. Hugo grabbed for him, but Eric hit his hand away.

Eric ran to the buttons and started to push frantically on all the ones to go up. He had to get away. Then, pain shot through his head as a strong and rough hand wove into his hair, took a firm grip, and pulled back hard.

"Stop," Eric cried. "You're hurting me." Eric reached up to knock Dodge's hand away.

Then the elevator started to move up. A sliver of hope filled Eric. *Up above there's a chance.*

Hugo stepped quickly past Eric and stabbed at a button and the elevator stopped.

Eric pushed Dodge away. "Leave me alone or my father will get you."

This brought a snicker from the two guards. "We don't take threats from brats." Dodge raised his hands and Hugo followed his actions. They cornered Eric.

Eric felt the cold wall of the elevator but didn't care as he pushed harder against it.

"Off with your pretty clothes," Dodge ordered.

"Why?" Eric asked, wrapping his arms around himself for protection.

"Take them off."

Without warning, Dodge gave Eric a cuff on the side of the head. The sudden stinging pain caused Eric's eyes to water. He felt Dodge grab his wrists and pin them against the wall.

Hugo ripped open the shirt and tore it off Eric's body. Then he was lifted from the floor.

"No." Furious, Eric kicked out at the nearest guard. He cried out as the large hand smacked him across his cheek.

When his clothes were on the elevator floor and he was in his undergarments. Dodge threw him down.

"Behave yourself or I'll show you how my old man kept me down." Dodge tapped his belt buckle.

twelve

Eric lay on the coarse elevator floor, his arms and legs exposed to the cold metal.

"First to the lowest level of the dungeon, level 101," Dodge said. "The B and F level."

"The B and F level?" Hugo asked.

"The *Banished* and *Forgotten* level," Dodge grinned wickedly. "Where the worst lots are. I want our Prince to remember his time in this awful place. Then we'll leave to Makemake."

Eric heard the click of a button being pushed and then the elevator engine groan into action. The elevator jolted sharply and started to move lower below the castle.

What am I going to do? Who will help me? Eric moved his body tighter into a ball. He wrapped his arms around his legs, pulling them closer to him. *What's going to happen to me? Will I ever see my family again?* His eyes welled up, the futility of the situation overwhelming him.

A soldier does not cry, a voice said in his head. *He stands tall no matter what life throws at him.* He recognized the voice. It was the voice that always spoke to him when he was looking at Victor's battle portrait in the western hallway. *Fighters do not give up.*

"Hey," Hugo said as he watched Eric get off the floor.

"Stay down," Dodge said.

Eric continued to get up until he stood in the center of the elevator. He stood rigidly at attention, staring forward.

"Okay," Dodge said, seeing the blazing gray-blue eyes fixed on the elevator door. "Don't give us any more trouble."

The elevator was silent except for the sharp *ding* signaling when a level passed. The sounds continued until it felt like they were a constant noise in the background.

Eric and the guards were thousands of feet under the Moon castle. The jarring of the elevator stopping almost knocked Eric off his feet. The elevator doors slid open. Eric gagged at the raw stench of the dungeon attacking his senses. He wanted to stop breathing, to stop the awful smell from entering his lungs.

Dodge jerked his head in the direction of the open doors. "Out."

Marching out of the elevator, Eric strained his eyes to look forward. One step into the opening Eric had to stop. He couldn't see and the room had a haunted feeling. Then, a hard shove sent him blindly further into the unknown. Eric froze, cautious, as there was no way of knowing what was ahead.

In the blackness, an abrupt bleakness filled him—a feeling so powerful it brought with it despair. It wasn't the misery of the situation. His mind told him. *This is the end. The life I've known is gone forever.*

The feeling of melancholy was replaced with anguish and sorrow when he thought of his mother. He was filled with a feeling of loneliness, and an immediate desire to be held in her warm and loving arms. But he would never know the cherished embrace of his mother again.

thirteen

Eric's eyes adjusted to the recessive light of a torch burning in the back. He and the guards stood at the entrance to a sizable room cut in a rough circular shape. The jagged walls had been hacked and blasted out of the inner moon's rock. The ground was formed of crumbled pieces of rock that hurt Eric's bare feet.

Shifting uneasily, he fought the urge to breathe as long as he could, knowing the stench would bring a terrible taste into his mouth. But Eric didn't have a choice. The thin oxygen on this level forced him to take several deep breaths.

"Hey!" Dodge yelled into the shadows.

Parts of the irregular-shaped fixtures at the far end started to move. Eric took an involuntary step backward. *The stories about monsters in the lower levels are true.*

Hugo drew his sword.

"Wuz this—" Eric heard something or someone muttering. Making slow progress out of the shadows, a hunched man and a thin woman came forward. Even though they spoke words, in the veiled light Eric wasn't so sure they weren't monsters.

The man's head was partially bald, and he had shallow eyes and only four teeth showing. His uniform was grimy and absent of any designation of rank.

"No children," the man croaked.

"Who are you?" Dodge asked.

"I'm the Emperor and this is the Empress." The man's voice was thick with sarcasm.

"No, you're not!" Eric said boldly, then leaned forward. He stared at the man's left eye that went in the opposite direction of the right.

"What's you looking at, boy?" the man demanded.

Hugo let his sword be seen. "You were asked a question. Who are you?"

The left eye looked at Hugo's sword, while the other circled around in the opposite direction. "I'm Jakey, the head on this level, and she's Megey." The right eye fixed on Eric while the left danced in the opposite direction. "No children on level 101. This here is for the scum of the empire."

"You'll take this one," Dodge said firmly. "The Emperor ordered us to bring him to this level."

"That's a lie," Eric said before feeling a knee at the back of his legs, sending him to the floor.

"He was caught impersonating Prince Eric," Dodge said.

"I am Prince Eric," Eric said, looking up at Jakey.

"Your lie brought you here." Dodge shook his head at Eric, then turned to the man and woman. "Don't listen to his lies."

"We don't have no cells for little rats like him," Jakey said, smacking his lips together like a fish.

"Don't treat him different than any other prisoner," Dodge said.

"But—" Jakey started again before being cut off.

"We're the Emperor's guards," Hugo said, placing the point of his sword on Jakey's chest. "Are you disobeying his direct order?"

The jailer's eyes moved rapidly in different directions. "No... no sir. We're faithful servants to the Emperor." He looked down at Eric, then kicked him. "Lying. Saying you was a royal prince."

"They're lying! I am Prince—"

Another kick from Jakey caused Eric to curl up. "Leave the little rat with us; we know how to treat his kind."

Dodge moved until he stood over Jakey. "You will keep him here until *we* come for him."

Jakey's lips smacked together several times before he said reluctantly, "Anything you say."

Dodge turned and walked to the elevator. Hugo again rested the point of his sword on Jakey's chest. "Follow our directions or there'll be one less jailer in the royal dungeons," he said before sheathing his sword and following Dodge.

Jakey stopped smacking his lips long enough to mouth a curse at the turned guards.

From the cold stone floor, Eric watched the two guards enter the elevator. Once inside, both turned and gave him sadistic smiles.

The elevator doors closed, taking most of the light with it. A shallow darkness surrounded Eric. He heard Jakey come closer. The jailer grabbed Eric by his hair and pulled up hard. Eric screamed out at the pain, working hard to get up quickly.

"Stop! I order you," Eric said and shook free.

"Order me. Hear that, Megey? He's telling me an order." Eric could see a mock bow. "Yes, my lord prince." The quick, rough hand against his head sent Eric across the room into the far wall.

"Leave him be, Jakey," Megey's dry voice pleaded. "He's only a little one."

"The cursed guards said *no different* than the other scum we have jailed here." Jakey moved over to Eric as his lips smacked together. "And I won't." A knee into Eric's side caused him to roll over.

"Stop. Please," Megey begged.

Eric felt someone close.

"There's a tear on his little face." The hand that wiped the tear away was cold and coarse, like sandpaper.

"I don't baby prisoners."

"Away, Jakey. I'll take him," Megey said. She put her arm around Eric's shoulder and helped him up.

"Far away," Jakey said with heavy disgust in his voice. "His blubbering will drive me bonkers."

"Come with me," Megey said. "What's our name, dear?"

"Eric Alexander von Battenburg."

"Stop with those lies, or learn why I'm hated and feared," Jakey said.

With her arms around Eric, Megey pushed Eric in front of her. "Be a good boy. Don't get on Jakey's bad side."

fourteen

Megey guided Eric to a large wooden door with rusted steel bindings and hinges. She released Eric and pushed hard on the door. It didn't move. She leaned into the door and pushed with all her strength.

With a groan, the door slowly opened.

"You stay here—far away from Jakey. I'll leave the door open. If you need anything, come find me."

Eric nodded.

"Now mind you, if you hear the smacking sound of Jakey's big lips, you come back here." She started to leave but stopped. "Wait, you need a blanket." Eric suddenly felt something draped over him.

"Keep you a bit warmer," Megey said, pulling the old blanket tight around Eric.

"Thank you," Eric said. "You're very kind."

She led him into the cell. "Sit down, and don't make a peep."

Eric sat down on the cold stone floor with the blanket wrapped around him.

"Think of something nice. Time goes by faster." A second later Megey was gone.

Eric pulled the blanket around him tighter. The old blanket smelled of dirty socks; he pushed it down away from his nose, then ventured a look around the cell. The rock walls were jagged and in the corner lay moldy straw. But the cell was private and quiet.

He felt not fear or terror, but a cold indifference. He forced his mind from the present torment to the massive portrait of his grand-uncle.

I have Victor's blood running through my veins. Despite the hopelessness which surrounded him, Eric somehow sensed that, like Victor, he was destined for greater deeds.

At the head of his own army, Eric would fly the same banner Victor had, an angry lion on a field of purple. Above the lion was a white swatch with a single word—a word made of random letters that was known only to him.

This was Victor's banner and would be his. They would share a great history of triumph different from all others in history.

Armies would tremble in fear when they saw Eric's banner. All would dread his coming, as it would foretell of defeat to come. All would bow to him for his greatness, including his father and older brother.

Another figure came to Eric's mind. This person would never bow to him. His mother to him was more than an Empress. In every manner, his mother was an angel.

A smile appeared on his face in this dark cell as the memory of his mother filled his mind. Every happy moment of his life his mother had been there—always playing with him as a young child, soothing his bruises after losing battles with Charles, and hugging him with such warmth that she seemed to hold part of the sun in her body.

No. She would never bow to him.

fifteen

The darkness surrounded him as if he'd lost his vision and cold moved through the old blanket like it was full of holes. Since he didn't have pants or a shirt, the old blanket's roughness attacked his body. Eric felt an itch, then a bump, he scratched it. Then he scratched the little bumps on his legs, arms, and back. *Are these insect bites?* He'd never had one before. It was madness; all the insect bites wanted to be scratched at the same time. He wanted to throw the blanket from him, but the cold was worse.

The woman, Megey. *Maybe she has a different blanket*, Eric thought. He started to rise, but then the thought of Jakey came to haunt him. *If Jakey catches me outside the cell he'll punish me.*

Twenty minutes later Eric couldn't take the torment any longer. He got up from the floor.

Is there a monster behind the door? Is the cruel Jakey waiting for me to leave and then he'll attack me? These and other thoughts ran through Eric's mind as he looked at the old door, the barrier that held him in. Or held the monsters out.

Eric dropped the filthy blanket and set about scratching every part of his body. When he had a minute of respite, the other enemy attacked him: cold. In only his undergarments, he started to shake, his teeth chattering.

Maybe Jakey's not so bad. Nothing could be worse than the cold and itching.

Eric leaned on the door; it made a screaming groan and then stuttered open. Without thinking, Eric put up his fist and closed his eyes. He stood in his mock battle stance, praying to survive. After a minute passed, he opened one eye and surveyed the entrance. His heart raced as he stepped outside the door with his fist still out in front of him.

The flickering torch gave gloomy shape to the objects outside. There was a lone desk against the far wall. He couldn't see the objects on the top of the desk.

Eric took a step and his hand flew to his mouth, but not quick enough to stop the cry of pain. A sharp rock had pricked the bottom of his foot.

"Who's there?" came a voice, breaking the silence.

The two words caused Eric to step back into his cell.

"Are you the accursed jailer?" the voiced boomed.

"No." Eric leaned out. Following the direction of the sound, he looked past the desk and saw another cell door.

"Who are you?" the voice asked and Eric realized it came from behind the other cell door.

He moved in the direction of the voice, slowly and on the tips of his toes, trying hard to make no noise as he stepped across the corridor.

"Who are you?" the voice repeated several times, each time rising in intensity.

Eric didn't respond but moved past the desk until he stood before the cell door. "Why do you want to know?" he finally asked.

"Are you a prisoner or jailer?" the voice demanded. "Answer me."

"Prisoner," Eric said.

"A fellow prisoner? Tell me your name. I'm Corcoran."

Prince Eric Alexander von Battenburg, Eric wanted to say. But he remembered how angry Jakey had become when he gave his real name and said, "Eric Alexander. Pleased to meet you."

"What false crimes were you accused of to be brought to this dreadful place?" Corcoran asked.

"None," Eric said, staring at the old wooden cell door.

"Wrongly detained," Corcoran said. "As I am."

"Yes."

"What has the solar system come to when there are no scales of justice that would balance action against the punishment?"

It was Charles' fault, but I'm the one who got sent to the dungeon. Father probably was mean to this man, too. His thoughts were interrupted as Corcoran continued.

"Why are you free?"

"I'm looking for Megey, the jailer," Eric said. "I need a different blanket."

"You have a blanket?" Corcoran said. "You're special." After a pause, he continued, "You sound young?"

"I'm ten."

"Ten—here on the B and F level—The worst level?" Corcoran's voice softened. "You must be scared."

"Yes, I—" Eric stopped himself. "No."

"I can help you find Megey," Corcoran said reassuringly.

"You'll help?"

"Yes, of course…get this cell door open and I will take you to her."

Eric looked at the door. "Megey left my door unlocked. Have you tried pushing your door?"

"Of course," Corcoran shouted. Then, in a softer voice he said, "Yes, it's locked. I'll show you." The door rattled and groaned but remained closed.

"How will I get you out?" Eric asked.

"Get the key."

"Key?"

"Search!" Corcoran bellowed. "Find the key!"

Suddenly, Eric's stomach rumbled. He hadn't eaten since breakfast. "Is there any food here?"

"I have lots here in my cell," Corcoran said. "Open the door and you'll have a feast."

Turning, Eric noticed across the room on the wall several keys on a hook.

"I see the keys," Eric said.

"Good," Corcoran said anxiously. "Get me out."

"I can't," Eric said. "They're too high for me to reach."

"Please, Eric, get the keys."

"There's a long pole against the wall."

"Good. Use it. Hurry."

Eric went to the pole. His fingers barely went around the thick wood. Eric's eyes traveled up the length of the pole. *It must be twenty feet long.* Eric lifted the long pole and it started to sway a little. The harder he tried to control it, the worst it swayed. Then, it was falling. The long pole hit the dungeon floor with a bang, like an explosion. Eric stopped and stood like a statue. *Did Jakey hear?* The thought of smacking lips approaching made him step back against the wall.

"Fool!" Corcoran hissed. "Quiet!"

Several minutes passed. No jailer, only silence.

"Hurry," Corcoran said again.

Eric bent away from the wall and peered down the corridor. There was only darkness. Relieved at the emptiness of the corridor, Eric shifted his eyes to the pole lying on the floor. He stooped and grasped the end closest to him, lifting the heavy pole into the air. Beads of sweat appeared on his brow as he fought to control the long pole.

First, Eric hit the key ring, hoping it would fall down. When it didn't, Eric tried putting the pole through the key ring and lifting the keys off the hook. But the ring was too small.

Eric let the far end of the pole fall to the ground. It was tiring and nothing he did seemed to work. "It's too hard."

"Don't give up," Corcoran pleaded. "You're a good boy. You can do it...and I have all this food for you."

Eric's stomach groaned and pushed him to lift the pole again and attack the key ring. On the third try, the keys came rattling to the floor. Setting down the pole, Eric picked up the keys. "I have them," Eric said.

"Quick, open the door."

Eric tried several keys before one worked. He quickly turned the key, releasing the lock. Grasping the handle, he began to pull. The door moved slightly. Then he jumped out of the way as it rushed at him. Eric backed away to the far wall and peered through the door's dark opening.

Eric held his breath as his eyes nearly popped out. *I've released a monster.* A beast twice his height, with long, tangled hair that covered the top of the head staggered out of the open door. The rags it wore were old and torn.

Run, Eric's mind shouted. He turned and took a step when a hand grabbed him around his neck, stopping him dead in his tracks. The thing turned him around.

"Where're you going?"

"Don't hurt me." Eric closed his eyes, not wanting to see the large fangs that were about to eat him.

The monster shook him until his eyes opened. It had broad shoulders and its dirty clothes clung to the outline of a strong man's body. But what caught Eric's attention was the roving eyes, like a hungry predator. Corcoran's voice was somehow deeper than it had been from the cell. "We must go."

Corcoran closed the cell door and locked it.

"What about the food?" Eric asked as his stomach rumbled.

"What I was fed can hardly be called food." He grabbed the long pole and examined it. Eric jumped as Corcoran slammed the pole against the wall. A four-foot piece broke off with a sharp tip. Corcoran swung it like a sword. "It'll do."

Corcoran turned his attention to Eric. "Which way is out?"

Eric shrugged his shoulders.

Corcoran gave Eric a hard stare before looking around. After a moment's hesitation, he moved to his left and went down one of the dungeon corridors.

Eric stood alone in the darkness. "What about me?" he called out.

There was no answer. The shadowy features of Corcoran had faded into darkness. Without thinking, Eric started to run after him.

Though the dungeon was like a maze, Corcoran quickly found the elevator. To Eric's surprise, the man hesitated in front of it. *He doesn't know how to work it?*

"I'll show you." Stepping past Corcoran, Eric pushed the button calling the elevator.

"Fool," Corcoran said quickly bringing up his sharpened pole.

"What's wrong?"

"Who will it bring?" Both heard the whine of the motor calling the elevator down to them. Eric stepped back as he watched Corcoran position himself for the attack. The thud of the elevator's arrival made them both jump.

The elevator doors opened and Corcoran swung his pole, shouting, "Die!" He leaped into the elevator, thrusting the pole forward—then silence.

Eric peered into the elevator. Corcoran was in front of the control panel and stood, statue-like, staring at the buttons. "Choose the wrong level and I will face hundreds of the Emperor's guards."

"Don't go to the third level, then."

Corcoran stepped out of the elevator and stood in front of Eric. He brushed the tangled hair out of his eyes and, looking down, searched Eric's face. "Who are you?"

Eric remembered Jakey's warning, but said defiantly, "I am Prince Eric Alexander von Battenburg."

"*Von Battenburg?*" Corcoran said, staring harder.

Eric did his best to meet Corcoran's eyes confidently. Corcoran's face broke into a wide grin. "The gods have changed my fortune. Prince Eric, we're going to be the best of friends." Corcoran put his hand on Eric's shoulders. "Friends stay together."

Eric walked toward the elevator, but Corcoran barred his way. "Now Prince Eric, let's have a little talk before we go up. Are you familiar with the different levels above?"

"Some."

"Tell me what you know."

"After the dungeon, the first level is storage; the second is the kitchens. The third floor is the garrison. On the fourth floor are the reception and dining halls, and above them is the office of the minister and government officials. The last floor is where my family lives."

"My good friend, let's go." Corcoran waved for Eric to go before him into the elevator. Turning to the control panel, Corcoran pushed the button for the first level. The doors closed and the elevator moved upward.

sixteen

Corcoran and Eric roamed through the food storage quarters, on the first level. While Eric discovered apples to eat, Corcoran opened bin after bin, gorging himself on anything he found. Corcoran grabbed a small bag and quickly filled it with food.

Next, they went to the armory. Corcoran smiled with delight as he found an officer's sword. He ran from aisle to aisle collecting more items, and placed them one by one on a table.

He tossed a uniform to Eric. "Put this on."

Eric did as he was told and watched as Corcoran started to hack off his long hair and beard with a knife. When he was done his hair was less than two inches long and his beard was almost gone.

Corcoran continued to move fast, as if he were racing someone or something. He put on a uniform and belted the sword he had found around his waist. He clipped on both a neutralizer pistol and personal force shield and finally slipped a dagger into his boot.

While Corcoran was busy, Eric looked at him. With his haircut and beard partially shaved, Eric was able to see Corcoran's face. He had brown eyes, a long nose with a strong chin. The left side of his mouth was constantly pulled up as if he was about to laugh.

Corcoran waved for Eric to follow him out of the weapons room.

"I don't have any shoes." Eric raised the long pant legs and showed his blackened socks.

"No small boots. You'll have to do without for now."

"If we go to my room, I have lots of shoes."

"Go to your room? You'd be seen and returned to the dungeon. Do you want that?"

Eric shook his head.

"Good, we leave."

"To where?"

Corcoran hesitated a moment before answering, "On an adventure. An adventure made for a prince, very special. Do you want to go?"

Eric smiled and nodded his head.

"Fine," Corcoran said. Then he slapped his palm against his head in frustration. "But the adventure is outside the castle. How can we get outside the castle without anyone seeing us?"

"I know," Eric said before thinking. He clapped his hand over his mouth.

"You know a way out?"

Eric bit his lower lip. "Father said not to tell anyone."

"Your father's right." Corcoran gazed down at Eric with an understanding look on his face. "So don't tell me, show me."

"Father said nothing about showing," Eric said. "Follow me."

Corcoran pulled out the extra force shield and clipped it to Eric's belt. "I need to protect my lucky charm." He stepped aside. "Lead on, Prince Eric."

seventeen

Why is he in such a hurry, Eric wonder as Corcoran pulled him quickly along.

"You're sure it's in this direction?" Corcoran said anxiously.

Eric pointed to a corner leading to another area. Eric felt his feet leave the ground as Corcoran lifted him up and started running to the corner. "Your princely adventure will start soon, I promise," Corcoran said breathing hard. "As soon as we are free of the castle."

Corcoran darted around the corner and stopped as if he hit a brick wall. It was a dead end. In front of Eric and Corcoran were dozens of large, marble, Greek statues, put on the first level for storage.

The pressure of Corcoran's arm around Eric suddenly increased until it was a vise.

"Oowww," Eric exclaimed, trying to squeeze free. *Why is Corcoran hurting me*?

"I must get out of here!" Corcoran said through a clenched jaw. "Freedom— I'll get it one way or another."

Eric leaned away from Corcoran, "We can. The tunnel's over there."

"Show me," Corcoran demanded, relaxing his hold on Eric and putting him down.

Eric ran from Corcoran to the statues. He stopped at several, *which one is it? They all look alike. Was it a man statue or woman statue? I don't remember.* After a minute of looking at the statues, Eric shrugged his shoulders. *"I don't remember,"* he said meekly.

The hair on the back of Eric's neck stood up as he heard Corcoran roar with frustration and march at Eric. Eyes wide, Eric stumbled backward. Abruptly his back collided with a statue's base. Eric looked up as Corcoran outstretched finger reached for him.

"It's this one," Eric said.

Corcoran stopped, "This one?"

Eric pointed up, "Hercules." To Corcoran's continued confused look, Eric reached over and pushed on the right heel of Hercules's statue.

Silently, the Hercules statue slid back revealing stair leading down.

"Eric, you are the best Prince ever!" Corcoran said happily as he grabbed Eric and rushing down the stairs. A few seconds later the statue slid back to cover the secret passage.

"What way to the princely adventure?" Eric asked after he led Corcoran out of the Moon castle.

Corcoran spoke haltingly and his eyes darted and stared nervously in different directions. "You must be quiet and follow close to me," Corcoran whispered.

In the town, Corcoran ran from wall to wall, like a spy in a game. Eric followed happily.

After a long time, Eric became tired of the game and was about to speak when Corcoran stopped. Corcoran placed his arm against Eric's chest and pushed him hard against the wall.

"Stay here."

Corcoran slipped out of the alley and into the shabby street. His movements were cautious, stopping every few feet to search the area.

Eric went to the edge of the alley and looked out. He'd never been out of the castle. The long street was dark, with a few lampposts giving off a weak light. The buildings of the village were odd shaped and packed closely together. The building's colors were hard to determine due to the dull light, and they were ripped and torn, as if hurt. Various objects were put over the rips and tears like bandages.

Eric noticed Corcoran stop by a window beside one of the most unpleasant buildings. From the building came shouts and laughter, just like Eric had heard from his father's parties.

Corcoran stood beside the window and stared in.

After a few minutes, Eric rolled his eyes and leaned against the building. *This isn't fun. I want to go on my adventure.* He took in a deep breath and let it out slowly. He looked out the alley again and wanted to go out, but remembered Corcoran's order.

Suddenly, Eric stood straight up and his back went rigid. *I'm the prince. I give the orders.* The thought still strong in his mind, Eric marched out of the alley toward Corcoran.

"Corcoran," Eric shouted, breaking the silence.

The enraged look on Corcoran's face stopped the rest of his words. It was the same look he received from his father when he was in big trouble.

Eric froze in fear. Corcoran ran at him, the look on his face having changed from rage to malice. Before Eric could move, Corcoran lifted him up with his powerful arms and threw him back into the alley.

Through gritted teeth, Corcoran said, "I told—" His words were cut off by the sound of a door closing.

Corcoran forced Eric deep into the alley before he moved against the inner wall to wait.

A small man with a large hat, who seemed to have problems walking in a straight line, passed the alley's opening.

Like a panther on the hunt, Corcoran slowly and cautiously moved behind the small man. Eric gasped as Corcoran pounced on the smaller man and dragged him deep into the alley.

The small man, at first caught off-guard, was struggling, but even Eric could tell it was in vain. Corcoran was too big, too strong.

"Empty all your pockets!" Corcoran said, towering over the small man with a dagger at his throat.

"Please," the small man pleaded.

"Give me your money or—" Corcoran pushed the tip of the dagger into the man's throat.

Eyes bulging, the small man moved his shaking hands. He had great difficulty opening his pockets.

Corcoran pushed his dagger enough to produce a trickle of blood. "Your money."

Hurriedly, a thick roll of money appeared in the small man's hand.

Corcoran's left hand put the stolen money in his pocket.

"Stop," Eric said when Corcoran took the money. "It's not yours."

Corcoran ignored Eric. A mistake.

"I said stop," Eric said, flexing his hands that finally formed into a fist. His gray-blue eyes blazed like a smoldering volcano.

Taking a deep breath, Eric dropped his head. He shot out at Corcoran like a battering ram. He pushed every ounce of strength he possessed to his legs.

Eric hit Corcoran like a cannonball. The impact sent Corcoran and the small man rolling to the ground.

Eric leapt up, fighting like a tiger, his fist striking out at Corcoran's head. Eric fell back when Corcoran pushed him away with his left forearm.

The small man jumped up. He started to run toward the street, but stopped, seeing his money on the ground. He ran back, diving for it.

Corcoran and Eric raced for the money too.

Eric was the quickest and he grabbed the money. The small man was on him, trying to tear his hands open. Then, Corcoran's hand clamped on his wrist.

"Leave me alone!" Eric shouted. He felt a hand go across his mouth that jerked away when Eric sank his teeth into it.

A moment later, Eric felt a sharp pain on the side of his head, then blackness seemed to take him.

eighteen

A loud gasp startled Megey. She stopped sweeping, listened, as more gasps followed. The gasps were followed by great moans. She'd never known fear in the dungeon until now. The sounds of pain continued, then became agonizing screams. Closing her eyes, she prayed that whatever it was would pass.

"Megey—"

Megey opened her eyes to Jakey running toward her in panic from the cell where they had put the boy. "Jakey, what's wron—"

"Where's the prince?" Jakey's right eye was fixed on her as sweat ran down his grimy face and his lips smacked together, hard.

"Prince?" Even in the gloomy darkness, Megey could see Jakey was stone white from fear.

"The prince! The boy those accursed guards brought down." He groaned. "Not here, not to our level...I'm cursed. I will suffer." The words echoed off the walls. "I kicked the prince!" Jakey shouted at Megey. "Tortured I will be, and jailed here on the B and F level."

"Jakey. You've gone bonkers; you make no sense," Megey cried, tears coming to her eyes. She began to back away.

"I went up, normal like, to have my monthly meeting with the head warden," Jakey said. "It was madness. They told me the mighty Emperor came here, here to the dungeons."

Megey's knees wobbled. "The Emperor...never comes... to the dungeon."

"His face was like a demon, red with rage and anger." Jakey's voice dropped as he looked away. "The lovely Empress, head down, tears streaming, begged for any word of her son."

Suddenly, Megey saw an amazing sight. Jakey's beady eyes stared forward together, as if they were normal. They stared straight into Megey's eyes as he whispered, "All the jailers and all the guards were searching for the prince...I ran away...They can't know the prince was here with us."

"That little boy was telling the truth?" Megey asked. Her legs started to shake, and then she collapsed onto the hard, cold ground.

Jakey sobbed.

"Jakey, you were so mean to the prince."

"He's got to forgive me." Jakey dropped to his knees beside Megey. "He liked you good, Megey. You's gots to say I'm a good man."

"I can't."

Jakey brought his hands together, begging.

"He's gone," she said.

"Gone?"

"I went back last night to give him a little food. He wasn't there. I thought you took him."

Jakey's lips smacked together several times before he finally said again. "He's gone?"

Megey moved her head up and down, then watched the jailer concentrating hard.

"The two guards are missing." Jakey got up and started to pace.

"The only other people who know the Prince was here on the B and F level is—" He pointed his finger first at himself, then at his assistant. "Yaaa!" He leaped into the air, whooping and shouting.

"The warlord," Megey said meekly.

"What?"

"The warlord is gone too."

63

"Smet de Corcoran is gone?" Jakey asked. He fell silent for a brief second, then burst out with a roar of laughter as he danced around happily.

Megey backed away. *Jakey's lost his head,* she thought. *Mad.*

"Good fortune," Jakey said, his eyes filled with happiness. "The warlord took the Prince with him. Takes away our problem."

"But he could hurt the Prince."

"So?" Jakey said with a shrug of his shoulders. "We'll keep quiet and no one will know. In a few weeks, I'll report the warlord's escape. It'll give him enough time to take that brat far away from the Moon castle and us."

"But Jakey—"

"If they go hard on me, they will go hard on you too," Jakey assured her. "You and me will be on the other side of these cell doors."

Megey's reluctant nod brought a smile to Jakey's face.

nineteen

All around them was total blackness, but on the horizon, the brilliant, bright stars shone like someone had gathered a billion sparkling diamonds and thrown them into space. Here and there the stars were arranged in swirling shapes, dazzling clusters, and magnificent, luminous clouds.

Eric was on the deck of the solar ship. Staring out, his imagination formed the stars into different shapes. He saw a dragon, elephants, and warships. His mind created whole armies. He pictured himself leading the army to great victories.

A shudder from the deck brought Eric's attention back to reality. He drifted away from the rail and looked up at the thousand-foot sail that towered above the deck. Three mighty sails carried the ship at light-speed across the solar system. Eric jabbed his arms above his head to feel as much of the wind current as possible. He was experiencing a freedom he had never known before.

Eric looked past the mighty sails with their centers pushed to the limit, and could see planets, stars, and far-off galaxies race across the horizon. Which distant planets were the ports of call where he would disembark?

Now Eric crossed his arms in frustration. In the four days since they had left the moon castle and boarded the ship he had asked Corcoran several times about their destination, Corcoran always said, "It's an adventure and I don't want to spoil the surprise." Today when Eric asked, it was dismissed with an impatient wave of Corcoran's hand. When Eric demanded to know, Corcoran threatened him.

Below deck, Eric shared a cramped cabin with Corcoran. Corcoran spent most of his time below gambling and drinking with the crew. Eric, free, spent his time exploring the ship.

Eric looked up again to the outstretched white sails. This was the first solar sailing ship which he'd ever been on—the first ship he'd ever been on at all, in fact. It was exhilarating. Here on the open deck, Eric felt part of a life force that connected all the stars, universes, and galaxies. The stars seemed to be looking at him, talking to him, and offering, "Come, ride the swift winds to us. See the wonders we possess."

"It's beautiful, isn't it?"

Eric turned around to see an old man standing behind him.

"I was about your age when I stole away on a freighter bound for a Jupiter moon." A smile creased his weathered face. "Most people would say my life traveling through the galaxies was a waste." He now looked down at Eric and pointed to himself. "I, Bart Jones, wouldn't want it any other way. To me, living life has never been tied to a dwelling with a bunch of squalling brats running amok. No, I say give me a firm deck and a star to set my course by and I'm as rich as the Emperor."

At the mention of his father, Eric looked down.

"I can see I've put you in a down spirit; it wasn't my intention."

"No." Eric shook his head, but the sadness stayed.

"I've seen you here on deck, looking up into the heavens. It reminds me of myself when I was a lad," Bart said in a gentle voice. "What do you see?"

Eric looked up, taking in the vastness of space and all its majestic objects. "I see freedom." Eric spread his arms wide. "An adventure."

A sparkle appeared in Bart's eyes and he gave a quick nod. "Freedom."

They both watched a sailor with arms covered in tattoos walk by.

Still watching the tattooed sailor, Bart asked, "Where are you going?"

"I don't know."

"Who's that man you're traveling with?"

"My uncle." It was the lie Corcoran told Eric to say.

The silence of space seemed to surround them. Finally, Bart said, "Your uncle gave us coordinates, but they must be wrong. We can't find anything on the charts at those coordinates other than empty space."

Eric jumped as a booming voice came from behind. "It's an old space station."

Bart and Eric watched Corcoran walk over.

"If there's a station it would be on the space charts. But as I was telling the boy—"

Corcoran cut Bart off. "There'll be a space station attached to a large asteroid. Few know of its location."

"What is the asteroid's name?"

"Vulcury."

The old man burst out laughing. "No such place. It's a fairy-tale that parents use to scare their children at night."

"I'm from Vulcury."

Shaking his head, a mocking smile appeared on Bart's face. "You're a warlord?"

"Warlord Smet de Corcoran."

"Never heard of you," Bart said.

"You've never heard of the Warlord Smet de Corcoran who fought in the fallow wars?" Corcoran asked amazed.

Bart looked down at Eric and brought his fingers a quarter inch apart. "A small skirmish." Then he folded his arms across his chest and asked Corcoran, "Which side were you leading?"

"I led the Wamu," Corcoran said.

"The losing side," Bart said, slipping a wink to Eric. "What happened?"

"The Wamu were not disciplined enough to implement my complex strategies. It was like leading blind men and women in a complex dance."

"Dance? From what I've heard, the Wamu stumbled into battle. A cross-eyed monkey could have beaten them."

"Your information's wrong."

Bart looked out into the stars. "From Vulcury, huh?"

"Vulcury," Corcoran confirmed.

"What's Vulcury?" Eric asked.

"The legends say it's the birth home of Death's son, the Grim Reaper. A world that worships death and the glory it brings."

"Death is a most passionate friend; defeat the enemy and glory will follow. The men and women who survive Vulcury are the most sought-after generals in the whole solar system," Corcoran said.

"A myth."

"Was Nicholas the Invincible, a myth? Or Ishaar the Supreme? What about Capriana the Wicked?"

"All great warlords."

"And von Stemann the Great?"

Finally, a name Eric recognized. "Von Stemann the Great. My great-uncle Victor defeated him," Eric said.

"Your grand-uncle?" Bart stared at Eric.

"Don't let the boy play you for a fool." Corcoran chuckled, but gave Eric a hard look.

Bart eyed Corcoran. "A warlord?"

"I survived Vulcury."

"*Survived?*" Eric asked.

"It's a school, an academy, a place to learn the art of war. Each student must survive five tests, called events. During the event, life is constantly challenged, and death comes to all but a few students."

"And you went through this academy with no problems?" Bart asked.

"I didn't say that. Each student is given one pass—a chance to cheat death during an event. But you must choose *before* the event."

"It's just school," Eric laughed lightly.

"To survive the events on Vulcury is no laughing matter," Corcoran said angrily.

"How did you survive?" the older man asked.

A broad smile appeared on Corcoran's face. "How did I cheat death?" He looked up at the stars above as if they held his memories. "How did I cheat the Grim Reaper when so many fell before his sword? I'm clever, smart in the tactics of war, and understand how to use it all to my advantage." Taking in a deep breath, he continued, "I chose the third event as my pass. I cheated death. It was my only defeat."

"Who could defeat such a *clever and smart* student like you?" Bart taunted.

"A green-eyed redhead," he said disgustedly. "A woman more cunning than the Gods themselves, more ruthless than the most savage predator, and more beautiful than the heavens above."

Bart looked up at the stars with Corcoran and nodded. "A woman can destroy the best of men."

Eric, who had followed Corcoran and Bart's stare, suddenly felt a hole in his chest. He averted his eyes to hide the tears. His mother came to his mind, the most beautiful woman in the universe. *She would never hurt anyone.*

No matter his faults, his mother had always been there with a kind word, a loving smile, and a warm embrace. He closed his eyes and could feel her presence.

"I speak of death and you smile." Eric opened his eyes to see the warlord looking down at him. "I tell you a woman slid her knife in me. I've a good mind to throw you over the rail into space."

Eric's face tightened with anger. Corcoran had disturbed his thoughts of his mother.

"Promise me, Eric. Swear to me. If you ever go to the events, you will take the third as your selection to protect," Corcoran said.

"Why?" Eric asked.

"Your manhood will be tested."

"I promise," Eric said.

"At the last port I saw you talk to Boris," Bart said.

"Boris?"

"Thin man, patch covering his left eye, speaks with a lisp," Bart said, staring hard at Corcoran. "He'd sell his own mother for a drink."

"You're mistaken."

Bart turned his stare on Eric and firmly held Eric's attention as he spoke to Corcoran. "You and Boris were whispering and looking at this boy."

Corcoran stepped in front of Eric. "Your eyes were lying to you, old man." Quickly, he added, "When will the ship be at our stop?"

"We'll be coming to the coordinates you gave us in a solar day and a half," Bart said.

"Very good," Corcoran said.

Corcoran stepped forward and put his arm around Bart. "I have some other questions for you." He led the old sailor away from Eric as he continued to talk.

Eric's mind returned to his mother. The thought of being without her made all the stars less bright.

twenty

"**There's nothing** here," Eric said, looking up at Corcoran.

Eric was left with Corcoran at an old and broken-down station, a desolate structure from the distant past. It had been used to refuel on long space journeys when travel was by propulsion engines.

For more than three hundred years it had floated in space, a hunk of metal attached to a large asteroid that now had little use. Thick dust covered everything.

Corcoran's reaction was different—he was like a child who had arrived home. His smile covered his whole face and he went in and rushed around inspecting everything. Now he sat on the floor, leaning against a wall with his feet up.

"This is no adventure," Eric said stomping his right foot.

Corcoran responded with a blustery laugh.

Suddenly, the space station was bathed in light. Then, they heard a great moan, as if the metal of the facility was being ripped apart. Eric moved to a steel beam several feet away and wrapped his arms around it. *I'll be thrown into cold, black space forever, drifting lifelessly in space.*

Eric was about to shut his eyes in fear, when a strange sight appeared before him. The wall across from him faded and became a window. His eyes opened wide as he watched several people in military uniforms studying him through the glass.

Slowly, Corcoran got up and walked over to the window. He raised his voice. "I must see the commandant."

One man shook his head; another turned to go.

"It's extremely important. I must speak to the commandant." Corcoran turned around and grabbed Eric under the armpits, shoving him toward the window. "The boy. The commandant must see the boy. He is…important."

Staring at Eric hard, the man behind the window searched for something. What, Eric didn't know.

Eric stood to the right of a large desk in an enormous office. On one side of the office there was no visible wall, just wooden bookshelves overstuffed with books of all sizes and colors, one wall hung antique weapons of war. On the far side, the wall had been painted in one large map of the solar system.

Lots of different-colored pins dotted the map. But it was the center of the painting which held Eric's attention. Here the Moon and Earth were depicted—as if they were the beginning of everything.

"I know I wasn't supposed to return," Corcoran said to the man sitting behind the large desk. "It was important, Commandant. Besides, Isuaro's returned."

"Warlord Isuaro von Stemann is back at our request." The commandant made a gesture to the other man standing behind the desk. "He will instruct half of this year's class for the event."

Eric's attention focused on the commandant. He was a rather plain-looking man of average height. Yet his presence dominated the room like a powerful lion. The only sign of age was his short, gray hair. His body was as lean and fit as a star athlete.

Eric shifted his sight to the other man behind the desk. Warlord Isuaro von Stemann was more like Corcoran, tall and powerfully built. Like the commandant, he radiated confidence and power. But while Corcoran stood at attention, Stemann stood carefree, almost arrogantly.

"I've heard of your exploits." Stemann's arrogant look turned to a sneer. "How can you bear to return in such disgrace and dishonor? Your tactics, strategies, and leadership have brought shame to Vulcury. You're no warlord."

"You have it wrong. I—"

Corcoran was cut off by the commandant raising his hand. "We are experts in the ways of war; we can see the truth. Your actions during the fallow wars were ill-conceived and lacked fortitude in execution. How you were able to survive the five events is beyond my calculations."

"He cheated," Stemann said, as if it was a challenge.

"You can't cheat the events or the action within," Corcoran said. "Death is in the events. I got through and earned the title of warlord."

"It's not too late to right the wrong," Stemann said, moving his hand to his sword. "Commandant, it would be an honor, if you would allow me."

The commandant gave a slight shake of his head. "Your sword cannot change the fact he did survive the events. He's stating nothing that is not true and is the law here." Then the commandant gave a sideways look to the warlord beside him. "Even you cannot disregard the laws."

"Let's just say I will bend them for a short time. A very short time." Stemann challenged Corcoran with a look.

"Enough," the commandant said. "The boy. Why is he important?"

Eric was pulled forward. "He must be part of your next class," Corcoran said. "He's an extraordinarily gifted boy."

"We have searched out young boys and girls, selected the most fit and through rigorous testing, selected the very best candidates," the commandant said.

"You missed one," Corcoran said quickly. "I hardly need to tell you we are bound by our pledge to bring a candidate to Vulcruy who shows greatness and to *stay here* until he or she graduates."

The commandant disregarded Corcoran and looked at Eric. "Are you special?"

Special. I'm not special. Father says Charles is the special one. He'll be the next Emperor. Eric looked down and shook his head.

"The boy will fail. He lacks confidence in himself," the commandant said.

Eric's back stiffened and he folded his arms in front of him. "Who are you?"

The man stood up, came around the desk, and stood in front of Eric. He looked down his nose at the boy. "I'm Romulus Victor Gnechko."

"Romulus Victor Gnechko," Eric echoed. The name was a legend. *Could this man be the famous warlord Gnechko?* "Did you fight in the Nidaros struggle for independence?"

The commandant nodded his head, and Eric took a deep breath to calm himself. The exploits of this famous warlord had been taught to him in history classes at the Moon castle.

Gnechko had been hired by a poor planet, a slave to the Zeiteman Confederation. Like Napoleon, Gnechko had devised an aggressive strategy and led the army personally. Because Nidaros had a small, ill-equipped, and demoralized army, everyone bet against Gnechko. In the battle on the plain of Dale, Gnechko routed the mighty confederation, and with the warlord's leadership, the lesser planet became master of the mighty confederations.

"It's an honor to meet you." Eric bowed his head in respect.

The compliment had no effect on the commandant as he asked, "Where did Corcoran find you?"

"At the Moon castle. Down in the—"

74

Corcoran cut in. "It's not important where I found him, but who he is."

"And who are you?" the commandant asked.

Eric pulled his shoulders back and said, "I'm Prince Eric Alexander von Battenburg."

The commandant stiffened. "von Battenburg?" A second later he shook his head. "Lies."

"I am Prince Eric Alexander von Battenburg!"

"False," the commandant said. "I know the Empress; you look nothing like her."

That's what Charles said. I don't have royal blood.

"How do you know the Empress?" Eric asked.

"Once I was a suitor to the princess Alisa Marie von Battenburg."

"Chasing Princess Alisa?" Corcoran chuckled.

Romulus Victor Gnechko's eyes narrowed, and his jaw tightened as his hand moved to his sword. "In my presence, she will be addressed as Empress Alisa Marie von Battenburg." He looked down at Eric. "The Empress is an incredible woman. She is a beautiful, highly intelligent, and passionate woman."

Eric nodded.

"Her only fault: lapse of judgment in a husband."

"My father?"

"A tall and handsome man who claimed to be an officer, but had no battle experience." The commandant cocked his head to the side. "You bear no resemblance to either."

Eric stared up into the eyes of Warlord Romulus Victor Gnechko and stated firmly, "I'm Prince Eric."

"I'm too busy for this charade," the commandant said angrily to Corcoran. "Get out, leave Vulcury, and take this imposter with you."

"My Lord Gnechko." Eric's voice rose, commanding attention. "Have you ever been to the Moon castle?"

"Many times," the commandant said.

"There is a large painting in a hallway."

"The Moon castle has many paintings in many halls."

"This one has a man on a gray horse."

The commandant's eyebrows furrowed together.

"Crushing his enemies," Eric continued. "Carrying his flag upside-down."

"Impossible."

"Describe him," Eric demanded.

"Thick black hair with light-olive skin." Eric could see the commandant noting the same features on Eric. "Gray-blue eyes that had the intensity of a wolf."

"Didn't he have von Battenburg blood running through his veins?"

The commandant slowly moved to his chair and collapsed into it.

"Who?" demanded Stemann. "Who's in the painting?"

The commandant stared hard at Eric. Finally, he answered, "Yes, Prince Eric. Victor had von Battenburg blood."

"Victor the Destroyer," Eric said boldly to Stemann. "The man who killed your father."

"A monster." Stemann's eyes flashed.

"Warlord Harada von Stemann was the first to fall to my great ancestor." Eric turned to Gnechko. "If Harada von Stemann is your measure of Vulcury's graduates, then you have a poor scale." Eric stood tall. "Yes, by your standards I am special."

"You dare—" Stemann lashed out.

But Eric exploded, cutting him off, "My great-uncle, Prince Victor the Destroyer, was only eighteen and untrained. But history clearly states who won their battle. He gave Warlord von Stemann his just reward: death."

Stemann once again reached for his sword. "If you were a man—"

Eric's insolent stare caused Stemann to pull out his sword and march toward the young prince.

Eric stood his ground, but Corcoran backed away.

"Hold yourself!" the commandant ordered. "Prince Eric speaks the truth." He looked at Stemann, red with anger. "You're a trained warlord of Vulcury. Control your anger."

Stemann bowed his apology to Gnechko, then turned to regard the prince. "He's no orphan."

"Orphan?" Eric looked past Stemann to the commandant.

The commandant nodded his head firmly. "All warlords from Vulcry begin as orphans."

"Why?"

"On the street, the orphan learns how to survive. Never giving up is an important trait." The commandant leaned forward, his expression uneasy. "The truth is very few survive the events. If an orphan is killed, no one cares."

"The fact remains he is a prince, not an orphan," Stemann said.

Eric walked up to Stemann. "You weren't an orphan."

"No. We do allow children who have the blood of great warlords to enter. They get no special treatment. Death is almost certain," the commandant said.

"I have royal blood: Victor's blood."

Stemann laughed. "There is nothing in the blood. The von Battenburg line is dying. Within two decades the Moon Empire will be no more. The Earth, for the second time in its long history, will be a subject planet to another galaxy."

"Never!" Eric said defiantly.

twenty-one

"**Isuaro is** right." The commandant got out of his chair and walked to the far wall with the painted map on it. He spread his arms to indicate the whole painting. "At one time the Moon Empire encompassed the whole solar system. Earth's history had not known such a vast empire since Genghis Khan. Elizabeth and her children were not only gifted generals but outstanding administrators. The empire flourished. But the latest generations are not so gifted."

Eric watched Commandant Gnechko bring his hands closer together. "For a hundred years the Moon Empire has been steadily shrinking. Now it is a quarter of its once greatness. If it continues to shrink, soon the empire will cease to exist." He turned and looked at Eric. "For the second time in history, the Moon and Earth will be defeated and under the rule of another planet."

"No," Eric said. "My father will stop it."

"With such weak leadership, it's only a matter of time before the Moon Empire is gone."

"It can't happen." Eric thought of his family.

Stemann laughed as if Eric had told the best joke ever. "It will. Soon your family will grovel, begging for their lives. The Moon Empire needs another Victor."

"My father—" Eric started.

"—is no Victor," the commandant said.

"But," Corcoran stepped forward. "If Eric was to become a warlord, he could save his family."

Stemann's head flew back and his roar of laughter consumed the room. "This pampered prince? This runt of a boy who doesn't even consider himself special?"

Eric looked at Commandant Gnechko, whose broad smile told him he agreed.

They don't think I can do it. They believe the same as Charles and Father: I'm not special. A beautiful woman came to his mind. *Mother said I'm special. She believes in me.* "I will become a warlord."

This brought a new fit of laughter from Stemann and the commandant shook his head.

"He can," Corcoran pleaded.

"Prince Eric. You will fail," the commandant said. "Do you want to die?"

I don't want to die. Eric shook his head.

"There is a little intelligence in him," Stemann said.

"I won't die. I will become a warlord," Eric said firmly.

"You will join the events?" The commandant asked.

Eric's thoughts came fast, making him dizzy. "I'll have to ask my father and mother first," Eric said.

Stemann looked at Eric. "Worthless."

Commandant Gnechko leaned forward, staring into Eric's eyes. "Eric, to survive the events you must be like the other orphans. You must forget your parents. Act as if they never existed."

Eric felt a chill run over his body as a sadness filled him. His eyes moistened and a tear made its way down his face. He looked at the map on the wall and his eyes fixed on the Moon. *If I don't become a warlord, they'll all die.* His heart was heavy as he forced himself to turn around and lift his face to the commandant. "I will become a warlord," he repeated.

"Let the prince come on the next event," Stemann said. "Cannon fodder for my students."

Eric wiped a tear from his face. "I will be your best student," he said to the commandant.

"Would you take on another student?" Gnechko asked Stemann.

"No," Stemann said reluctantly. "I would love to see this *useless* prince from a dying empire fall, never to rise. But I have too many students already."

"Warlord Tangen Santos will decline also. I've already given him an extra student." The commandant turned and walked back to his desk. "You will not be trained."

"I will lead him through the events," Corcoran said.

"It must be a warlord who is trained as an instructor," the commandant said. "Only through correct mentoring can a student hope to survive the events."

In exasperation, Corcoran ran his hands through his hair, making it stand on end. "There must be another."

"The only warlord-instructor other than myself would be Shinichi Markov."

"Is he still alive?" Stemann asked. "He was an instructor of events when I was studying here."

"He's perfect," Corcoran said. "I'll go speak with him."

"The students leave tomorrow morning on the first event," the commandant said.

"No worries," Corcoran said confidently.

twenty-two

"**I'll do** the talking," Corcoran said, walking quickly. His large strides made Eric run to keep up. "He's old and set in his ways."

It really is a school. Eric passed several large rooms filled with young children who were sitting at desks, listening to a teacher. He briefly leaned into a gymnasium and saw a group of students exercising. There was even a cafeteria where a few students ate at long tables.

Everyone was in uniform. The teachers wore black, and the students were in different colors based on age, Corcoran told him. The youngest, who seemed to be about six years old, were in white; eight-year-olds wore yellow, and the students his age were in orange. Eric noticed only a handful of purple uniforms and two brown on older students.

Corcoran and Eric left the main buildings. Eric saw dorms, then apartments, before coming upon private, walled-off compounds.

"Hurry. There's little time." Corcoran increased his pace and Eric began to fall behind. "He must take you."

"If he doesn't?"

"I won't have a place to hide...er, stay," Corcoran said anxiously. "I mean, you won't become a warlord and help your family."

Eric was twenty feet back when Corcoran made a sharp turn, going into a compound. Legs aching, breathing hard, Eric pushed himself to catch up. Hurriedly he turned the corner and saw Corcoran turn another corner farther up, an entrance. Gritting his teeth, Eric pushed harder following Corcoran into a temple-like building.

Past the next turn, Eric jerked up hard, trying to stop. He rammed into Corcoran—like hitting a brick wall. The impact spun Eric around, sending him past Corcoran and falling to the ground.

Every part of Eric's body sent urgent signals of pain. He rolled to his hands and knees, trying desperately to stop some of the pain. Then, he froze like Corcoran, all pain forgotten.

Help! Eric's mind screamed. Wide-eyed, Eric stared at a giant black king cobra. Like a thin branch in a strong wind, the snake's body swayed back and forth, coming toward Eric. The snake's black eyes looked directly into his, but Eric's eyes were fixed on the two enormous white fangs and the dancing pink forked tongue.

"Do as I say or die," Eric heard a soothing voice say.

"Okay," Eric said without moving his lips.

"When I clap my hands you must leap back," the soothing voice continued. "If you're not quick enough, you will feel the sharp fangs of Khan here."

"Okay." Eric panted with anxiety, his adrenaline-filled body starting to shake.

"Khan, it's me you want," the strange, soothing voice said. "To feast your sharp fangs and send your deadly poison to take my life."

Eric felt the figure come closer, wondered who he was, but his eyes were still fixed on the swaying cobra and the white fangs.

A booming clap made Eric jump. He pushed his hands hard against the floor, sending him backward. Then he used his legs to scramble back faster, but his left foot slipped and he went down again.

Khan's head launched forward, stretching the black, scaly body to sink his fangs into Eric.

Eric screamed as the cobra widened his mouth.

Like a deadly mongoose, a hand darted out from a black-robed figure and grabbed the cobra's spread hood. The hand pulled back. But the cobra's body twisted, eyes still fixed on Eric. Khan was fast, whipping his body hard, forcing the hand to let go. Khan, suddenly free, slithered swiftly after Eric.

I'm going to die, Eric's thoughts screamed as Khan hurdled his powerful body into the air, mouth open, straining to reach Eric.

A surge of energy filled Eric's body. *I don't want to die*. He darted left, avoiding Khan's snapping jaws. Then he ducked his body away from Khan, allowing the black-robed figure between them. Eric was too slow and Khan struck out, fangs extended toward Eric's bare leg.

A thin, silver streak arced through the air, attacking Khan.

Eric's eyes followed Khan's head as it flew through the air. The cobra's head landed on his lap. Eric's body tightened as Khan's eyes gazed up into his, life still flowing in the severed head. He scrambled back, throwing his body in several directions, trying desperately to throw Khan's head off him.

Thin fingers extended from the black robe. A hand picked up the cobra's head and from within the robe, Eric heard a deep voice. "Does it scare you?"

"No, not at all," Corcoran said. Eric whipped his head around to see him scrambling from the top of a table at the far side of the room.

"Were you frightened?" the man asked Eric.

"Yes," said Eric.

"To conquer fear you must feel it and understand it first."

"Warlord Markov. I urgently need to talk to you," Corcoran said as he stepped around the still-twitching body of the cobra. Then, as an afterthought, he said, "Eric, this is Warlord Shinichi Markov."

Eric fought hard to control his shaking body and bowed. "An honor to meet you, Warlord Shinichi Markov."

"Please, call me 'Shinichi'.

Shinichi stood with the cobra's head in one hand and a samurai sword, slightly turned from them, in the other. "I'm very busy."

"I have a student for you," Corcoran said.

"I no longer teach."

"He is an exceptional student."

"All who come here are exceptional students," Shinichi said. "I will not take another to his death."

"You must," Eric said.

Shinichi stopped and raised the severed head of Khan. "I have taken students through three series of events," Shinichi said. "I have never brought one through. Khan has joined them."

"Few survive the events regardless of instructor," Corcoran said.

"Not one student survived," Shinichi said.

"I'll be different," Eric said.

"What makes you so special?"

Eric walked over to stand in front of Warlord Markov. He looked at the ground. "I don't know if I'm special, but I have the blood of Victor the Destroyer in me."

The robed figure stiffened, leaned forward, and looked deep into Eric's face. "You're not one of his children!"

"Victor had none," Eric said.

To Eric's surprise, the warlord suddenly looked sad. "Elitsa had three," he whispered.

"Who's Elitsa?" Eric asked.

The hooded figure stared off into the distance for a second, then shook his head.

"I have to become a warlord."

Shinichi opened a straw basket and added Khan's head to the others that were revealed inside. He pulled out a white, square cloth, wiped his sword, and put it away. He lifted his hands and threw the black hood back. "Come with me."

Eric looked up into a lean face with high cheekbones and doe-shaped eyes.

twenty-three

Eric and Corcoran followed Shinichi past a hut and into a Japanese garden. Eric recognized it from a picture he'd seen in his history book. Gray pebbles covered the ground, different-sized boulders were scattered about, and meticulously trimmed trees were placed throughout. A red bridge in the center of the garden arched gracefully over a small, clear pond.

They followed Shinichi through the garden and over the bridge. Eric looked over its rail to see several orange koi fish swimming lazily about.

Shinichi approached a small wooden Japanese-style temple. "Take off your shoes."

After removing their shoes, Eric and Corcoran entered the temple.

Shinichi stopped beside a low table. When Eric stopped beside him he asked, "Do you know this game?"

Eric looked down at the table and noticed there were lines carved into its surface. The lines intersected, forming squares. On top of the corners of some of the squares were white or black thin, round stones. Eric shook his head.

"It's called 'Go'. It's a game of strategy played in Japan and China centuries ago." He motioned for Eric and Corcoran to sit at another table that was set with silverware.

After Corcoran and Eric seated themselves, Shinichi poured hot water into a teapot. As the warlord set out cups, Eric studied him, thinking he'd encountered figures like him before in his history books. "Are you a druid?" Eric asked.

"Yes, in a way." Shinichi poured tea into the three cups on the table and sat down. "Like a druid, I'm knowledgeable in many areas. Druids used their knowledge to teach and guide others."

Corcoran cleared his throat. "Eric wants to be a warlord. But the commandant said you must be the instructor."

Shinichi took a sip of his tea, then set his gaze upon Eric. "Why do you want to be a warlord?"

Eric looked up into Shinichi's eyes, hoping he would understand. "To protect my family."

"Your family—the von Battenburgs?"

"Yes. I must save the Moon Empire."

Shinichi looked down and shook his head.

Eric leaned forward. "I have to."

"We cannot make you into a miracle worker. Do you know what Vulcury is?"

"A school."

"Yes, in simple terms."

Eric took a drink from his teacup. His body tightened. *It's awful.* He returned the bitter green liquid to the table and nudged it away.

Shinichi pushed the tea closer to Eric. "In the century past, a place like Vulcury would be called a war college, a place to study the discipline of war. Over and over, the students would be tested and disciplined. This is critical because, after graduation, the students would lead men and women into battle. Without training the outcome was often death."

Shinichi stopped for a sip of tea, then continued. "For the past two hundred years, every great battle has had one of our students leading one side, or both."

"Not true."

"Don't argue," Corcoran said.

"My great-uncle never came here."

Shinichi looked off into the distance and after a few silent seconds said serenely, "No. Prince Victor von Battenburg never came here. The destroyer was never a student at this academy. But Victor was an anomaly; a gifted person like Victor comes once every thousand years. A man like Victor needs no training." He looked down at Eric. "You are not Victor."

"I want to be." All his life, this had been Eric's dream. To change from the small, heavy, boy to the tall and powerful man who leads armies. *I must become Victor.*

"Why does Vulcury exist?" Shinichi asked him.

Eric shrugged his shoulders.

"Several centuries ago, the human race began to expand through the solar system. In many ways, this was very bad."

Shinichi took a deep breath, released it slowly, and stared into his teacup as if he could read man's history in the tea leaves. He continued, "There are certain characteristics that make mankind special. One is the need to be challenged and grow. Like a determined locust, humans spread quickly from planet to planet. The technology had been developed to make any planet habitable for men and women. Soon there were trillions of humans inhabiting hundreds of planets, moons and asteroids."

Shinichi peered at Eric as if to see whether any of this was sinking in. "There is another characteristic of the human race which isn't so noble: the need to continually fight, conquer, and destroy. Humans must take away what another has. If another has more a human can't be at peace until he possesses it."

Shinichi paused to pour himself more tea. "Because of this fact, war is a constant event. Death, destruction, and mayhem are parts of our solar system. It was from Earth that a man and woman came to travel throughout the distant planets. Both of their families had a long history of war. For several generations, their families had studied at Earth's great war colleges like West Point, Sandhurst, and the Prussian Military Academy. Both were experienced veterans of numerous battles and conflicts. They left Earth set on making their fortune leading armies."

Shinichi stopped to take another sip of tea. To Eric's frustration, he pushed Eric's teacup closer until Eric finally took a drink. Eric swallowed it with difficulty—it tasted worse than before.

"The tea's good for you," Shinichi said.

Taking a deep breath Eric finished the tea, disregarding the rebellion in his stomach.

The warlord looked at him, smiled, and nodded.

The smile made Eric feel good. He thought back to his days at the Moon castle. *Shinichi is smiling proudly just like Father did that one time my instructor praised my work.*

"Good. You can follow instructions even if you don't want to," Shinichi said.

Eric suddenly realized that he'd been tested. He nodded, smiled back, and was rewarded with the warlord continuing.

"Their names were general Taylor Kitsch Ingram and General Nicole Marie Aragon. Within a short time, after leaving earth, both Ingram and Aragon were famous, revered and wealthy. Because of their many victories, they were both given the title of warlord."

Shinichi poured more green tea into Eric's cup. "How do you think they felt?"

The great painting of Victor the Destroyer came to Eric's mind—the pride he showed as he defeated his foes. Eric sat up straight, smiling. "They felt awesome."

"No... Horrified."

Eric's eyebrows came together in confusion. "Horrified? Why? They won. Everyone wants to win."

"In their great victories, they witnessed tragedies on every battlefield. War, for the past several centuries, was again savage, brutal, and cruel as a caveman beating his victim with a club." Shinichi sighed heavily. "The art of war, the warlords found, had been lost to the outer worlds. Strategy, planning, and execution are important to defeating an enemy in battle. When applied correctly, these aspects allow a warlord to quickly overcome the enemy and save many lives."

"Because the art of war was lost, armies were thrown at one another like the battles in World War I. The result is a massive killing field where the winner is the last one standing. In this method of fighting, it is common for whole armies to be destroyed, for millions to die on the field of battle."

"To warlords Ingram and Aragon, this wasn't war. It was butchery. With their wealth, they established this academy to bring back the art of war. Deep in man's DNA is the need to fight, attack, and wage war. This will never stop. But it doesn't have to be barbaric. Not if its participants are trained correctly."

Eric nodded his head in understanding.

"To obtain victory," Shinichi concluded, "it's not necessary to kill needlessly. Except for Victor the Destroyer, every great warlord since Ingram and Aragon has come from this academy."

Eric thought of what Shinichi was telling him. This academy had produced, except for his great-uncle, every victor in every war for three hundred years. Then, finally, the question came. "How are the warlords trained?"

Shinichi gathered the tea set and put it aside. He collected his thoughts, folded his hands together and after studying Eric for a second started. "There is constant academic study and training of the body. But to become a warlord, you must experience the harsh realities of life through constant conflict, battles, and leadership decisions. This experience is obtained from living through five events. Each event is designed to test the student to the fullest. As you've no doubt already been told, death is common. Only a few have the courage, intelligence, and discipline to survive the constant trials. Every day is a test of their will, drive, and survival skills."

"Where are the events held?"

"On the most savage planet in history...Earth," Shinichi said.

"Earth? My father and mother are the Emperor and Empress of the Moon Empire. This includes Earth. I've never heard of these events."

"Our students go back into Earth's history."

Eric shook his head, trying to understand. "Earth's history?"

"There is no other world whose history is filled with such conflict, pain, and suffering—the ingredients to build character in an individual destined to lead men and women in battle."

Shinichi looked at Eric. "If you can survive the events—if you can live through the tests—you will be a great leader."

twenty-four

The great portrait came flooding back to Eric's mind. His mind redrew the painting. It wasn't his great-uncle on the great horse, but himself. He glanced at Corcoran first, who looked like he was waiting with baited breath, then at Shinichi. "I will join this academy. I will become a great warlord."

The man across from him shook his head. "You must survive to become a great warlord. But probability says you will die during an event."

"When I'm in trouble," Eric said, "will the other students help?"

Shinichi sighed deeply. "No one will help you. The other students will strive to quicken you to your death. They know it is best to take you out as soon as possible. They know that if you are not killed, you may kill them in the future."

Disregarding Eric, Shinichi got up and moved to the 'Go' game. He picked up a white stone and stood, pondering where to place it.

"May I ask a question?" Eric ventured to ask.

"Yes." Shinichi continued to study the 'Go' table.

"I was told there is one pass on an event. What does it mean?"

"For one event, you may be killed physically during the event, but you will not truly die." He looked at Eric. "Each event starts and ends at random—it may be for one month, or for over a year. The only constant is that after every event, fewer students return than began."

Corcoran leaned forward. "Can I tell the commandant you will be the prince's instructor?"

Shinichi regarded Corcoran and shook his head slightly. "Didn't you understand I have never had a student survive the events?"

Eric snapped to attention. "I will be your first. What must I do?"

Shinichi looked off, deep in thought. *"What must I do?* He asked me the same questions. I failed him." His head and voice both dropped. "He died too soon. And with him went all our hopes and dreams."

"What was that?" Eric asked, puzzled.

Shinichi looked into Eric's eyes. "I pray the gods give me strength to guide you to fulfill his hopes and dreams."

"I swear I will," Eric said returning his stare, still wondering who the warlord was talking about. *Why do adults always leave out important information?* "Guide me."

Eric watched Shinichi put down the white stone in a corner. It and several other stones the same color surrounded the black stones.

"You must learn 'Go'."

twenty-five

Shinichi and Eric had entered a large chamber where two large groups of children sat. Impatiently, everyone turned to look at them.

"We're late," Shinichi whispered.

A man got up and marched toward them, followed by another man who walked slightly behind him.

"It's good to see you, Shinichi," the first man said.

Shinichi bowed. "Tangen Santos, you're a welcome sight."

Eric looked at Warlord Tangen Santos. He didn't look like a warlord to Eric. *He looks like a…*a word finally came to mind. *Teacher.* Standing at average height, Tangen was thin, pale-complexioned, with glasses resting halfway down his nose.

The man who walked with Santos was Eric's idea of a warlord. Stemann was tall with a strong, square chin. His long, brown hair was pulled back into a tight ponytail. His long strides brought him beside Santos.

Eric wasn't surprised by the cold look he received from Stemann, and he returned the look as best he could. The sudden expression of anger on Stemann's face made Eric smile.

"You're late," Stemann growled at Shinichi.

Shinichi bowed. "I apologize. I wasn't planning to come to the event today."

"A mistake. He's not worth your time," Stemann said.

"Yes, he won't last long," Shinichi agreed.

Eric stiffened. *Won't last long? What?*

Stemann's eyes fell upon Eric and he nodded in agreement.

"I was bored. This gives me something to do." Shinichi turned to Eric and winked. "For a little while anyway."

"Shall we start?" Tangen asked.

"Yes," Shinichi said.

Tangen and Stemann walked away.

Eric watched them go, then looked around the chamber. There were a hundred boys and girls his age standing beside large, glimmering poles. All looked at him. *Why are they staring at me?* Eric smiled and gave a little wave. None of the stares changed. *They don't like me.* He stepped back, closer to Shinichi.

"Move over to the pole on your right," Shinichi directed Eric.

Eric moved to the right and came to a metal pole that had lights moving throughout it as if was alive.

"Place your right hand on the pole. Do not let go!"

Eric placed his right hand on the pole and felt the smooth, shiny, vibrating metal.

"Do not let go," Shinichi repeated before walking toward another pole across the room.

The chamber's thick door closed with a bang that made Eric jump. Almost immediately, the pole under his hand began vibrating harder. With the passing of each second, the vibration increased until it became audible—a horrible screech. It pierced him, agitating his body. His body tensed to protect itself, and Eric started to move his hands to protect his ears, but suddenly he remembered Shinichi's warning.

Eric's mind was pulled away by a sudden physical coldness. It consumed his body like thousands of swords continuously being stabbed into his body until he completely forgot the unbearable screeching.

Eric's eyes sprang open to look for help. But he was surrounded by total blackness, like a black hole.

His senses rebelled. Eric screamed, giving voice to the horror and pain he was feeling.

twenty-six

"Why are you screaming?" a tall girl asked.

"It was scary and painful!" Eric said, his body still shaking.

Eric found himself on hard, cold, dirt with his right hand extended. He looked up; the tall girl was looking down at him. A look of disgust was clearly spread across her face as she chewed her lip.

Eric looked around. All the students were staring at him. *They're looking at me with disgust. Like I don't belong. Charles said I didn't belong at the Moon castle. Their eyes are telling me I don't belong here, either.*

The tall girl rolled her eyes and moved away. *Who is she?* Eric wondered.

Slowly his body was heating up and the pain receding.

It was painful, the crossing over to the event. What happened? Eric rolled over in the opposite direction to find Shinichi standing over him.

"Did I forget to mention to you the black, pain, and numbing cold of the cross-over?" Shinichi asked.

Eric nodded.

"Did I also forget to mention that if you had taken your hand off the pole you would have died?"

Eric's eyes widened.

"Get up; the others are already leaving."

Eric looked at the other students. Most had indeed started walking away, but several, including the tall girl, tossed back looks of anger. *I'm an outcast, just like I was at the castle.* His father's word haunted him. *Why can't you be more like Charles?*

"Why isn't anyone else affected?" Eric asked as he fought to get to his feet.

"They've been practicing the cross-over for several months." Shinichi brought a pack forward. "Here, put this on and start following the others."

"Wait. I have to rest."

Shinichi shrugged his shoulders and walked off.

After several minutes of silence, Eric looked around him and suddenly realized he was alone. The other students, their instructors, and Shinichi were already a hundred yards away.

It was then Eric noticed his clothes had changed. He no longer wore an orange uniform. His pants and shoes were gone, replaced by brown leather leggings and moccasins. His shirt and vest were made of deer skin.

Eric leaned over, grabbed the pack, and pulled up. He grunted. *It's so heavy. Shinichi must have given me the wrong pack; this must be his.* Fighting the weight of the pack, he finally got it over his shoulders. Then he moved out to follow the others.

twenty-seven

Eric looked to his left, then to his right. He was in open country, flat land as far as he could see. Although there were a few tall oak trees scattered about, it was the vast sea of brown, dry, knee-high grass that held his attention. He looked up at the clear blue sky and saw no clouds. *It's amazing.* It brought a happiness to Eric as he continued to gaze around at the beauty of nature.

He checked ahead and realized he'd fallen further behind the moving group. Eric wanted to quicken his pace, but the pack was so heavy. The heat of the noon sun tortured him with every step he took.

After an hour, Eric's body was covered in sweat. His mouth was dry like a desert. He wanted to throw off the heavy pack and take off his vest.

For the next hour, Eric was in constant pain. His shoulders ached and his legs fought him every step. *I shouldn't be here. I should be in the cool Moon castle.* He thought of how easy it had been to call a servant and be brought a tall, cold, delicious drink.

By the third hour, Eric cursed himself. *I'm so stupid to have helped Corcoran. I should have stayed in the dungeon. Mother would have gotten Father to release me.*

Time passed and Eric, head down, trudged on. His mind was blank except for the labored thought of making the next step.

His head slowly came up as he heard noise ahead. He saw the students and instructors standing in a river.

Eric's legs started moving faster as if the water was a magnet pulling him hard to it. He panted and his tongue was already out at the thought of getting the refreshing water. He pushed through the students, knocking over the tall girl, and fell flat into the water.

Ahh, this is awesome, Eric thought as the cool water surround his body. His skin was happy, but his insides suddenly shouted, *I want some too*. He lifted his head partially out of the water and opened his mouth. Water rushed in.

He relaxed and let the wonderful feeling invade his body. Eric froze; someone had grabbed his head and was forcing it under the water. *Someone is trying to kill me. Help!* Eric fought desperately to get his head up, but the pressure increased. Eric's lungs demanded air; he thrust up with all his might.

His head came to the surface and he gasped for air. But he got none as he head was pushed back under the water.

Eric fought with all his might, but the strong hands were keeping him down. *I'm going to die*. Abruptly, the pressure on his head vanished and his body reacted, pushing out of the water. His mouth opened, taking in great gulps of air.

"Karro, the event doesn't start until we get to the village; control yourself," Santos said.

Through water streaming down his face, Eric saw the same tall girl. *Why did she try to hurt me?* Never had he seen such hate in a face.

Finally, Karro looked away and Eric let out a sigh of relief. She picked up a pack, placed it on her back, then turned abruptly to look at Eric. Her eyes blazed as she chewed on her inner lip. She raised her index finger on her left hand and slid it across her throat.

Eric took a step back, understanding the message.

Several students smiled. *They think it's funny. Me dying. The others who are looking don't care.*

The students started walking again.

Eric scooped up several quick handfuls of water to drink while he walked out of the river to follow.

It didn't take long for Eric to fall behind. The pack was too heavy, and his legs refused to move any faster.

Eric watched a boy stop a hundred yards ahead, turn around, and look at him. To Eric's surprise, he stood still and waited.

"You have a problem keeping up?" the boy asked.

"Shinichi gave me the wrong pack," Eric said.

The boy extended his right hand. "I'm Sami Khan. Who are you?"

Eric shook Sami's hand but hesitated. *Shinichi said not to tell anyone I'm a Prince.*

"Don't you know your name?"

"I'm Eric…Eric Alexander."

"Eric, I can help you."

"Really?" Eric stopped. Sami was a thin boy, with lots of black hair and a broad smile with thin lips. "It so nice of you." He began to take off his pack.

"How much money do you have?"

"Money?" Eric shook his head. "I don't have any."

"No money, no help."

They walked in silence for a while before Eric asked, "What's wrong with that girl, Karro? She almost killed me."

"To start with you're a boy, a male. Amazons hate males. You should never push an amazon into the water and expect to live," Sami said.

"I didn't mean to."

"She doesn't care." Sami eyed Eric for a few seconds. "Is there anything in your pack that I can sell after Karro kills you?"

Eric's eyes widened. "Kills me!"

The silence returned and soon Sami shrugged, leaving Eric to fall further behind.

twenty-eight

The sky turned dark when Eric climbed over a ridge. Breathing hard, he stopped and looked out. Two miles ahead, beside a small creek, was a village. In the distance, he could see the students and instructors walking into it.

It was over an hour later, and the stars were shining brightly above, when Eric finally stumbled into the village. Arms hanging limply at his sides, shoulders slumped, and head hanging down, he staggered on. Two women in knee-length buckskin skirts passed Eric without looking at him.

Where's Shinichi? He has to send me back to Vulcury.

He stopped at a large clearing within the mass of teepees and looked. The village was filled with people moving around doing various chores. A young man was walking in Eric's direction. Eric grabbed his arm and pulled him to a stop. "Where's Warlord Shinichi Markov?"

The young warrior looked at Eric's hand holding him back, and his face reddened. He jerked free. Then, with surprising quickness, he pushed Eric, sending him to the ground.

Eric lay on the ground. He could feel his eyes moistening and a tear run down his cheek.

"That's not a very dignified position for a future warlord." Shinichi walked up to Eric.

"I was wrong. I don't want to be a warlord. I just want to go home…I want to see my family. I want my mother." The thought of his mother made more tears run down his dirt-stained face.

"How quickly you have forgotten your purpose. Do you no longer care about your family?"

"But—"

"You, Eric, may be their sole hope—regardless, you need to understand. There's only two ways to leave an event—when it ends or when you die." Shinichi reached down and helped Eric up. "Every day on an event is hard. It must be to build the character of a great warlord."

Eric nodded, feeling another tear slide down his cheek. Shinichi walked away. Eric followed.

In the center of the village burned several fires. Eric realized he was hungry. As quickly as his feet would move, he went to the cooking pots. All seemed to be abandoned but one, which was still over the fire, and the aroma of cooked food pulled at him.

Eric walked to the pot and stood by it. He did not recognize the food, or its aroma, but at the moment his stomach didn't care. He looked at the woman stirring the pot. "Please give me some."

The woman ignored him.

Eric moved in front of her. With animated signs and motions, he mimed eating. Then, as the imaginary food went down to his stomach, he rubbed his stomach in a circular motion and smiled broadly.

The woman stirred the pot.

"She won't give you any food," Shinichi said.

Eric looked up from his knees where he'd been begging. "Doesn't she understand I'm hungry?"

"I can assure you she is quite intelligent," Shinichi said.

"Why won't she give me any food?"

"She's cooking for the warriors on guard. If they come back and there isn't enough food, she will be disciplined," Shinichi said.

Looking up into the face of the woman Eric resigned himself, got up, and walked away.

Shinichi followed him. "I can tell you Shoshone women are excellent cooks. Tonight, they truly outdid themselves with succulent deer meat and wild turnips." Suddenly, Shinichi burped loudly. "I did help myself to several extra servings."

"I'm tired. Where's my bed?" demanded Eric.

"My lord." Shinichi bowed mockingly to Eric's demand. "There's no accommodations to meet your high standards. Therefore, you shall have none."

"What?"

"You must be present when the beds are assigned. You were not here, so you have none."

"Where do I sleep?"

"You are asking me something I can't answer. You won't be allowed in any teepee," Shinichi said. "I myself was barely able to secure a place for myself." With this said, Shinichi left Eric standing alone.

twenty-nine

Emperor Archibald slumped in his throne. *Where are you, Eric?* Suddenly, unable to control his emotions any longer, he leaped off it. "Eric, where are you?" he screamed. When the silence returned to the empty room, he dropped his head and collapsed back onto the throne.

It had been ten days since he'd ordered his son to be taken to the dungeon. *Eric needed discipline, he had to grow up, start—"* His thoughts died. *Why couldn't you be more like Charles?*

The Empress' words came to him as if lashing him, tormenting him. *Charles is Charles. Eric is Eric. Do not judge one's action by the other.* He rubbed his temples in the hope of releasing the tension. *Was she right?*

Suddenly, his back stiffened. *No. We are royalty. We must set an example. Weakness couldn't be tolerated. Eric must learn.*

Why won't Alisa understand? She still confined herself to her suite of rooms, and every hour on the hour she sent out a handmaiden to ask if Eric had been found.

"She is distraught, frantic, depressed. The Empress has cried until there are no more tears," the last handmaiden had told him.

Alisa bars me from her room. She only allows Charles and George. She holds onto them like they're ghosts and if she releases them they will fade into nothingness.

"My lord Archibald."

"I told you I was not to be disturbed!" the Emperor shouted as his jaw tightened.

"News of your son, Prince Eric," the Chancellor said meekly. A man the Emperor had never seen before stood at his side.

"What?" Archibald leapt up once more. "You've found Eric. Come, we must tell the Empress at once."

"No...No, he's not found," the Chancellor stuttered. "This officer has something for you."

The officer came to attention. "Lieutenant Evens, Outer World Army, third division. I have received a message for the Emperor." He extended the envelope toward the Emperor.

Archibald yanked it away and ripped it open. He stared down into perfectly formed penmanship.

Cousin, I write you to tell you your future. To tell you about the destruction of what was the most powerful empire in history, the Moon Empire. I, Lord Darko Sumonja, will destroy the Moon Empire and the von Battenburg Dynasty. My army is attacking your outer planets. Soon they will be under my control.

The Emperor tightened his grip on the paper.

You will disregard my declaration as that of a madman. As proof, I will send the body of your son. Prince Eric will be the first to die. I will parade his body, so you will know I speak from a position of power. My sister Zemfira and my brother Madhu will whip my armies into a blood lust and take away all your subject planets. You and the Empress will face me not as royalty, but as my slaves. Your execution will not be swift.

Enjoy the short time you have left.

"'The future Emperor Darko Sumonja,'" the Emperor spat out. He looked at his Chancellor, his body shaking in anger. "What is this rubbish?"

"My lord, I believe it's important," the Chancellor said meekly.

The Emperor turned on Evens. "Where did you get this? These lies." He threw the papers at the officer.

"Lord General Molender brought the envelope with him when he was returned."

"Returned?"

"He was defeated on Vannum. He returned with the message while the rest of his army was destroyed."

"So, this message means nothing?" the Emperor asked, dismissing it with a wave.

"My Lord," the officer shuddered. "A whole army was slaughtered and Vannum taken. It means everything."

"I have other armies and Vannum is a minor planet," the Emperor said.

Evens' face turned red and his neck muscles bulged. He took a deep breath and released it slowly. "Many soldiers died for this *minor* planet." Before the Emperor could respond, Evens snapped to attention. "May I be dismissed? I must return to my men."

"Go," the Emperor ordered. He looked at the Chancellor and pointed to the paper on the floor. "Never, ever, bring rubbish like this to me again."

The Chancellor bowed his head. "Another matter, my Lord. The Empress has instructed me to cancel her birthday celebration."

"Cancel the party?" the Emperor asked. "Why?"

"The Empress says she cannot celebrate without Eric."

Emperor Archibald wagged his finger at his Chancellor. "This is all for nothing. I tell you Eric is probably laughing right now. He has hidden himself in one of the far bedrooms and is sleeping on a luxurious bed and eating cakes and pastries."

"Of course, my Lord. Eric is a foolish child." Seeing the Emperor nod in agreement. The Chancellor stated. "Eric should be more like Charles, the future Emperor."

"Precisely," the Emperor said. "And we *must* organize a grand birthday party for the Empress. A party so majestic, magnificent and glorious Eric will have to leave his hiding place and join the celebration."

thirty

The shadows caused by the sunrise were receding when Eric opened his eyes. The night before, he had walked behind two teepees, leaned over, and collapsed. That was when he felt the cold night. He curled up as best he could and fell asleep on the hard dirt.

He could feel a cool morning breeze, but he now felt comfortably warm. Eric noticed a brown arm surrounding him. He shifted and turned around to look into a woman's face. She released her arm as a concerned look filled her face. Quickly she moved away and stood up, keeping her eyes cast down.

"Thank you for helping me," Eric said, getting up as well.

When she didn't respond, Eric examined her. The young woman had thick, black hair parted down the center, golden skin, and a slender build. He looked into her large, golden eyes and oval face and smiled.

Eric noticed her clothes were old, with many rips and tears. She wore no moccasins on her feet.

Not knowing what to do, he reached down for his pack. Her body abruptly hit his. Eric looked up.

Stemann stood over both of them. "Don't help him," he shouted at the woman.

The woman's face turned white with fear.

Eric's hands balled into fists and he stepped forward.

"Ah, Eric, there you are."

Eric, the woman, and Stemann turned to see Shinichi walking between two teepees toward them.

"Thank you, Isauro, for waking my student. But you needn't trouble yourself; I'm sure you have plenty to do with your own students."

"You should never have brought him. It's a mistake. I can remedy the problem quickly." Stemann reached for his war tomahawk.

"Perhaps you're right, but since I have started already, I feel an obligation to try and finish." Shinichi turned to Eric. "Did I tell you that Stemann was a student on my first event as an instructor?"

At this statement, Stemann's demeanor became cold. He eyed the old instructor with clear malice.

Eric shook his head, still watching Stemann closely.

"Oh yes," Shinichi said to Eric. "Although he was arrogant and self-centered, somehow he did survive all the events."

"The standard was low," Eric said.

Stemann's hand moved quickly to his tomahawk.

"Well," Shinichi said, quickly moving in front of Stemann. "Eric, you must go and help take down the village."

"Eric will follow in the steps of all the rest of your students," Stemann told Shinichi. "He won't last through this event." Then he turned and marched away.

Suddenly, the Indian woman stepped in front of Eric, making wide gestures with her hands. She pointed in the direction Stemann had departed, then to his head several times.

"She's telling you to think," Shinichi told Eric. "It's dangerous to antagonize Stemann."

"Why doesn't she just say so?" Eric asked.

"She can't; she's a mute. She cannot speak, and her hearing is poor."

"Can't speak?"

"A problem with her vocal cords."

Eric looked at the woman. "Thank you for taking care of me last night."

The woman relaxed, and a smile appeared on her face reminded him of his mother's.

She signed to Shinichi.

"Kamani says you're welcome." Then, after more signs from the woman, Shinichi nodded his head and signed back. "She said you better go get your breakfast before all the food is gone."

Without warning, Kamani ran away from them.

"Kamani's right." Shinichi said. "Let's go get breakfast."

thirty-one

Eric forced himself to try a bite of the brownish-gray paste. It reminded him of thick mud. He scooped a lump into his mouth and was surprised at its sweetness. He ate three bowls full. For the first time since entering the event, he was content.

"The village is breaking camp. Help where you can; I will meet you on the trail," Shinichi said, then walked past him toward the horses.

Eric looked around and noticed several women and girls working on a large teepee. He walked over to them.

The women and girls were struggling to bring down the tee-pee. Eric examined it and noticed they'd missed a line tied to a stake. Eric stood over the spot where the stake was stuck in the ground. "Don't worry," he said. "I know the problem."

He reached and pulled at the knot. Continuing to pull, he looked up to find the women and girls screaming and waving their arms. Then Eric felt the knot release, and the line pulled taut and yanked free of his hand. The teepee collapsed with a crash—all the poles escaped the leather covering and fell in disarray on the ground.

An angry yell came from under the teepee. A woman rushed forward and pulled the teepee flap up.

"What happened?" Karro demanded.

All the women and girls pointed at Eric.

"Sorry," Eric said smiling sheepishly. *Can't I do anything right?*

When Karro saw Eric, her jaw tightened, and her face turned bright red. "You!"

Eric started to backpedal when Karro, eyes blazing, dashed toward him. Her knife was in her hand.

She's going to stab me. "I was trying to help." Eric's apology had no effect on the charging Karro.

Then Kamani sprang in front of Karro, holding up her hands to stop her from passing.

"We must finish," the women ordered Karro to return.

Karro pointed her knife at Eric. "I'll take care of you later."

Eric didn't like the sound of her threat. *She's serious. Why don't people like me?*

thirty-two

Eric looked up. The sky was a deep blue, and it surrounded a blazing yellow ball of light. The sun beat down on him like a hammer, heating his body. Droplets of sweat ran down his face and body. Dry flatland stretched as far as he could see, covered in grass that waved in the slight breeze like ocean waves.

The village had begun to move twenty minutes ago, but it already felt like hours. The heavy bag on his back reminded him of its weight after every step. To get his mind off the strain, Eric looked ahead. The tribe was stretched out—most of the men on horses, and the women walked in groups; a few dozen led horses which pulled the teepees behind them.

Eric noticed two large groups, ahead and off to the side: one led by Stemann and the other led by Santos. The groups were their students, and the two teachers were giving instructions. He gazed at the students. *How can I make friends*? He remembered their angry looks from the crossover. *Do I really need friends*? He thought of his family. *I wish I could see them.* Eric spotted Shinichi and waved.

Shinichi stopped and waited for Eric to catch up. "I think we should start with any question you might have," the warlord said.

Eric looked at the olive-skinned, black-haired people in front of him. "Who are these people?"

"They are one of the twelve Shoshone Indian tribes. Did you ever study American Indians?"

"Yes, briefly in my history class."

"Were you a good student?" Eric remembered the rare proud smile on his father's face when his instructors had praised him. Usually his father frowned at his average marks. When Eric didn't answer, Shinichi continued, "When the Western Europeans came to the new world and moved across the land, they found it inhabited by an indigenous people, the American Indians. A great race of people who segregated into different groups. There were the Shoshone, Ute, Apache, Blackfeet, Cheyenne, and Sioux. These are some of the better-known tribes, but there were hundreds of them."

Shinichi indicated the people around him. "The American Indians are amazing beings. By their hard life they're made tough. Indians are fierce in their beliefs, efficient in their resources, and ferocious in battle. Each individual learns throughout his or her life how to be self-sufficient or die. To grow to an adult as an American Indian is quite an accomplishment."

"Why were the students brought here?"

"We must weed out the weak students as quickly as possible. Concentrate all our teaching resources on the best candidates to become warlords."

"But—"

"To survive, a student must learn to adapt. Only the strong and resourceful can learn to live by the Indian ways." Shinichi looked down at Eric. "To survive this event, you must push yourself by acting and thinking like an Indian."

"I will," Eric promised him. Shinichi gave him a weary smile.

Eric looked at the two groups of students. "The Indians don't mind us being with them?"

"The Shoshone don't know we're any different."

"What? We look so different." Eric stared at the group of students. Most had dark hair, though several boys and girls had blond or light brown hair, and a few had red.

"When the Shoshone look upon us, they see boys and girls who look like them. When we talk, they hear their language and we hear them in ours. Quick, pick it up," Shinichi suddenly told Eric.

Eric's eyes followed Shinichi's extended finger to look at a rock. The rock was a light gray, almost white. Picking up the rock, Eric examined it more closely. It was about an inch and a half across, oval, and flat. Finishing his inspection, Eric offered the rock to Shinichi.

"Keep it," Shinichi said. "As we walk I want you to collect one hundred and eighty stones similar to this one. Also collect one hundred and eighty-one similar stones, as close to black as possible."

Shinichi pointed to another oval-shaped rock for Eric to pick up. After Eric did so, he noticed a woman far off in the distance by herself. "Isn't that Kamani, the woman who took care of me last night?"

"Yes."

"What's she doing way out there?"

"She's an outcast."

"Outcast. Why?"

"The tribe thinks she's cursed," Shinichi said. "The Shoshone feel Kamani must have done something evil to their Gods for them to make her voiceless."

"They're wrong."

Shinichi shrugged, looking at the woman. "Nevertheless, that's their belief. Without a warrior to care for her, she has to work hard to survive."

Before Eric could ask more questions, Shinichi turned off to talk to a Shoshone brave.

thirty-three

Eric **was** doing his best to keep up with the tribe.

To his left he saw Santos still talking to his students. Trailing the group by twenty feet was Sami. Eric altered his course to intercept the trailing boy.

When Sami saw Eric he asked, "Get any money?"

"No," Eric said. "Why aren't you with the other students?"

Sami looked forward to Santos and his students. "I'm not like them."

"I don't understand."

"I'm no warrior."

"Don't you want to become a warlord?" Eric asked.

"No, I want the easy life."

Yes, the easy life. I want to be at the Moon castle, out of the sun, eating cake and ice cream, Eric thought.

Sami began, "I was an orphan, living on the streets of Wearter, the capital city of the planet, Zazar. I was doing all right, surviving. Four years ago, I was running for my life through the outdoor market when I spied a ship ready to leave. Running aboard I overheard someone saying they were testing kids from the street. Like me. They would take whoever passed, and through specialized training they would have fame and fortune. I went and entered the line for testing. But it was too hard. For the boy in front of me the test was easy. At the end, I gave him all my money to change tests with me."

Eric started to laugh. "You didn't know?"

"No, I didn't know it was a test to become a warlord." Sami laughed with Eric. "A big mistake."

"If you try—"

"I know my limits."

"You never know."

"Oh, but I do," Sami said confidently. "I'm no match for anyone, even you."

"I won't hurt you," Eric said. "I give you my word."

"Don't make promises you can't keep."

"Oww!" Eric suddenly cried as pain shot through his left leg. He looked down to see a rock laid next to his leg.

"Watch out!" Sami warned.

Eric's head shot up, looking for the danger. *Wham*, something hard hit Eric in his chest, causing him to fall.

"Karro's throwing rocks," Sami shouted.

Eric turned to see Karro pulling back her arm to hurl another rock.

"Sami, help me up," Eric said. But Sami was already running away. Jerking his head back, the rock missed Eric face by only an inch. With a sudden spurt of energy, Eric leapt up and started to run after Sami. But with the heavy pack, Eric was too slow, and he felt the pain of several more rocks hitting their mark.

thirty-four

There was a constant battle going on in Eric's mind. *I'm so tired... Quiet, you have to keep on walking...But the bag is so heavy...You have to carry it.*

One, two, three... Eric had to count to keep his mind off the pain. He counted all the people; then he counted all the men, and then the women. He heaved a great sigh when he counted the last horse.

Sami walked with Eric for a while, but Eric's pace wasn't fast enough, so Sami strolled off with the rest of the tribe.

An hour later, Eric looked up. The Shoshone tribe had vanished. The only evidence they had passed was the trampled grass before him.

Sweat ran over his body like great rivers. His breath was labored, and he leaned forward from the weight of the bag. Never in his memory had he been so tired. Every cell in his body screamed for him to stop. But he continued to walk.

Eric suddenly stopped. All around him, small birds were taking flight. He jumped. Hundreds of squirrels came out of holes, running past him toward a distant oak tree.

He heard faint sounds of roaring thunder and the earth below his feet trembled. Eric looked left and right, alert for danger. His head spun around, and eyes widened in panic. He turned and ran.

"Help," Eric started to scream. *I'm going to die.*

He stared at the squirrels scampering and scurrying up the oak tree and longed to be one. *I'm not going to make it.* With each passing second, the thunderous noise seemed like it was going to devour him.

Thick dust surrounded Eric as he reached for the tree. With his heart slamming against his chest, he leapt up into the lowest branch.

The squirrels, agitated, moved from branch to branch ahead of him. Twenty-five feet above the ground, Eric threw his arms around the trunk and held on with all his might, finally daring to look down.

Hundreds of horses crushed the dry grass where he had stood moments before and sent great clouds of dust up into the tree.

One horse raced a hundred feet ahead, leading the herd. The stallion was as black as night, tall, and broad shouldered. It ran like the wind. Under its thick coat, Eric saw powerful muscles flexing and straining as the black beauty flew like a tornado, charging across the plain.

After twenty minutes, the wild herd of horses began to thin, and finally the stragglers ran by. Eric exhaled and relaxed, but still kept his eyes on the majestic creatures that had just passed.

Eric looked up to see hundreds of beady little eyes glaring at him. One broke away and ran at Eric, teeth bared. The squirrel stopped two feet away, chattering like a madman. A second later more squirrels followed angrily, chattering like the first.

The first squirrel darted forward and snapped at Eric's exposed arm.

"Stop!" Eric shouted, waving his fist at the squirrel. It dashed back with the others.

Now more darted forward as Eric quickly worked to get down.

"Back," he screamed as squirrels scurried all over him. He waved his arms, fighting back. He lost his balance.

"Nooo—" Eric fell backward out of the tree. He threw up his arms to cover his face as the army of squirrels scurried down the trunk, storming after him.

"Get off me." He rolled over and knocked several squirrels away as he got up, jumped away from the tree, and out of their path. "Haha!" Eric mocked them. The squirrels dashed around in every direction in search of their holes. But there were none—the stampeding horses had crushed them.

He looked at the large dust cloud in the distance. Then, with a deep sigh, Eric resigned himself to continue his march after the Shoshone.

He looked down to the ground. *Where's the trail?* Now, like the squirrels, he was dashing in different directions, searching. It was gone.

thirty-five

Eric weaved his way between the teepees. For the past twelve hours he'd walked without stopping, until he saw the village fires warm and bright against the dark night sky.

Half of him was grateful to be among the teepees; the other half didn't care. Dog-tired, he was about to drop to the ground and go to sleep, when the strong aroma hit him. His hungry stomach hollered out to his weary brain, *Food!*

He took in several deep breaths of the strong smell of cooking meat. Like a magnet, the aroma pulled at him, making him walk toward it.

Eric stumbled into an opening to find a crowd of Shoshone. With each step, the aroma became stronger. All he could think about was the cooking meat. Resolute, he walked past the line of waiting children and women and received several hard stares from Shoshone men, but he didn't care. All that mattered was getting food.

A man with several eagle feathers in his hair stood by the cook fires. He was older and chief of the Shoshone, Angry Bear. Around him waited the elders and leaders, a dozen men similar to the chief. Shinichi, Santos, and Stemann were among them.

Eric was in agony. The aroma drove him mad with desire. Nothing else mattered but getting food into his mouth. Ten feet away, a woman was bent over a roasted turkey, cutting a large piece. She put it into a bowl, then got up and walked to Angry Bear, handing him the bowl.

The roasted turkey looked tender and juicy. *Why do I have to wait?* Eric thought. *Back home, in the Moon castle, I would be served first, along with the royal family.*

He walked up to Angry Bear. "Chief," Eric said. "I'm a prince of the greatest empire in the solar system." Out of the corner of his eye, he saw Shinichi drop his eyes and shake his head. But he didn't care. "I will eat first."

The look of horror on the face of the Indian woman serving Angry Bear should have warned Eric. *She doesn't know who I am.* He dismissed her.

Angry Bear's face tightened, stretching the skin taut across his high cheekbones.

"Angry Bear," Eric said with force, "I'm of royal birth. It is your obligation to show me the courtesy of my rank." Eric held out his hand for the bowl.

Face red, eyes blazing, Angry Bear looked at the other leaders around him.

"I will eat, now!" Eric said, pulling Angry Bear's attention back to him.

Eric noticed some movement among the circle of leaders. Santos' face tilted, puzzled; Stemann smiled broadly. Shinichi was turning away.

Angry Bear smiled like Stemann. With a bow of his head, Angry Bear extended the bowl of meat toward Eric. Eric took it. Smiling, he raised the bowl in salute and thanks to the chief. In triumph he looked at Shinichi. But his instructor just looked down.

His mouth watered as he looked down at the tender meat. With his fingers, he scooped up a portion of the meat and put it in his mouth. His mind leaped in pleasure as his tongue caressed the food.

Then a great sting of pain killed the pleasure of the food. Looking down, Eric gaped at a red welt across his arm. He dropped the bowl of meat as another sharp pain and another welt appeared above his wrist.

Eric's head shot up; first he saw Angry Bear's red face, then his right arm pulling back. In his hand was a leather thong used to whip his horse.

The leaders laughed—Stemann loudest of all. "Stop!" Eric screamed at Angry Bear.

"Slow Weasel needs to learn respect."

Eric felt the whip again. Before Angry Bear could raise his whip one more time, Eric turned to run in the direction he'd come, but wasn't quick enough as he felt the leather thong across his back. The villagers started to laugh as a foot shot out and tripped him. He looked up into a young boy's black eyes and a face bearing the same smile as Stemann's.

thirty-six

"**That was** foolish." The voice came from behind him.

Eric recognized the voice and turned away, wanting to be alone. The crackle of leaves told him Shinichi was still walking toward him. Head hung in shame, his eyes cast down, he saw Shinichi's moccasins come to stand before him.

"Why does everyone hate me?" Eric said through a sob.

"Eric—" Shinichi said gently.

He lifted his face, tears streaming down his cheeks. "Why am I cursed? Why does everything always happen to me? Charles is right: I didn't belong in my family. I don't belong anywhere."

Eric stepped forward, throwing his arms around Shinichi, pulling him in tight and crying freely into his vest. He couldn't help himself. "I want my mother."

"She's not here," Shinichi said softly, patting Eric on the back. "She cannot come." He allowed Eric to cry for a few minutes. "Eric, be strong."

Reluctantly, Eric released Shinichi and looked up into his face.

Shinichi wiped away Eric's tears and stared deeply into his eyes. He smiled brightly. "I'm proud of you."

"Me, Why?"

The other students came from a hard life. It's easier for them to adapt to the rigors of the Indians' tough life. But you have come from a pampered life, one of royalty. It is a hard change. You have not given up—you have a lot in you."

"Really?" Eric said hopefully.

"Yes. Now, listen. Most of my teachings are on one of the greatest generals of all time. Sun Tzu was a Chinese general who lived in ancient times. He proposed thirteen rules for war. You disregarded one of his most important ones," Shinichi said. Then he spoke slowly and distinctly. "Know your terrain. In this situation, know your environment."

When he got no response from Eric, he continued. "In your exhausted state, you forgot the environment you're in. The consequences were, shall we say, painful."

"It was only a bowl of meat."

"Yes, this time. But one day it may be an army. Thousands, millions, or perhaps billions of lives could hang in the balance of your actions. You must understand your environment here, at this time, the rules of the village and its leadership. Who are the knights and rooks and who are the pawns?" Shinichi put his hand on Eric's shoulder. "Do not assume anything."

Eric nodded his head in understanding. "Everyone laughed when I left."

A hearty chuckle escaped Shinichi's lips. "When they see you again, they will continue. Right now, you are considered the court's jester."

Eric remembered the court jester at the Moon castle—his antics were so stupid they were funny. Like the others at court, Eric had laughed. Now, he compared his actions to the jester's, and within seconds, Eric was laughing.

Shinichi watched his student and gave a smile of approval. "It's your pride that really hurts," Shinichi said. "Within hours those welts will go away. But when they go away you cannot forget the lesson."

Then, in an amused tone, Eric's instructor asked, "Did you know the chief's name?"

"Yes."

"You didn't understand it?" When Eric gave him a blank stare, the warlord continued, "Shoshone names convey meaning about actions or personality. Angry Bear. The chief has a quick, hot temper."

"I understand now," Eric said. "But why did he call me Slow Weasel?"

"Really, you have to ask?"

The next day there was a gray tint to the sky with several ominous rain clouds. The wind was brisk. Eric pulled his leather vest tighter against the cold.

Ahead, Shinichi was waiting for him.

"How do you feel today?"

"The welts still hurt."

"After an hour on the trail you will forget them."

Eric and Shinichi walked together in silence for a time.

"Last night when I ran away from the chief, all the Shoshone were laughing, but the students weren't. Why?"

"They are different from you, Eric. All of them have lived on the streets, been orphans. All have experienced the pain of hunger."

"Were you ever hungry?"

"Yes. There were days I was so hungry I would rather die than go on."

"I'm sorry."

"It's not your fault. It was an accident that changed my life."

"An accident?"

"I'm from Ogleday. A small moon on the near side of Neptune." Shinichi's eyes brightened. "I was part of a good family—loving father, mother, and a younger sister. My father was an architect and my mother a doctor. Both were very good at their jobs and well paid. I remember running around a large house filled with numerous toys my sister and I played with."

Shinichi fell silent.

I was part of a good family too. Eric's eyes shifted to a young boy and girl running and playing. Each had a stick and took turns hitting an acorn, then laugh and chase after it.

"It was a day like today. Dark clouds filled the sky, there was a bitter wind, and the sun was growing dim. I remember clearly the knocking on my bedroom door. Knocks, light and spaced far apart. I opened the door to see my grandmother standing outside. Her eyes were red, and her face drawn. When she saw me, she burst into tears. The funeral for my father, mother, and sister was a few days later."

"Were you sad?"

"Not sad…I was numb. I was six and didn't understand. My grandmother was too grief-stricken with the loss of her daughter to talk to me."

"Did she put you out on the street?"

"No, Eric." Shinichi's lips edged up in a partial smile. "She was a sweet old lady. That was her problem."

"I don't understand."

"After the funeral, my grandmother came to live in the house. My parents had left a sizable amount of money. It would be enough for me and my grandmother to live well. Life, no matter the tragedy, goes on."

"What happened?"

"A man came into my grandmother's life. He was handsome and spoke sweet words to her. It wasn't long before he moved in. When he did, everything changed. There were constant visitors who ate and drank all the time. I would lock myself in my room to keep out of everyone's way. It was a year later my life really changed."

"How?"

"They had spent all my parents' money. There were no more parties, just screaming and shouting. One day I arrived home from school and the man and my grandmother were gone. The next day, a woman pulled me, crying, out of the house and locked the door."

"No one helped you."

"I was alone. Wandering the streets, trying to understand why it was all happening to me." Shinichi looked down at Eric. "If it wasn't for Vulcury, I would have died before I was ten."

"It's not right."

"I'm sure if you talked to the other students, you would hear similar stories. Tragic circumstances, surviving on the street, and constant hunger and danger."

These were all foreign feelings to Eric. He had only known excess in the Moon castle.

Eric suddenly stopped, eyes wide. "Kamani."

"Yes, Eric." Shinichi said. "She is alone, without a home. She is truly a remarkable woman to have survived so long."

"It stops today."

"Have you forgotten the lesson already? You will be going against the ways of the tribe."

Eric pulled back his shoulders, standing taller. "Today!"

thirty-seven

"**I want** them." Sami stared greedily at the dozen eagle feathers Eric presented. "What do I have to do?"

"Talk to Karro."

Sami shifted his eyes away from the feathers to look at Eric. "Why?"

"Does she hate all boys or just me?"

"She hates all boys—especially you."

Eric had had a hard start with the Shoshone tribe, but every day it had gotten better. He had stopped falling behind. His body toughened, no longer hurting at the end of the day. But not everything had gotten better.

Karro's greatest ambition was to torment Eric. She constantly threw rocks at him. When she walked by, she would push him over, and she took great delight in calling him Slow Weasel.

Several times, Eric had tried talking to Karro. Each time he tried, she would ignore him, walk away, or taunt him with his new nickname until he left.

If I can get Karro to like me, I can get anyone to like me. I know if I talk to her, I can make her my friend.

"All you have to do is get her alone and I'll talk to her." Eric waved the eagle feathers in front of Sami.

"Okay, when?"

"When we stop for lunch."

"Deal," Sami said, holding his hand out.

"*And* new moccasins for Kamani."

"How about, just the moccasins?"

"No. Both or no deal!"

"Fine," Sami said as he took the eagle feathers.

thirty-eight

The noon sun cast shadows around the grove of trees and bushes, shading the pond they surrounded. Eric stepped into a small clearing beside the pond where animals came to drink and rest.

Two beavers played at the edge of the pond by a patch of tall reeds. Eric slowed his walking to study the two furry balls with big teeth. A small branch snapped under his foot. One beaver cocked its nose, sniffing the air. A second later, he chattered, and both dived into the pond, swimming away.

Eric heard a knock and looked up. Fifty feet up, perched on a branch next to the trunk, was a medium-sized bird. It had a gray-black body with a white chest. But what caught Eric's attention were the bright red feathers on its head. *Like the red hats used at the Moon castle parties.* The bird shifted it body to face the tree trunk and started to hammer its beak into the wood.

He leaned against the tree and listened to the woodpecker and his mind reassured him. *Karro and I will talk this out. After this, everything will be fine. We'll become good friends.*

"Tell me!"

Eric dashed to the other side of the tree, hearing Karro's voice coming along the trees on a path directly from the Shoshone camp.

"It's instructions from Santos. He didn't want the other students to know," Sami said.

"Know?" Karro asked suspiciously.

"How he thinks you're his *best* student. He wanted me to tell you about the special project."

Sami stopped on the other side of the tree. He had to keep Karro facing him.

"Now is the best time," Sami said.

"Best time for what?" Karro demanded, taking a threatening step toward Sami.

"Now. Now is *really* the best time," Sami started to shout.

Eric came quickly behind Karro and wrapping his arms around her.

"Let me go," Karro roared.

"No, not until you agree to talk," Eric said.

"Slow Weasel?" Karro screamed.

"My name is—ahh!" Eric groaned. His back slammed against the tree. "Just listen—" barely escaped his lips when Karro snapped her head back, hitting Eric hard in the face.

Karro whipped her body around and dived to the ground, landing on Eric.

"Stop," Eric said, gritting his teeth against the pain. Now they were rolling. It was like trying to hold onto a tornado, thrashing about in every direction.

Karro shrilled with anger, "Slow Weasel, let me go or else!"

"I won't."

"You will." She fell into a thick bush trying to break Eric's hold.

In the bush Karro's rolling, wiggling, and thrashing caused the rough branches to rub through Eric's skin. The leaves sliced his shoulders and back. *If I let her go, it will be worse.*

Karro rolled to a stop. She pulled her head back to help her rapid breathing.

Eric took advantage of the tired Karro. "All I want to do is talk."

"No," Karro said between gasps of breath.

"I won't let you go," Eric said. "You'll be late returning to the village and punished."

Karro answered Eric by grunting, tightening her body, and pushing out her arms, trying desperately to break Eric's hold.

Eric was surprised at her strength, but held on tight.

Karro finally relaxed. "Okay."

"Promise you'll talk and not hurt me."

"No." Then, after a long few seconds, "Yes."

Not yet, an inner voice told him. "I want you to swear as an Amazon."

Karro tried again to break Eric grip, but after a minute relented and said, "I swear."

"Me too, me too," Sami pleaded.

"You won't hurt Sami either."

"Fine, let me go."

Eric let Karro go and got up, quickly backing away.

Karro got up, red-faced. Her hands were balled into fists, body rigid, and she glared threateningly at Eric. Without a word, she turned toward the village.

"We need to talk," Eric said.

Karro turned to look at Eric. "If I stay, I'll do something you'll regret. We'll talk tomorrow night in the woods." Karro turned and marched toward the camp.

"We're dead," Sami said.

thirty-nine

The next day, like every other day before, the Shoshone tribe stopped to eat in the mid-afternoon. Instead of waiting for the women to bring water, Eric walked to the stream. When he arrived, the women were already there with their water skins.

Eric went down on his knees and, cupping the water in his hands, drank deeply.

"Hello," a sweet voice came from above.

He looked up to find a girl beside him. "Hi," Eric said as he got up. She was a student like him, with alluring light-brown eyes highlighted with jade-green flecks. The smooth, radiant skin of her face was surrounded by long, black hair. Like Kamani, she had a dazzling smile.

"My leg hurts." She gestured with her hands to her left leg.

"What's wrong?" Eric asked.

"Does it matter?"

Eric was about to say he didn't understand, when her eyes started to flutter.

She moved closer, starting to pout, and stroked his arm. "Would you help me?" she said meekly. "Carry my water skins to the village?"

"Okay," Eric said.

"My name is Isabeli. What's yours?"

Eric opened his mouth, but the word Isabeli heard was "Fool."

Eric turned to see Karro walking toward the stream, carrying several empty water skins.

"My name is Eric," he said sternly.

"No, it's 'Fool' if you carry Isabeli's water skins," Karro said.

"Don't listen to Karro." Isabeli moved closer to Eric. "She's jealous."

"Eric, don't carry her water," Karro said.

"Forget about her," Isabeli said. She pointed a short distance away. "My water skins are over there." Before Eric could answer, she started to walk in that direction. "I didn't get a chance to fill the skins." The dazzling smile returned. "Do you mind?"

Eric picked up the water skins, went to the river, got to his knees, and started to fill the skins.

"Don't listen to Karro," Isabeli said. "She's an Amazon. All those females want to do is make trouble for everyone. As you can tell I'm not like her."

He looked up to see Isabeli in a pose, her eyes fluttering and a wide smile. Eric got up with the water skins full. Isabeli started to walk back.

When Eric caught up to her, Isabeli was talking as if he had been with her the whole time. "I'm from Wek on the far side of the galaxy. A planet known for beautiful women who live their lives to the fullest. Men treasure us."

Isabeli didn't stop talking until they were at the center of the village's cooking area. Here, she ordered Eric to empty the water skins into a large pot. Isabeli looked down at the empty skins. "I have to bring more."

"I can't," Eric said before running back to the stream.

A few yards further downstream was Karro with her skins. Eric walked to her.

Karro finished filling up her water skins and got up to find Eric had already picked up the others.

"I don't need—" Karro started.

"I'm going to the village; there's no reason I can't help," Eric said.

Karro opened her mouth to respond, but then looked over Eric's shoulder.

Eric turned to see Isabeli standing with her arms crossed.

"What are you doing?" Isabeli demanded. A step behind her was a boy carrying her empty water skins.

"I'm helping Karro."

"She doesn't need help. She-an-Amazon." When there was no reaction from Eric, Isabeli smiled and said softly, "Eric, please help this boy. The water skins will be so heavy."

"I can—" The boy started.

"Shut up," Isabeli ordered.

Eric looked at Isabeli. "I took your water skins earlier." Eric noticed the boy stiffen. "This time I'm taking Karro's."

Then he walked past the shocked Isabeli.

After several yards, Karro caught up to him. "She can't believe you didn't follow her commands."

"Remember, I'm Slow Weasel."

"You understand I don't need you to carry the water."

"Yes, I know," Eric said.

"You won't get a pretty little smile from me."

"I'm sure I won't," Eric said.

They walked in silence the rest of the way. Eric walked to the cooking area and set down the water skins. He began to leave when he heard, "Thank you."

Eric looked at Karro. He couldn't read her face. Nodding in response to her thank you, Eric turned.

"Be careful of Isabeli," Karro warned.

Eric turned back. "She's not an Amazon."

"Worse. She's wants to be a spy. Like Fia."

"Fia?"

"She's a student of Stemann."

"Spy? Why does Vulcury train spies?"

"Throughout the river of history women have changed its course," Isabeli said, stepping abruptly in front of Karro. "Not with a knife, spear, or gun. It's with perfume, smiles, and the imagination of what dreams they can fulfill."

Isabeli stopped an inch away from Eric.

Eric swallowed hard. Isabeli smelled of cinnamon; her smile was wide, and her eyes were moist. She leaned forward and her soft skin brushed Eric's cheek as she whispered into his ear, "Have you never heard of Antonia Ford, Mata Hara, or Valerie Plame? Through their sexuality they controlled men, conquered enemies, and ruled empires—women who were more than women. The woman I will become."

When Isabeli stepped away, Eric felt a sudden emptiness. Hypnotized, he started to follow, but a sudden pain in his arm stopped him. Eric looked down at Karo's balled fists.

"I want to talk now," Karro said, stepping in front of Eric.

"Okay," Eric said, rubbing his upper arm. "First, stop hitting me."

forty

Eric's life was becoming routine. When he wasn't with Shinichi or Kamani, he was with Karro and Sami.

There was so much to talk about. Life with the Shoshone, becoming a warlord, and what it was like out in the solar system.

The discussion of the solar system was a tough subject. When talking with Karro and Sami, he began to realize how little he knew of the world beyond the moon and earth. All his knowledge came from books.

He couldn't help grinning and thinking, *I have friends.* At least he thought he did. Sami would still ask for things. And Karro—she'd stopped hitting him and they talked. But sometimes when they argued, he could see her eyes light up and she chewed on her lip. Like she was a dam ready to burst. But she held it in.

Today, Eric felt a chill in the morning air. The seasons were changing and so had the landscape. The flatlands changed to hills, with large patches of tall trees.

He bent down and picked up the round, white rock that was smooth on both sides. When he confirmed it met Shinichi's criteria, he put it in his pouch.

A shadow fell across his body. He looked up to see a gray horse standing over him. The horse's head moved to one side and Eric looked at a boy seated upon its back.

Eric recognized the boy who tripped him after his trouble with Angry Bear. The boy stared at him.

Even on the horse Eric could tell the boy was taller than him. He had black, lifeless hair upon a square face, bushy eyebrows, and black eyes.

"Out of my way," the boy ordered.

"I was here first," Eric said.

The boy pulled the horse's reins, forcing the horse's head at Eric.

The big head pushed Eric back. Then, it jerked upward as Eric rapped it on the snout.

"Hit my horse again and I'll kill you."

"If it gets in my way again, I will," Eric said defiantly.

The boy kicked the horse hard and it rammed Eric, knocking him over and spilling the rocks out of his pouch. He kicked the horse again, riding away at a trot.

Eric grabbed a rock and jumped up. He threw the rock, hitting the horse's left rump.

The horse leapt up, its front legs reaching for the sky. The boy threw his arms around the horse's neck. Then, he held on tight as the gray horse bolted away.

His name is Bolek Maubourg," Shinichi said after Eric had described the boy.

"Stay away from him," Sami said. "He's mean."

"He's serious about becoming a warlord," Karro added.

"Yes, Bolek is Isauro's best student," Shinichi said. "He has several characteristics that make him a natural leader."

Eric looked up into a tall pine tree he was walking past. Sami and Karro walked beside him and Shinichi was slightly ahead. Eric thought for a few minutes.

"Why does Bolek hate me?" Eric asked.

"Isauro hates you, so Bolek hates you," Shinichi said. "He will hurt you to please his mentor."

"Hurt him first," Karro said.

"He can't," Sami said. "Bolek is seldom alone. There's Malek and Kirill. I've even seen Raica with him."

Eric noticed Karro's face darken at the last name.

"Eric, to survive you must become like Bolek. Remember Sun Tzu," Shinichi said.

"I understand," Eric said. "Let's go."

Eric veered off away from Shinichi and the two other students followed.

"Who's Sun Tzu?" Karro asked.

"A famous general. He said to be great, we must know the terrain or environment we're in. How the tribe is made up, and how people interact."

"It's easy and I don't even want to be a warlord," Sami said. "At the top of the village is Angry Bear, the chief, and under him are his elders, who help him govern. Then, he has a group of leading warriors. The best is Stomping Horse."

"No, it's Fast Deer," Karro said.

"Have you seen the muscles on Stomping Horse? He could whip anyone." Sami said.

Karro snorted. "Fast Deer is too quick for him."

"You're both wrong," Eric said. "It's Calm Cougar. He's patient and thinks before he acts."

"By the time he's done thinking, Stomping Horse would have beat him," Sami said.

"What's wrong, Eric?" Karro asked.

"Sometimes when Calm Cougar passes me he gives me a strange look."

"It's your imagination. Why would he bother with a nobody like you?" Sami said.

"Thanks," Eric said, annoyed. *No, he does look at me. Like I've stolen something from him.*

forty-one

Eric was walking through the village when Shinichi marched toward him. He was startled as Shinichi was suddenly thrust aside and Kamani came rushing to him. She threw her arms around him and pulled him in a tight hug like his mother used to after a fight with Charles. *I miss Mother.* Eric hugged her back, enjoying her warmth.

Kamani pulled away and looked at him, wiping a tear from her cheek. Then she signed abruptly, "You were gone too long!"

Eric smiled. Pleased Shinichi had begun teaching him sign language. "You didn't have to worry. Nothing happened." To his surprise, Kamani's face tightened in anger. She signed again with more force. "Never walk in the forest alone. Always have someone with you."

"I'm not a baby," Eric signed back with equal force. "I'm old enough to do what I want."

Kamani dropped her eyes and shook her head.

Her response angered Eric even more. He was about to continue the argument when Shinichi stepped forward. "Kamani, can you please bring some water?"

She looked at Shinichi and nodded her head. "Talk to Eric," she signed before she left.

"I will," Shinichi promised. "He's back. That's what's important." He looked down at Eric. "Let's take a walk." They headed toward the forest.

"Fine," Eric snapped and marched ahead, his back stiff and arms crossed.

Before they reached the forest, Eric heard Shinichi shout, "Eric. Stop."

Eric whirled around. "I'm too old to be mothered. I won't be told what to do."

To Eric's surprise, Shinichi didn't turn red with anger. He simply took a breath and said, "This morning, one of Isauro's students was found dead in the woods."

Eric's mouth dropped open in shock. "Dead? How?"

"He'd been strangled."

"Who?"

"His name was John Wheats."

The face of a boy a little taller than him with dusty blond hair came to his mind.

"When it was first announced this morning, we didn't know who it was. Kamani thought it was you. It hit her hard."

Eric stomach soured, and he dropped his head. "I'm sorry. I shouldn't have talked to her like that. I'll make it up to her, I promise."

Shinichi's face darkened. "There's more. Follow me."

They walked through the forest in silence, crossing a river, and on the other side came to a heavily bushed area. Shinichi stopped.

Eric stopped beside him. "Is this where John was found?"

"Yes. In the bushes."

Eric nodded.

After a moment of silence Shinichi said, "Go in and look around."

Eric hesitated. He didn't feel very old now. He didn't want to go in.

"Go in," Shinichi said again.

Eric stepped forward and parted the branches. He lifted his leg and extended it to get through the thick bush. In the center, the shrubbery wasn't as thick, and Eric could move around.

He surveyed the area. There were broken branches, crushed leaves, and trampled grass. It was clear there had been violent activity. Eric thought of the young boy. Swallowing hard, his spirits sank.

Something caught his eye, he gasped and stepped forward. Falling to his knees, he pushed aside a broken branch and, with mouth agape, looked at the fresh carving on the tree trunk, two feet from the ground. Eric stuck out his hand and touched it. It was crude and out of proportion. But he had seen it all his life. There was no mistaking the crest of the von Battenburgs, his family crest.

Eric stepped out of the bushes to a waiting Shinichi.

"Did you see it?" Shinichi asked. "At the base of the tree?"

"Yes. Who carved it?"

"You. According to Isauro."

"Me…Why?"

"Isauro is taking this as a personal insult against him. You remember he was in the commandant office when you declared you are Prince Eric Alexander von Battenburg. Since John Wheats was his student and you took the time to carve the von Battenburg crest, he considers it a slap in the face."

"It's true. I don't like him," Eric said. "He's dimwitted to think I'd hurt a boy to get back at him."

"Did you?"

Eric looked at his teacher. "You have to ask?"

"I must. You were gone this morning, you don't like Isauro, and it is your family's crest beside the dead boy."

"I didn't do it," Eric said. "I swear it."

"Eric, where were you this morning?"

His face turned bright pink and he looked at the ground. "I got lost."

Shinichi looked into the distant trees' foliage as Eric told him of wandering into the woods and following the wrong stream.

"Really," Shinichi shook his head. "It's a tall tale."

"I'm not lying. Why don't you believe me?"

"Actually, I do," Shinichi said, putting a hand on Eric's shoulders. "Eric, you are a strange boy. In the turbulent current of life, you are a bobbin with a string and a hook. Fate is the fish who's taken the hook. He pulls you up, down, and all around, but somehow you always rise to the surface."

"I'm telling the truth."

Shinichi shook his head. "No one else will believe you. You must lie. As I told you, death is common to the Shoshone. Although tragic, John's death has not raised many eyebrows. If you say he insulted you, none of the Shoshone will question his death."

"I don't want to lie."

"A bigger question is who carved the von Battenburg crest into the base of the tree?"

"Isauro von Stemann," Eric said firmly.

"Isauro? Why?"

"He's trying to get me into trouble. Get me thrown out of the tribe."

"John Wheats was his student."

"I bet he tricked John. Told him lies to get him here and then snuck up behind him and took him out."

Shinichi looked down at Eric with concern on his face. "I could be wrong, but I think John Wheats' death and the crest was for you, Eric. Whoever carved the crest is used to taking lives. You must be on guard at all times."

forty-two

This morning, the Shoshone tribe was at a junction where the vast grass plain met the rugged mountains. Eric's eyes traveled slowly from right to left along a clear-blue river of melted snow that wound its way south.

To Eric's joyful surprise, the march had stopped temporarily. The Shoshone made camp beside the lazy river—the teepees were erected in organized circles with a large clearing in the center of each. The women went around removing bushes and cleaning up around the camp, and Angry Bear sent out warriors to scout the area for enemies.

Over the next two days, the village fell into a rhythm. In the morning, the women were up early fetching water and cooking the morning meal. The men worked on weapons and broke in young horses. When the sun set in the evening, the village would eat their final meal. The men huddled around the fire and told stories, and the women gathered by the river and talked.

Eric noticed each of the warlords went off with his students, taking them out into the wilderness. Like the other warlords, Shinichi would lead Eric out. But it wasn't for instruction; it was to play 'Go'.

The third day began with a windy morning. The camp filled with men on horses forming into bands, fully armed and anxious to ride out. The warlords, including Shinichi and all the male student, were among them.

Shinichi trotted his horse over to Eric, and Sami followed. Eric noticed his teacher was heavily armed. Even Sami had a bow and a quiver of arrows across his back.

"I'm going," Shinichi said, looking down at Eric.

"What about me?" Eric nodded toward the other male students mounted and armed.

"Do you have a horse? Do you have a bow and quiver full of arrows or a lance?"

"No."

"Then you must stay with the women."

"Eric can have my horse." Sami began to dismount. "I'll stay with the women."

"Stay on your horse," Shinichi ordered. "Eric, help where you can and look for more stones."

"Where are you going?" Eric asked.

"To hunt buffalos. The meat is almost all gone. We must bring back buffalo meat as soon as we can."

"How long will you be gone?"

Shinichi looked off into the distance and heaved a great sigh. "The scouts haven't found any close by. We may be gone for a few weeks." His gaze turned to the village. "It's not good to leave the village so few warriors, but we have to find the buffalo trail quickly."

The buffalo hunters started to ride out. Shinichi gathered up his reins and turned his head in the direction of the retreating warriors. "Let's go, Sami."

Sami's shoulders slumped, and he gave a little wave to Eric before he pulled his horse's reins to follow Shinichi.

Eric stood watching the riders disappear into the distance, longing to join them.

forty-three

The Shoshone had made camp in a wide, open field with a river running through it, surrounded in every direction by forest made up of ancient trees that were tall and had trunks as wide as four men.

Disregarding Shinichi's warning and Kamani's concerns, Eric spent the afternoon wandering through the woods. He enjoyed the solitude and the beauty the trees provided, and quickly became familiar with the animals and plant life around the camp.

Two days after the warriors left, Eric was making his way through the woods to the north late in the evening, when he heard a muted thump. Half a minute later, he heard another thump. Wondering what creature had made the noise, he walked toward the sound.

Venturing into a clearing, he again heard the noise distinctly. At the far end of the clearing stood Karro with a bow and a small quiver of arrows. He leaned against a tree and watched her silently.

Eric admired Karro's gracefulness. In one fluid motion she took an arrow, notched it to the bow string, and raised the bow. With little effort, she pulled back the string and fired.

At shoulder height on a tree fifty yards away hung a leaf. The recently fired arrow was stuck through the center of the leaf, along with several others. A few minutes later he watched Karro put another arrow into the center of a leaf.

Amazing.

Eric walked toward her, then stopped abruptly, his heart racing. Karro had swiftly turned and aimed the arrow straight at him.

His wide eyes focused on the tip of the arrow targeted for his heart. Slowly, he raised his hands.

She's going to shoot me, he thought. *I thought I could trust her. I want so much to be her friend, but she's just playing at being mine.*

"An easy shot," Karro said. It seemed like a long time before she lowered the arrow. With hands still in the air, Eric walked cautiously toward Karro.

"You're an expert with a bow." Eric fought hard to smile because he still felt scared.

Karro turned back to face the tree with the leaf. She brought up her bow, pulled the string back, and released the arrow. Within a heartbeat, it struck the center the leaf.

"Amazing." Eric turned to her, incredulous. "How?"

"I'm an Amazon. Our history is full of war and conquest. We are taught the bow starting at the age of three. It develops hand-eye coordination, strength, and focus." Karro's jaw tightened and her shoulders went rigid. "*I should be with the warriors in the hunt.*"

Something within Eric told him to nod and keep quiet.

"I'm here to learn the art of war, to become a great warlord. Why am I left to fetch water and cook? I can bring down a buffalo with one arrow."

Eric nodded again.

"Can you shoot?"

"Shoot? . . I'm very good," Eric lied.

Karro pushed the bow toward him. "Show me."

Eric reluctantly took the bow. It was heavier than he'd thought. Turning, he looked at the leaf against the tree trunk. *It's so small.* But a grin appeared on his face. *How hard could it be?* He extended his hand for an arrow.

Eric stepped over a little to align himself to the far tree. He spread his feet like Karro had done, then notched the arrow. Eric brought the string back, pulled hard, and aimed the tip at the leaf. He let go of the string.

The arrow dove to the ground halfway to the tree.

"It slipped," Eric said quickly.

"Try again." Karro handed Eric another arrow.

Eric took the arrow and adjusted his stance, pulling his feet closer together. This time he pulled the bowstring as far back as he could, grunting at the effort. Looking down the shaft of the arrow, he made sure it was aimed at the target and opened his fingers. The arrow flew upward and disappeared somewhere past the target.

"A five-year-old Amazon can shoot better than you," Karro said. She moved over to him. "You're standing wrong. Face the target with your side. Your legs are too close together." She kicked Eric's legs further apart.

"Bring the bow up," Karro said as she moved around him.

Eric brought up the bow, then nearly jumped as Karro grabbed his wrist. He could feel her whole body as she pushed up against him.

Moving her other hand to rest on his she said, "Keep your back arm level when bringing the bow string back."

Eric did as he was told.

"Now, don't breathe as you release the string."

Looking at the hanging leaf, Eric let go.

Thump! He'd missed the leaves by four feet, but hit the tree.

Eric and Karro heard loud, slow, and distinct claps. "Holding tight to a male, sister."

A close replica of Karro walked slowly into the clearing, her face full of contempt. "I see Mother's weak blood runs through your pathetic veins."

"Take care with your words, sister. They may be your last." Karro's right hand rested on her knife.

"Threats are just words unless there's action," the girl said, circling Karro and pulling out her knife.

Karro likewise pulled out her knife and moved to the girl's left. "I only wish, Raica, that you were a worthy opponent."

"Stop." Eric moved between them. "You're family."

"Not by choice," Raica said.

"Did you see? Karro's an expert with a bow," Eric said.

Raica threw back her head and laughed. "An expert... compared to who? You?"

"Eric, stay out of this," Karro demanded.

He ignored her and pointed to the arrows in the leaf. "Look, all the arrows are perfectly placed."

Raica followed Eric's finger. "Let's see how good." She turned, and Eric watched her walk slowly to the tree.

"I told you," Eric said with satisfaction.

Raica pulled the arrows from the tree. "What can she do with a real target?" She bent over and picked up a pinecone. "All or nothing. Right, sister?" Raica put her back to the tree and placed the pinecone on her head.

"Right." Karro lifted her bow.

"Wait," Eric said anxiously. "What are you doing?"

Karro respond by removing an arrow from her quiver.

"No, she's your sister."

Karro notched the arrow.

"Raica, please don't do this," Eric shouted.

Raica laughed. "Karro's a coward. She won't shoot."

Karro's eyes narrowed as she raised the bow. "We'll see who's the coward?"

"Put down the bow," Eric pleaded.

"I won't be the coward. Raica must walk away." Karro pulled back the bowstring, but Eric clamped onto her wrist.

"Wait. Let me talk to her." Eric didn't wait for a response but ran toward Raica. He kept his body directly between the two sisters. "Raica, stop taunting Karro. She might shoot."

Raica raised her voice. "No. Karro's pathetic. Listening to a male, just like our disgusting mother."

"Out of the way Eric," Karro demanded.

Eric stood in front of Raica. *I can't let Karro kill her sister. It would destroy her.* "Give me the pinecone."

Raica reached up. "It doesn't matter. Karro's weak, only good for fetching water." She extended the pinecone to Eric.

Eric gave a sigh of relief. "You're wrong." He stepped forward but suddenly two strong hands pushed out hard, catching Eric in the chest. He fell backward.

Raica put the pinecone on her head. "Shoot."

"Don't—" Eric screamed.

Karro released the arrow.

Eric whipped around, wide-eyed.

"You missed," Raica yelled. "You couldn't do it. You're weak. You'll never be a warlord, you'll never be an Amazon, and you will die soon."

Eric looked at the pinecone with an arrow buried in its center before watching Karro turn and walk away.

As dusk fell, Karro stood by the river, the swift current thrashing about in front of her. The air was clear and cold.

"Are you crazy?" Eric yelled, marching up to Karro.

"Why?"

"Why?" Eric threw up his hands in frustration. "Raica's your sister."

"You shouldn't have interfered."

"You were wrong." Eric moved in front of Karro. "Why?"

"When I look at her or she looks at me, we are reminded of what could have been…and what actually happened." Karro looked past Eric at a lone mountain in the distance. "You wouldn't understand. How could you?"

"Tell me."

Karro took a deep breath and released it slowly. "Raica and I are…were…Amazon princesses. Our mother, ZKarivich, was queen of Spartic, a powerful Amazon city-state, and was feared and respected for her cunning and ferocity in battle."

"What happened?"

"He came."

"Who?"

"A man," Karro cursed as her jaw tightened and her eyes narrowed.

"So."

"An Amazon is brought up to despise men. A man's only value is as a slave, to serve a woman."

"Doesn't sound right," Eric said watching the moon begin to rise.

"It's our way."

"Men shouldn't go to Spartic." Eric said.

"He did."

Eric noticed Karro move her shoulders back and her eyes sparkled. "His name was Richard Wolfe. He was caught, by Spartic warriors, walking across the flat shishir plain alone; an act of madness. He had walked into a den of lions."

"Was he mad?"

Karro shook her head. "Richard was brought before my mother. She told us the first time she saw him, she knew Richard was different from other men. He was tall, lean, and handsome— traits Amazons prize in their male slaves."

Karro looked into Eric's eyes. "But there was more. He was strong, noble, and confident. *And* a warlord from Vulcury with many victories over enemies."

Eric watched as Karro's shoulders dropped and her head hung down. "Queen ZKarivich, my mother, committed the ultimate crime: she fell in love."

151

"Crime?"

"My mother made Richard her personal servant. A year later I was born, and a year after, Raica."

"Do you remember him?"

Karro nodded. "He was always with us, playing silly games he knew. Raica and I were very close and very happy. Then I—"

When the silence seemed to last too long Eric asked, "What?"

"A fight with Raica; she had a toy I wanted. When my father pulled me away I screamed, 'Slave, take your hands off me.' First, his face showed shock, then hurt, and finally, devastation. The next day he escaped and we never saw him again."

"It's another reason Raica hates me. It was the juncture when our happy lives changed. Without Richard, my mother changed, became a tyrant. Life in the city became hard. Eighteen months later she left to find our father."

"Did she find him?"

"I don't know—she never returned," Karro said. "My mother's cousin, Belen, took over stewardship since Raica and I were too young to rule. Behind our backs, she turned the council against us. My mother had left to follow a man. Her blood was bad. We have the same blood."

Karro's eyes narrowed. "The council agreed with Belen and we were thrown out of our home and onto the streets." She shook her head at Eric, who suddenly felt guilty of something, though he wasn't sure what. "You cannot begin to understand what we went through."

Eric looked up at the full moon in the dark night's sky.

"Understand the loss of your world and everything you've known," Karro said.

Eric's body tightened.

"Understand how cruel life can be."

Eric looked away.

"Understand the loss of a mother, a woman so precious that thinking about her brings pain."

Eric abruptly turned away from Karro, his face sad, eyes filling with tears, and walked away along the river.

forty-four

"**Alisa, you** must come to the ball," the Emperor demanded as he paced in her royal bedroom suite.

"I cannot. I will not!" the Empress shouted back.

"Why? Tell me why?"

Alisa's eyes narrowed. "How can you ask such a question?"

"You are the Empress and as such, you have duties."

"I'm a mother first." the Empress said, collapsing into a chair. "I have a hole in my heart and it is filled with pain. My son is gone."

The Emperor stomped his right foot and raised his voice. "He will return! I have sworn an oath to bring him back."

"They are words—promises with no results."

The Emperor's eyes bulged and his breath came heavily through clenched teeth.

There was a knock on the door.

"That must be your handmaidens. You will go to the ball. You will talk to people and you will dance and be merry."

"Never!" the Empress said evenly. "What will you do—send me to the dungeon like you sent Eric?"

Suddenly, the Emperor dropped his head. "You use Eric like a whip, lashing me constantly. I can't change the past."

The knock on the door became louder and more urgent.

"Enter."

The door opened and the Chancellor came in with large, quick steps, throwing himself into a deep bow before the Emperor and Empress. "News of Prince Eric," he said anxiously.

"News of my son?" The Empress rushed forward.

"Guards."

Four guards pushed in a man and woman wearing dirty, old uniforms, and who quickly dropped to their hands and knees in front of the Emperor.

"Speak," the Chancellor demanded.

"Me? I don't know nothing," Jakey spat out, then edged back, still on all fours. One eye was fixed on the Emperor's shoes, and the other darted around.

"You swore to the men in the tavern that you kicked the Prince," the Chancellor accused.

Jakey's lips smacked together nervously. "They lie. I'd never kick a child. I love little rats that squeal and holler. I would never hurt one." He raised himself up and brought his hands together. "Please, your graces. I done nothing. Let me go back to the dungeon," Jakey begged.

The Empress stepped forward. "Please, I beg you. If you know anything. Anything at all."

"Lies." Jakey's lips smacked together again. Now one eye was looking at the Emperor, the other at the Empress. "I'm a faithful servant."

"Nothing?" the Empress moaned, a tear running down her pale face.

"Now, Alisa," the Emperor said condescendingly.

The woman spoke up, "Two guards brung a boy." Everyone looked toward the ancient jailer's accomplice. In her hand was Eric's uniform.

The Empress gasped and reached out. She took the uniform and pulled it to her as if it still held her son.

"You knew, Megey, and you didn't tell me?" Jakey said. "For shame. For shame."

The Empress helped Megey stand. "You saw my Eric."

Megey nodded her head vigorously.

The Empress took her hand and squeezed. "Tell me."

"Two royal guards told me and Jakey to take him."

"She lies, too." Jakey smacked his lips. "Me…me never saw the little rat."

"We must take him. They told us." Megey looked at the Emperor. "A direct order from the Emperor."

The Emperor moved uncomfortably.

"We have to obey," Megey said sadly to the Empress. "The Prince trembled, scared he was."

"But now he's not scared. You've been hiding him. His holiday is over. Bring Eric here." The Emperor pointed his finger to the floor directly in front of him.

"We's don't have him anymore. Right, Jakey?" Megey said.

"Guards." The Emperor shook his fist at Jakey. "Make sure he's telling the truth."

The guards brought out their swords and held the tips inches from the jailer's roving eyes.

"Oh…That little rat." Jakey scratched the stubble on his chin with a thumb. Then a smile leaped to his face. "Oh, the Prince. Yeah, I done treat him special. Like he's me own brat."

"Where is he?" the Emperor demanded.

"Smelt de Corcoran stolen him," Jakey shouted quickly. "The warlord yanked him away from our loving embrace."

"Smet de Corcoran, who led the Wamu during the fallow wars?" the Chancellor asked.

"That's the scum, the lowlife, the wicked." Jakey eyes were focused on the Emperor. "A shiftless bum."

"No," the Empress wailed. "Eric's in danger."

The chancellor opened his mouth to speak, but he was cut off by the Emperor. "We will search and find this Corcoran. By my word, he shall be here within the week."

The Chancellor turned his face away.

"He's a good boy, a strong boy," Megey said to the Empress.

"He's a little boy." The Empress closed her eyes and a tear slid down her cheek. "In my heart, I know he's alive. But he's in grave danger."

The Emperor turned his face away like the Chancellor, and the room fell silent except for the sound of smacking lips.

forty-five

It was ten days since the men had gone hunting for buffalo. Life around the village was uneventful, even boring at times. Promptly finishing his chores in the morning, Eric spent his time looking for small, flat rocks and exploring the land with Karro.

Today he and Karro were climbing in and out of tall ravines—a maze of deep trenches that ran in every direction. It looked to Eric as if some giant had taken a knife and cut deep grooves into the earth's surface.

He was enjoying himself. *It's good to have someone to talk too, someone my own age.* Karro reminded Eric of Sarah, his closest friend back at the Moon castle.

"My mother's family has a long history," Karro said, bringing Eric's attention back to the present. "I can trace my bloodline back to the Amazons of Earth."

Eric scanned his memory. "In Northern Africa?"

"Yes, along the Mediterranean Sea. It was a hard life and women—"

Suddenly, Eric began wiggling and performing little hops. His face twisted in agony.

"What's wrong?" Karro demanded.

"I'm going to burst; I have to go."

"Are you waiting for me to take you by the hand and lead you?" Karro pointed to a grove of trees. "Go."

Eric ran, praying he would make it to the trees. He went around the first tree and stopped. He looked back to confirm Karro wasn't looking and lifted his flap. He released a great sigh as his overfilled bladder emptied.

Relieved, Eric stepped out of the trees and looked around. The sun was a bright yellow ball with dozens of fluffy-white clouds dancing around it. The large cloud above him looked like a turtle with a long head and stubby legs.

The mountains in the distance were green with trees. He felt a mild breeze pushing the long, slender weeds in motions like hands waving goodbye.

Eric stopped and stared. A few minutes ago, Karro had been moving. Now she stood in an awkward manner as if she was a statue. Not a single muscle twitched. As he moved closer, she stayed motionless, but her eyes were wide.

"Karro, I'm hungry. Let's go back." When she still didn't move, Eric shouted louder. "Let's go back."

Movement caught Eric's attention—a brown dirt mound behind a tall bush thirty yards away, started to move. *What, the earth's moving?* Like Karro, Eric froze when two other mounds moved behind the first.

Suddenly, his eyes focused and he realized what he was looking at. He could see the beasts' whole, massive bodies—the creatures were six feet off the ground at the shoulder. A ton of powerful muscles lay behind those shoulders; in front of them, giant monster heads with sharp horns.

The lead buffalo leaned forward, its front hoof digging anxiously into the hard dirt and its big, black eyes fixed on Karro.

It's going to charge. Stomp Karro to death. Why doesn't she run?

Eric started to yell, "Buffalos…buffalos look at me," waving his arms vigorously. Two of the buffalos turned to face Eric, but the lead buffalo with the great horns continued to stare at Karro. Its head dropped, ready to charge. *Karro's my friend,* Eric thought. *I can't fail her. I won't fail her.*

Quickly, Eric reached into his pouch and took out a rock. He threw it from his side, like skipping a rock across a pond. The thin rock spiraled, cutting the air and hitting the buffalo behind its shoulders. It bounced off the thick hide, not causing even a flinch from the beast. Anxiously, Eric pulled another rock and threw it as hard as he could.

The rock slammed into the big buffalo above its right eye. The monster turned its enormous head and black eyes toward Eric. The creature swung its front legs around to face him.

"Yeah, I did it! You stupid buffalo!" Eric roared.

The buffalo jerked his head up and down in fury, his front feet digging up the earth below him.

Eric matched the buffalo's aggressive motions, moving his head up and down, swinging his right foot back and forth, kicking up dirt.

The buffalo bellowed in rage. When Eric hit it with another rock on its nose, the beast leaped into the air and charged.

Uh oh. The charging buffalo drove at him like a speeding rocket. But he couldn't move. *If I move too soon, it might turn back on Karro.* Determined, Eric stayed where he was, staring hard into the eyes of the beast.

Every cell in his body pleaded for Eric to move, to save himself. *Run away.*

But he stood firmly in place.

Karro broke out of her stupor. "Eric, run!" she screamed. "He'll kill you!"

His throat was dry, sweat was collecting on his brow, and his stomach was turning summersaults. But he didn't move. As if it had a mind of its own, his right hand reached into his pouch and brought out a rock. The earth shook under him as his hand caressed the rock. With every second passing the beast's speed seemed to increase. Its black eyes fixed upon Eric's small body.

When the buffalo was mere feet away, Eric fired the rock, hitting it between the eyes. The buffalo shifted and Eric dived to his left. He rolled up into a ball and watched the mound of muscle speed past him.

"Yeah!" Eric shouted, throwing his hands into the air. But the ground below him continued to shake. Eric turned to see the other two buffalos charging at him. There was only one way to run, and he took it. Without hesitating, Eric ran forward toward the oncoming buffalos. *It's my only chance.*

The buffalos altered course and converged. The gap narrowed fast. He lunged forward, running between the buffalos a second before they collided. A hind leg brushed Eric, sending him tumbling to the ground. Eric looked up in barely enough time to see the lead buffalo charging, horns pointed directly at him.

Eric sprang forward like a sprinter dashing out of the starting block. *Run faster!* His mind screamed. He looked over his shoulder. The lead buffalo had exploded forward, the distance between them disappearing.

This was a deadly game Eric knew he couldn't win. The buffalos were mad with rage. Their only purpose was to crush, gore, and trample his body.

"Run away, Karro!" Eric shouted. *She doesn't have to die, too.*

The enraged buffalos gathered and struck as one. Together, they charged, and Eric started to sprint away from them. His right foot stepped into a gopher hole, causing him to fall. He didn't have to look up; he could hear the pounding hooves coming closer. Springing up into a run despite the pain in his ankle, the thundering hooves stomped right behind him.

Giving himself one last chance to live, he focused all his energy into a final burst of speed. He pumped his arms hard and jumped high into the ravine.

But his tired legs failed him, and Eric fell short, hitting the other bank hard. Stabbing out his left hand, Eric captured a thin tree root sticking out of the ground.

The buffalos' momentum took them into the deep ravine. Eric heard a bellow that sounded like a curse as the beasts fell to their deaths eighty feet below.

I'm alive. But it was only a second of reprieve, as the tree root Eric hung from started to tear. Wide-eyed, Eric looked down at the dead buffalos on the ravine floor. *I'm going to fall. I'm going to die, too.*

A shadow appeared, his eyes shifted, and he glimpsed a pair of legs flying across the ravine. "Give me your hand." Karro bent down over the ravine's lip and extended her hand. As the root tore, Eric shot his hand up and Karro grabbed it, leaned back, and started to pull up. Slowly, with Karro's help, Eric climbed out of the ravine.

Eric fought to catch his breath. Karro's eyes blazed and she bit her inner lip before shouting, "I didn't need your help."

"What?!" Eric threw up his arms and said sarcastically, "Sorry for interfering. Next time I'll just watch you get trampled to death." Before Karro could respond, Eric turned his back and limped back toward the Shoshone camp.

forty-six

It was late afternoon the next day when all the warriors returned. No buffalos had been found. The village would go hungry until they could go out again.

When the warriors were a few hundred yards from the village, they caught the aroma of a familiar scent, and their stomachs growled at the thought of the succulent meat cooking. They looked at each other. *Could it be?*

The women and children ran out to greet them. "I smell cooking buffalo meat." Angry Bear leaned forward on his horse toward the camp fires to better enjoy the aroma. The rest of the hunting party dismounted, handing their tired horses off to boys and girls who would take care of them, and followed their noses to the cooking pots. The women quickly served the hungry men.

After the men and young braves were full, the questions started. When were the buffalos found? Who hunted them? Who had taken the large beasts down?

At night when the fire blazed high in the center of camp, an elderly man was brought forward. Everyone bowed their heads to him. Angry Bear stepped aside to give the elderly man a seat by the warm fire. He was the man who held the history of the Shoshone tribe. The Shoshone way was for a man to memorize the passing of time through events and recite them in verse. This man could recite the history going back hundreds of years.

Now in front of the fire, with the women chanting quietly around him, he began.

It was the time for the buffalo hunt. No meat in the village.
All the warriors mounted their horses. Find buffalo they must.
One warrior was left behind. Young in years was this Shoshone warrior.
The sun was high, the winds lazy. The young warrior prayed to the spirits to guide his steps as he moved through the brush, across the land.
Then the warrior stopped and listened. On the wind was the word, 'buffalo'.
Around he did search. But he could see nothing. Only mountains were around him. Then three mountains moved.
The warrior looked in fear as the great beasts' black eyes stared at him.
It was then the young Shoshone warrior gazed up. Into the blue sky above, he called upon the great warrior spirit.
Make his legs swift. Make his arm strong. But most of all he called to the warrior spirit to take the fear from his heart.
The mighty buffalos gave their war cries and charged. The earth shook.
The mighty spirits had listened to the prayers of the young warrior. With the power of the spirit, the warrior shook his fist at the beasts and shouted the Shoshone war cry in challenge.
At the buffalo did the warrior run. Two great powers coming toward the same spot.
The warrior spirit had not only taken away the warrior's fear, the spirit had given the warrior the wisdom to fight the beast.
A beat before the beasts were to crush the young warrior, he leaped to one side. The battle began, and he fought the buffalos.

With the speed of the panther and a fearless heart, he drove the beasts into the canyon to their deaths—their spirits leaving and entering the young warrior.

The Shoshone had meat again to stop the moaning of the stomach. Happiness filled the Shoshone village. And in the night, around the fire, during the celebration, the young warrior danced like a man without sense.

When the elder finished, it was quiet throughout the village.

"Who is this young Shoshone warrior?" Angry Bear asked, breaking the silence. "Who is the young warrior who brought the great beast down and delivered meat to the village to feed the empty stomachs?"

The village remained quiet. "Who is the young Shoshone warrior who is now remembered forever in Shoshone history?"

Karro elbowed Eric, who sat beside her. "Stand up."

"No," Eric said, trying to make himself smaller.

"Eric, you're a hero," Sami hissed from his other side.

The chief looked in the direction of the noise. Then as he watched, Eric slowly rose to his feet.

"Come forward that all can see." He looked hard at Eric before he bowed his head slightly in honor. "You have done well, Quick Coyote."

Great shouts and cries erupted from the people. Though Eric tried to sit back down, men's hands pulled at him. He was raised onto the shoulders of warriors and paraded around the village as they shouted, "Quick Coyote, mighty buffalo hunter."

But when Eric's eyes met Bolek's eyes, there was no joy there.

forty-seven

Later under the star filled night Eric, Sami, Karro, Kamani, and Shinichi were in a little clearing with a small campfire. Kamani picked up the empty bowls.

"Life is strange that way." Shinichi shook his head in disbelief. "I left here concerned you would come to some harm. I come back and you're a hero." He stared at Eric. "The story the elder told to chronicle the event was a mighty tall tale. How much is true?"

Eric shrugged his shoulders. "I wasn't alone; Karro was with me. She saved me from falling into the ravine," Eric said.

"It was Eric who stood against the buffalos," Karro said.

"I think we should call him Eric the Dumb," Sami said.

"No," Karro said. "Eric the Brave."

"You tell me the story in your own words," Shinichi said to Eric.

For the next half hour, Eric talked.

When Eric completed his story there was silence. Sami, Shinichi, and Kamani stared at him. Karro smiled. For a brief second their eyes locked before both looked away.

How can I explain how much Karro means to me? She likes me for me. Sami too. If Sami was in danger I would fight for him, too. I'm not a bad boy like Charles always told me. He looked first at Shinichi then at Kamani, Karro, and Sami. *You all mean so much to me. My family is gone. You are my new family.*

Feeling uncomfortable with these self-revelations, Eric started to explain again. "As I said, it wasn't just me. Karro was there, too."

Shinichi took a deep breath, then asked, "Are you telling me three large male buffalos which weigh more than two thousand pounds each charged you, so you charged them back?"

Eric nodded his head.

"Why? What insanity possessed you?" He looked up to the heavens. "I've only one student and he is mad as a hatter." Shinichi stared at Eric for an answer.

Eric remembered back to the event. The massive buffalo had turned away from Karro and toward Eric instead. Its nostrils flaring and its hooves pawing the ground in fury as it built up energy to charge Eric. The thick horns and head had come up and the anger showed in the creature's eyes.

"It angered me," Eric recalled. He had looked into the eyes and his mind had erupted. "The buffalo's eyes were like Stemann's, mocking me. Rage filled me, driving out any fear. So I fought them. All three."

"Yes," Sami confirmed. "Eric the Dumb."

Eric shrugged his shoulders and his eyes caught a flashing meteor across the night sky. There was no sight of the Moon tonight, but he thought back to life at the Moon castle. *They would have described it dumb to antagonize a buffalo. Over and over, Charles would have called me dumb as he sat on me.*

A screech owl in a nearby tree reminded him he wasn't in the Moon castle. He was in the wild. This gave him a sense of freedom. It was a different type of luxury than what the Moon castle afforded him.

"Well, in addition to being a celebrity you now have some wealth," Shinichi said.

"Wealth?" Sami put his arm around Eric's shoulders. "My good friend Eric the Brave is wealthy?"

"Yes, a little," Shinichi said. "Since you are given the credit for bringing down the buffalos, all the valuable parts are yours: horns, heads, and furs. These are considered costly by the Shoshone."

"I—" Eric started.

"I'll take care of everything. I'll be your personal banker," Sami said.

Karro grabbed Eric's arm as she stared at Sami. "Don't trust him, Eric."

"Karro, relax." He looked at Shinichi. "Can Sami trade the buffalo valuables for other things?"

Shinichi nodded.

"What do you want?" Sami asked.

"A teepee," Eric said.

"It won't be very big," Shinichi said.

"How big?"

"Sleep four to six people."

"Perfect," Eric said.

"Who will sleep in it?" Shinichi asked.

"Me," Eric said, and then he looked to his left. "Kamani will sleep in the tent, too."

Kamani vigorously shook her head and waved her hands.

"You will sleep within the teepee," Eric said. "It will make me happy."

Shinichi frowned. "The tribe will not like it. Kamani's an outcast. But that shouldn't bother a young warrior who stares down buffalos." After a second, Shinichi added, "I to shall move into your teepee. Student and teacher should be together. Besides, the snoring in the elders' teepee is like constant thunder."

"Good," Eric declared. "Sami, Karro, you can come at any time."

He watched Kamani hand out more bowls of meat to everyone. Eric took a piece of meat and put it in his mouth. "Very good.

THE FIRST EVENT: SURVIVAL

With Kamani cooking, we'll eat well every night." He smiled up at her. "By the way, what part of the buffalo is this?"

Kamani looked at Eric, then pointed to her chest.

"Yes, you," Eric said to Kamani. "What part of the buffalo is this?"

With more emphasis, Kamani pushed her finger toward her chest.

"She's pointing to her heart," Shinichi said. "You're eating buffalo heart."

Eric's eyes widened. He turned to Kamani and she nodded.

Suddenly, Eric didn't feel so good. "You're turning blue," Shinichi said.

Getting up quickly, Eric ran to a clump of bushes.

"I wouldn't tell Eric about the brains he had for lunch," Shinichi advised Kamani.

By early afternoon, Eric was the proud owner of a medium-sized teepee. With the help of Kamani, Sami, and Karro, he set it up at the outside boundary of camp.

"This teepee is half yours," Eric said to Karro.

"Why?" Karro asked suspiciously.

"You were there, too."

Karro folded her arms across her chest and kicked at a rock on the ground. "Women can't own property."

"Half yours," Eric said.

Karro shifted uncomfortably, looking away. "I froze. I was so scared when the buffalo's black eyes stared at me."

"Karro, the buffalo could have crushed you."

"You saved my life."

He shrugged. "We're even. You pulled me out of the ravine."

Raising her head, Karro stared hard at Eric. "When you charged that buffalo, your eyes were on fire as if they were blazing diamonds. For a brief second, I was as afraid of you as I was of the buffalo."

Eric waved his right hand dismissively, "I would never hurt you, Karro."

"I cannot make the same promise to you."

Later, after the evening meal, Eric pulled back the flap covering the entrance to his new home and let Shinichi in. Shinichi pulled out a long knife and handed it to Eric, "Cut a slit in the back big enough for Kamani to get in."

Eric took the knife and punctured the valuable leather, sliding the blade down in a vertical motion. He parted the slit and let Kamani in.

"Thank you," Kamani signed.

"You're welcome," Eric signed back.

A little while later, Kamani had a small fire burning inside. Its flickering light sent shadows against the teepee walls in constantly changing shapes.

Eric and Shinichi watched Kamani place a little branch on the fire. "How many stones have you collected?" Shinichi asked Eric.

He thought of the pouches that grew heavier every day. "I have half of the black ones and a little less of the white ones."

"It's enough to have a small game. Get the stones."

Eric returned with two leather bags and handed them to Shinichi.

Shinichi emptied the bags in front of him. Looking over the stones, he smiled in satisfaction. Then, getting on his knees, he started to draw lines in the dirt. In less than five minutes he had drawn a series of horizontal lines, and a matching number of lines going perpendicular to them.

Shinichi sat cross-legged on one side of the lines. He indicated to Eric to sit opposite him. "We will play 'Go' every chance we get."

"Why 'Go'?" Eric asked, finally able to get to the question he'd wondered so many times.

"Go's Chinese name is translated to mean 'encircling game.' It is a strategic game that has been played for over four thousand years. Two players are pitted against each other, and they take turns placing stones on intersections of the two sets of lines. To win, a player must surround a larger total area than his opponent."

Shinichi organized the white rocks in front of him. "I have found 'Go' mimics the progression of battles. Battles are simple in nature: advance or retreat. It is the strategy, how troops are positioned and moved, that can bring victory. To win a 'Go' game, you must think ahead, anticipate your opponent's moves, and guard your pieces and territories. No two battles are fought the same. In 'Go', every game is different."

Eric nodded.

Shinichi gathered the black rocks and handed them to Eric. "We'll play until you can beat me."

The fifth game was over as quickly as the first, with Shinichi easily winning them all. Eric didn't care; he was tired and wanted to go to sleep.

Shinichi handed Eric a bag to put his rocks in.

Eric was beginning to stretch out to sleep when Shinichi said, "I will leave tomorrow."

"Where?"

"Tomorrow the warriors will leave to find the buffalos. Although you supplied much-needed meat, we need more to survive the winter."

Eric turned over on his side to look at Shinichi. "How many?"

"Sixty to seventy. The Shoshones' life is built around the buffalo hunt. The buffalos must be found."

"How long will you be gone this time?"

"Not long, I hope. This time the students and the young Shoshone braves will stay with the village." After a second Shinichi threw a small branch on the fire and added. "While I'm gone, do nothing to earn the title of Eric the Foolish. Stay away from buffalos and trouble."

forty-eight

As Shinichi foretold, at the break of dawn the next day the warriors gathered supplies and weapons needed to find the buffalos. Shinichi waved goodbye to Kamani, then turned to Eric. "It is very rare that a story marking an event in Shoshone history falls on one person." He mounted his horse. "Be safe. One history note is enough for you."

Sami walked up and stood beside Eric. Shinichi nodded to both boys as he pulled on the horse's reins to move in line with the other riders.

Sami and Eric watched the rest of the warriors mount up and start their horses to the north. Eric looked up into the morning sky and saw three hawks circling above. The hawks were great hunters like the Shoshones. Eric was sure the warriors would be back soon.

He pointed west along the river toward the woods. "I have to find more 'Go' rocks. Let's try over there."

An hour later, Sami and Eric looked down as they went through the forest along the river bank.

"Where's Karro?" Eric asked, picking up a thin black stone.

"She's studying. Tangen left instructions to study Shoshone battle tactics."

"Aren't you supposed to study, too?"

Sami shook his head. "Why waste my time studying?"

"Well, what do you want to be?"

"I want to wander freely through the solar system, learning the history of the different worlds."

"Like an adventurer?" Eric raised an eyebrow. "Dangerous."

"Adventure without any danger," Sami said quickly. "Do you really want to be a warlord?"

No was the first word coming to Eric's mind. At the Moon castle he had only thought about eating dessert, playing with Sarah, and avoiding Charles. But Stemann's laughter and words had stirred something in him. *"The von Battenburg line is dying,"* Stemann had told him. *"Within two decades the Moon Empire will be no more."* His stomach knotted with the thought of the fall of the Moon Empire—the destruction of his family. *I must become a warlord. Protect my family.*

"Yes, I do," Eric said reluctantly to Sami.

Just ahead of them, between the trees to his left, a movement caught Eric's attention. Curious, he moved in that direction, quickening his pace. Eric saw movement again, something brown, maybe a deer. Moving quietly, he waved to Sami to follow.

"What do you see?" Sami asked suspiciously, leaned back ready to run to the Shoshone camp.

Eric raised his finger to his lips, signaling Sami to be silent. Three boys, hunched over, moved cautiously among the bushes and trees. Their footsteps made almost no sound.

"It's Bolek with Kirill and Malek," Sami whispered anxiously. "Let's go back."

Eric shook his head. *Kirill, Malek and Bolek are up to something. But what?*

Eric bent at the waist, mirroring the boys' stance, moving in a parallel path behind them. Suddenly, a light crackle in the otherwise silent forest brought everyone to a sudden stop. Eric's eyes shifted down and he saw a small, dry tree branch under his left foot. A second later, the three boys started walking again, but after a hundred yards, the boys slowed down, moving even more cautious.

Eric wondered what they had seen to give them such a pause and noticed something ahead. It moved into a clearing. *It's a student, a boy.*

"It's Omar," Sami whispered.

Bolek made hand signals to Kirill and Malek, and the three boys separated. It wasn't hard for Eric to guess they were moving into position to surround Omar.

Eric set his own path where he estimated Bolek, Kirill, and Malek would encircle Omar. He waved for Sami to follow.

Sami stopped and shook his head. Eric again waved Sami forward, but Sami took a step back.

Bolek, Kirill, and Malek ringed Omar. They hid, ready to spring on Omar as he passed.

Eric quickened his pace. The three boys were already in position, and Bolek was raising his hand to signal the attack.

"Watch out!" Eric yelled. Omar stopped, and Eric waved his hands as he ran quickly in Omar's direction.

Bolek's eyes narrowed as he caught sight of Eric. Eric was still fifty feet out when Kirill and Malek sprang on Omar, attacking.

Because of Eric's warning, Omar wasn't caught off-guard. He ducked under Kirill's swing and kicked out at Malek, causing Malek to step back. Bolek shifted his direction to get a better angle to attack.

Omar was tall and strong, and he moved quickly in the fight. But it was three against one, and the attackers used this to their advantage: Kirill and Malek struck from the front while Bolek attacked from behind. Bolek hit the backs of Omar's upper legs, sending him off balance. Kirill slammed his fist into Omar's ribs, causing him to lower his arms. A grin crossed Bolek's face as he steps in front of Omar and jabbed his fist into his victim's face.

Malek's fist to the side of Omar's head sent Omar down.

Eric ran as fast as he could, but not fast enough as Kirill brought out a knife. Kirill struck, but Omar slid under the knife and rolled away.

Malek, hearing the approaching footsteps, turned to face Eric. Eric ran so hard he hit Malek and sent him flying backward, then leapt forward and swung his pouch of rocks, knocking the knife out of Kirill's hand. Eric picked up the knife and threw it into the fast-flowing river.

A fist smashed into Eric's chest, and before he could recover another fist sent him falling backward into a tall redwood tree.

Omar recovered and hit Malek's jaw so hard he wavered. When Kirill stepped forward to help Malek, Omar brushed his outstretched hands aside and grabbed Kirill's head. Omar whipped his head forward and head-butted Kirill.

"Help!" Kirill cried. His head was still locked in Omar's hands, who was jerking his head back for another head-butt. Bolek pulled out a knife and bounded forward. He pushed his sharp blade forward to stab Omar. But Eric's rock-filled pouch caught Bolek above his right eye, sending him down.

Quickly, Eric turned to give battle to the other boys. But Kirill and Malek were already running away. Bolek got up and his hand went to his right eye, which was turning bright red.

His eyes showed no fear about this change in odds. "You'll pay for this interference," Bolek promised Eric.

"Anytime you want another black eye, come see me," Eric said with a grin.

Bolek bent down and picked up his knife. To Eric's surprise, Bolek looked back at him without malice, only amusement. Slowly, without worry, Bolek turned and walked in the direction of the other two boys.

"They're gone," Eric called out to Sami.

Cautiously, a minute later, Sami came into the clearing.

A gasp of air escaped Omar as he fell to one knee.

Eric moved to Omar. "Are you hurt?"

Omar turned away, his face twisting in pain. "I'm still able to fight," he grunted defiantly.

"Eric, why are you helping him?" Sami asked.

Abruptly, Omar fell to his knees.

"Where are you hurt?" Eric asked.

"My left rib."

"Lie back; it'll take pressure off of your rib," Eric said.

Omar shifted his weight, relieving the pressure. He looked up at Eric, his face a mixture of gratitude and distrust. "Why are you helping me?"

"Because you're hurt, and it wasn't fair—three attacking one."

Omar stared at Eric. "Thank you. I'm glad you did. My name is Omar Vasa."

"Eric Alexander. I'm pleased to meet you."

Omar's face tightened, telling Eric he continued to be in pain. Eric bent down and grunted with the effort of lifting Omar up. "Sami, help."

Sami was shaking. His eyes darting left and right, as he helped Eric lift Omar.

Once Omar was upright, Eric looked at him. He was tall, a half-foot taller than Eric, and muscular, almost like a man. His skin was black, as were his eyes. His face, although highlighted with pain, was strong and confident.

"We should go. It's a long way back to the village."

Omar nodded. Eric couldn't help but notice he gritted his teeth with every step, and to distract him, he asked, "What can you tell me about Shoshone battle tactics?"

Omar started to explain as Sami stuck close, looking warily behind every tree and bush. Together, at a slow pace, they went back to the village.

Two days later, when Eric and Karro had finally convinced Sami to join them, they ventured deep into the forest again. When they happened to see a large cougar walk across their path ahead, Karro laughed when Sami ran away and climbed up a tree.

"It's a female cougar. You should be scared," Karro said after she stopped laughing. Ten minutes later, when Sami still hadn't come down, she rolled her eyes. "I say we leave him."

Eric, caught a glimpse of the village, about two hundred yards back. He jutted his chin toward the village. "Something up?" Eric said. *Everyone is running around agitated.*

"The cougar's in the village!" Sami shouted from up in the tree.

"No. Look, the warriors have returned," Karro said.

"Let's go!" Eric said. Together they ran back, leaving Sami to scramble down out of the tree on his own.

As Eric, Karro, and Sami moved through the camp, Eric noticed many familiar warrior faces. When they passed Santos, Karro and Sami left to join him and his other students.

Everyone seemed happy. But then, Eric caught sight of Stemann off to his far left. He was standing over Bolek, pointing to his blackened right eye, and his face was red with anger. Bolek caught sight of him and nodded his head in Eric's direction. Stemann turned and saw Eric.

Eric stopped and crossed his arms, staring back at Stemann. *That's right, I gave it to him. He deserved it.*

Stemann's face became even redder and he turned back to Bolek. Whatever he said caused Bolek to tighten up and look again at Eric. Suddenly, Stemann dismissed Bolek, pointing out, away from the village.

Eric and Bolek again made eye contact, and Bolek's look of malice was startling in its intensity. In return, Eric smiled and winked at him, only adding fury to the malice.

Turning his back on Stemann, Eric came upon Shinichi a short distance away standing in front of his horse. His instructor's shoulders drooped, dark circles were under his eyes, and his clothes were dirt-stained. Clearly, he was tired, but Eric still received a large smile when Shinichi glanced up seeing him.

"It seems the search went well," Eric said.

"Yes, we found a small herd of twenty to thirty thousand."

"*Small* herd?"

"Yes," Shinichi said, handing Eric his horse's reins and stretching. "At this time in Earth's history, there are more than fifty million buffalos in this part of the United States. But in a hundred and fifty years, after the American West opens up, there will less than a thousand."

Eric's jaw dropped. "How?"

"It's not uncommon. Animals, trees, and sea creatures all gone because of man," Shinichi said. "It's the failing of man, that he destroys more than he creates."

"What's next?" Eric asked.

We shot three small buffalos and brought them back. We left a dozen warriors to watch the herd's movement, and in a few days, we'll break camp to move closer to the buffalos."

"How long will it take for us to meet up with the herd?"

"About ten days," Shinichi said. Then, eyeing Eric, he asked, "Will I be hearing another story about you tonight around the campfire?"

Eric couldn't help but grin. "Only if giving a black eye is important to the tribe."

"Black eye?" Shinichi said, shaking his head. "I can't wait to find out."

forty-nine

The Shoshones were happy. The warriors had found the buffalos, and everyone enjoyed the meat brought back. Eric enjoyed the delicious buffalo meat as well, but he was cautious. He always asked what part of the buffalo he'd been served before eating.

Wood brought from the forest and stacked in the center of camp blazed like a volcano. When the darkness of night came and everyone finished eating, the singing and dancing started.

Eric caught sight of Isabeli. She looked beautiful—her hair, thick and shiny, was parted in the middle and framed her oval face. Her eyes sparkled as she went from group to group, talking and laughing. She was one of the first to dance, and her fluid motions were a pleasure to watch. Fia was the only one who rivaled Isabeli in attention from others.

An hour later, Shinichi and Eric returned to Eric's teepee, where Kamani greeted both of them happily. Eric handed Kamani a bowl of hot buffalo meat. "This is for you."

Shinichi sat and made the lines in the dirt, and the two began a game of 'Go' in the light of the teepee's fire.

Shinichi cleared his throat. "Now tell me about the black eye. I noticed Bolek has a black eye?"

"Yes, I gave it to him."

"What happened?"

Eric spent the next ten minutes talking about the fight in the forest with Bolek.

"It was unwise for you to interfere," Shinichi said.

"If I hadn't, Omar might have been hurt or worse," Eric said.

"I'm sure he would have," the warlord said. Seeing the startled look on Eric's face, he continued, "The events are not only to develop the students' awareness in the art of war but to test their survival."

"But Omar's a student." Dumping the black 'Go' stones out of their pouch.

"Yes, some will perish at the hands of fellow students," Shinichi said as he removed a few white 'Go' stones from their pouch.

"It's not right. I wouldn't attack another student."

"You'll have to if you are to survive all the events."

"No," Eric said firmly dropping his black 'Go' stone on two intersecting lines. "I will find another way."

"Better men than you and I have made vows which they have broken later. Do not set yourself on a course you cannot follow," Shinichi warned Eric.

"I will survive, but not on those terms."

"How will you protect yourself?" Shinichi asked. "I cannot interfere."

"I'll find a way."

Shinichi placed a 'Go' stone on one of the intersections of two lines. "Eric, what is the purpose of Vulcury?"

"To make great warlords," Eric said as he placed a matching 'Go' stone on the board.

Shinichi nodded his head slowly. "You are not my first student. I have taken more than two hundred students through the events. None have become warlords." He now looked solemn. "Several were strong candidates, talented in so many ways. But they were consumed by the events, as I fear you will be unless you change your standards."

"I will not."

"Do not answer so quickly."

A silence fell between them as they both concentrated on the game, quickly placing dozens of stones on intersecting lines. Within a few moves, Shinichi defeated Eric. He started to put the stones back into his pouch. "One piece of advice that may help you live longer: if you must make enemies, do not make them with students like Bolek."

Eric looked firmly at Shinichi. "I won't back down from him." An idea was brewing in his mind.

fifty

The next night, Eric asked Shinichi and Kamani to stay away from his teepee for a few hours.

This has to work.

He sat in front of the fire with Karro on his right and Sami behind him.

Across the fire from him sat Omar, Isabeli, and a student he'd never talked to named Abbas Han. Omar had asked to bring him when Eric briefly explained his reason for the meeting.

Eric stared into each of their eyes to gather their attention.

"There are five events. These events are meant to push us, test us, and make sure only the best make it through. Chances are, not even one of us will make it through to become a warlord."

"I will be a warlord," Abbas said confidently.

"I will!" shouted Omar.

"No. I will." Karro flashed red with anger and her hand reached for her knife.

Eric reached over and pushed Karro's hand back down. "What about you, Isabeli?"

She gave her dazzling smile. "I'm a sure bet. While all these other baboons kill each other, I'll pass right through."

"Why does it only have to be one? Why can't we all become warlords?" Eric asked.

"There are five of us. How can we *all* make it through?" Omar asked the group.

"Six," Eric corrected.

"Who's the sixth?" Abbas asked.

"Sami doesn't count. He'll never become a warlord," Omar said.

"I'll be surprised if he survives this event," Isabeli added.

"I told you, Eric, they don't want me here," Sami said, still cowering behind him.

"Sami's part of it," Eric said.

"Part of what?" Omar asked impatiently.

"An alliance. We help each other become warlords."

Abbas snorted. "I have enough trouble watching my own back. You're asking me to watch five more?"

"Everyone is already watching my back." Isabeli smiled mischievously.

"I'm not," Karro said.

"Listen," Eric said, raising his voice. "We all have a pass, so there are only four events we must survive. I believe the events will become harder, with the final one taking most of us out."

"I agree," Omar said, absentmindedly rubbing his rib where Malek had punched him.

"We save our pass for the hardest; the last event. For the other events, we help each other get through." *I have to convince them. We must work together.*

"But what if—" Abbas started.

"We must totally trust each other, never doubting each has the other's back. We must become like a family who would die before seeing another of its members hurt."

"Yeah," Omar said, looking at him in understanding. "You saved my life; there's strength in numbers."

"For me, it doesn't make a difference; I'm the sure bet," Isabeli said. "Then again, why not?"

"Okay, I'm in," Abbas said, glancing at Omar.

"Let's seal it and find out who is the weakest," Eric said.

"It's Sami," Karro said, and they all looked at Sami, except Eric.

Eric threw more wood on the fire, building it up. "Clasp my hands over the fire. The weakest will pull his or her hand out first."

Eric stuck his hand out about twelve inches above the hot flames. Karro quickly grabbed it. Then, to Eric's surprise, Sami locked onto his hand. Omar, Abbas, and Isabeli all joined in.

The heat was intense. Eric saw Abbas' jaw tighten in pain, but he didn't move his hand. Isabeli's eyes moistened but her grip stayed strong. Karro shifted her position. Eric's whole body tightened as each second brought more pain. After the first minute, Sami was breathing hard, looking scared, but his hand held firm.

Eric released his grip and pushed the others away from the scorching flames.

"You're the weakest," Abbas said to Eric.

"I'm the weakest and I will never break the alliance. You can't either," Eric said.

The next day, Eric walked through the village, his thoughts still on the alliance among Karro, Omar, Isabeli, Abbas, and Sami. It was good, but he knew the pact must be more than just words. He'd talk to Karro about it the next time he saw her. Having spent more of his time with her than anyone else in the group, he knew of her growing knowledge in planning and strategy.

Just past the woman cleaning and tanning a buffalo hide outside a teepee, he stopped abruptly. About fifty yards away, at the edge of the camp, he watched Bolek, Malek, Raica, and Kirill running from the woods. He watched as both Malek and Kirill fell to the ground, fighting for breath. Raica dropped to one knee, her long brown hair plastered with sweat to the side of her face.

Bolek bent over, holding his side. Even from this distance, Eric could see the black eye was almost gone. He stood his ground with his legs braced, not falling to the ground as the others had a determined look on his face.

A minute later, Stemann rode up on a gray mare. Not disguising his anger, he shouted for Raica, Malek, and Kirill to stand. At that moment, Bolek caught sight of Eric, and, following his gaze, Stemann turned to look at Eric as well. His anger seemed to multiply as he made wild gestures toward Eric. Malek and Kirill stood up shakily and nodded in agreement with Stemann. B o l e k ' s expression never changed—his stare fixed, shoulders back, and fist clenched.

Bolek finally shifted his eyes when Stemann pointed out to the woods. Eric watched Bolek grit his teeth, then turn and sprint into the woods. Slowly, Raica straightened up and jogged after Bolek, and Malek and Kirill stumbled away in the direction of the others.

Stemann turned his head to face Eric. Eric quickly acted like he was running hard, then fell to his knees like one of Stemann's students, and followed it up with a comical death scene. Then, Eric sat up and pointed at Stemann, working his body hard with mocking laughter.

Eric got off the ground and ran as fast as he could when he saw Stemann turn his horse his way and start toward him.

fifty-one

It was still dark inside the tent when he heard his name being called. The tone was direct and loud. Through the dim light, Eric could see Shinichi get up and go toward the opening. Slowly, Eric got up as Shinichi left the teepee. Half a minute later, unable to help himself, Eric went out.

He was confronted by three men—a Shoshone elder, Shinichi, and Stemann stood outside the tent. He looked from face to face. All of their faces were stern, but Shinichi's eyes were laughing.

The elder spoke. "This morning, rabbit droppings were found in Stemann's moccasins."

"Really?" Eric said. "Who did it?"

"You did!" Stemann yelled, stepping forward.

"Let me see your right-foot moccasin," the elder said, extending his right hand. Eric did as he was told. The elder turned over the moccasin and presented it to Shinichi and Stemann. Stemann smiled with satisfaction. "Follow me, Eric," he said.

"No. I will take care of this," Shinichi said.

But—"

"He's my student," Shinichi said evenly.

Eric watched the muscle bulge on Stemann's neck as he fought back his wrath. Abruptly, he turned and stormed away.

The elder stepped toward Eric, and brought up the bottom of Eric's moccasin, pointing to a ridge on the heel. "It left a mark. Next time hide your tracks."

"Thank you," Eric said.

"Shinichi," the elder said, "it will be a hot day. The horses will need much water."

"Yes, they will," Shinichi replied.

The elder walked away.

Shinichi let out a heavy sigh as if he was tired. "Eric, why must you antagonize Isauro? Did you make fun of him yesterday?"

"It's his fault. He started it," Eric argued.

"Eric, Isauro von Stemann is—"

Eric crossed his arms before cutting Shinichi off. "He did it right outside our tent."

"What?"

"He drew the crest of the von Battenburgs in the dirt. He drew two lines through it as if the von Battenburgs are all dead," Eric said defiantly. "You're always taking his side."

"I'm not."

"I told you Stemann had carved the von Battenburg crest into the bottom of the tree where John Wheats died. You defended him. He's the enemy."

"Isauro didn't do it." Shinichi started rubbing his chin. "But whoever did is certainly sending a message. Eric, make sure you're never alone."

"Why?"

Shinichi bent down and stared into Eric's eyes. "Both messages were the same."

After a few seconds of silence, Eric shrugged his shoulders.

"Both are of death."

Eric sneered. "A true Prince doesn't worry about such things."

Shinichi watched Eric stroll off, and his heart skipped a beat. *I fear death will strike you soon, Prince Eric. I will see another von Battenburg buried in a grave.* He dropped his head. *How can I get Eric to understand the danger?*

fifty-two

The following night it happened again.

Eric tried several different positions on his buffalo skins to fall asleep. It was hot, and the teepee was stuffy and humid. Finally, Eric couldn't take the heat any longer. He put on moccasins and quietly went out.

It was dark, but the breeze felt good against his skin. Eric winced as he stretched out. *I'm sore. Omar pushes us today in hand-to-hand combat training. He want's everyone in the alliance to be ready for any danger.*

Eric's mouth opened wide in a lazy yawn. He groaned inwardly. Now that he was up, he got the urge to relieve himself. Hearing the deep breathing of the braves within the other teepees, Eric moved off to his right to go outside the campground. If he made any noise, one might wake up, come out and Eric knew he would feel his anger. He walked until he stood within a gathering of trees and got into position to relieve himself.

The crack of a dry twig got his attention. A few seconds later, another twig crackled further into the trees. Without hesitation, Eric moved in the direction of the noise.

His eyes adjusted to the darkness and he walked rapidly. Eric bent low to the ground, watching the path for any dried twigs or leaves that would betray his movements. He heard another crunching sound and adjusted his direction to follow it. At the edge of a clearing, Eric stopped behind a large tree trunk. He looked out and viewed the outline of a body moving across the opening. Then, as if hearing a noise, the person stopped and turned. Eric almost fell over in shock.

Karro, not seeing anyone, turned away and continued in the direction she had been going, away from the village. Eric jumped up and followed, trying to understand. *Why is Karro out here so late?*

Eric kept his distance. Then, a thought came to him. *Maybe she's going to bathe in the river.* An uncomfortable feeling came over Eric. He'd be ashamed if she caught him. He started to slow up, convinced Karro was out for a bath. *A waste of time. I could have been back in my tent sleeping.* He yawned and was about to go back when he noticed Karro reach into a bush and bring out a knife and tomahawk.

With the tomahawk held firmly in her right hand, and the long knife in her left, Karro dashed off again.

Eric moved rapidly to follow her tracks again. *Is something wrong? Why the weapons? There's no reason for Karro to go in this direction.*

He heard Karro further off and increased his speed until he was almost at a run. She was moving as if to escape. If she was caught far from the village, the discipline would be harsh. *What if I'm caught, too?* Eric thought. *My discipline could be worse— especially with Stemann's wrath so close upon me.*

Fifty minutes passed and Karro was still heading away from the Shoshone village. *We've traveled miles. Is Karro running away? Is she fed up being looked down upon because she's a girl?*

Checking himself, he slowed down. Karro's movements were getting harder to hear. He used all his senses to try and locate her, but there was nothing. Desperate, Eric continued in the last direction he had heard her.

Eric froze. There was light ahead—manmade light. A fire. He dropped to the ground. When he sensed no sound, he crawled slowly in the direction of the light. Below a bushy tree, he cringed in shock. *Cherokees, one of the Shoshone's greatest enemies.* If he were caught here, the event would be over for him.

Eric started to edge back. *I must warn the tribe.* Then, he thought of Karro. *If she's caught by the Cherokees, she'll be taken.*

Backing away from the camp, Eric tried to orient himself to the last place he had heard Karro. It was off to the left, parallel to the Cherokee camp. Moving close to the ground, he left the light of the camp behind.

Suddenly, he spotted Karro again. She was bent over close to the ground like he was, moving slowly. *If I speed up, I'll catch her. We can still escape and warn the Shoshones.*

Too late.

A shadow of a man stood in front of Karro.

Eric was about to shout a warning but stopped. *The Cherokee warrior hasn't seen Karro. There's still a chance.*

Eric gave a silent gasp of elation. He could see Karro looking up in the direction of the Cherokee warrior. She had time to stop and move away. Then, Eric could meet up with her and together they would return to the Shoshone village.

Instead, something else happened that made Eric want to scream. Karro moved closer to the warrior.

fifty-three

Eric's eyes jerked away from Karro to the warrior. He watched the warrior lean against a large rock and stare off in the distance. His bow was off to the side, knife sleeve was empty, and his war club rested several feet away. The warrior shifted his attention to the stars above, deep in study.

The Cherokee brave is a foot taller and outweighed Karro by more than a hundred pounds. A chill went through Eric as Karro grinned confidently. *Karro's going to attack the Cherokee warrior. She can't! Like the rest of us in the allegiance, she's been practicing hand-to-hand combat with Omar. But she's crazy if she thinks she can beat this warrior.* Eric watched Karro grin grow. *Yea, Karro's crazy.*

Eric watched Karro take a deep breath to focus herself. She slid in the direction of the lone warrior. He was the northern sentry, left to guard against enemies of the Cherokees.

Karro may have a slight chance. The Cherokee warrior has foolishly left his weapon away from him.

It doesn't matter. Karro, please walk away.

There was only a tree between them. She leaned over and kept as close as she could to the ground. Continuing around the tree, she was now only five feet away.

Wait, the Cherokee warrior has gray eyes. He must be a student from Vulcury on his last event. If he's on his fifth event, he'll be highly trained. Doesn't Karro realize that?

Karro stood up to her full height, bringing up her long knife as she tiptoed within striking distance of the warrior. In her

192

other hand, the tomahawk was pulled far back so she could build momentum and drive it into the Cherokee brave.

She swung the tomahawk forward with all her might.

The brave turned, smiling, and shifting into a fighting stance. Like a cornered rattlesnake, he struck quickly, grabbing Karro's wrist. Her eyes widened. His hand tightened like a vice. He squeezed so tight she was forced to drop the tomahawk. Twisting her body, she swung hard with her knife, but he caught her left wrist, too.

The malicious smile on the enemy's face told Eric everything he needed to know. *Karro's going to die.* The warrior lifted Karro off her feet like a little rag doll. Shifting, the Cherokee warrior swiftly pushed her down as he brought his knee up savagely into her stomach. He let go, and she dropped like a rock. As Karro fought for breath, he grabbed her hair and jerked it back hard.

"You thought you were silent, unnoticed, and could attack me, the fierce Ebru Subutai? Do you really think I'm a fool to leave my weapons thus?" Ebru said. "I did it to trap you." Viscously, he kicked out and struck Karro cruelly on her side. She rolled over but couldn't move quickly enough as another came right after.

The warrior called Ebru now leaned down over Karro as she grabbed her side. "I haven't called out because it would shame me. A small, feeble girl attacking me—I would be laughed at. Why didn't your warlord send out a worthy warrior, one who would test me and bring honor when I killed him? My warlord would expect nothing less."

"Yes, I am a small, feeble girl. A true Amazon would never be so easily caught and handled like a child. I *should* die. I bring shame to my Amazon sister. Kill me!" Karro begged, her head down in defeat.

The Cherokee warrior gathered his war club. "I will and leave your body for the scavenging coyotes to eat." He pulled the club back to his right.

fifty-four

Wake up, Eric's mind begged. *End this dream.*

It was a bad dream turned into a nightmare. When the Cherokee warrior turned and grabbed Karro, Eric's heart stopped. With surprising strength and quickness, Ebru disarmed her.

I'm going to see Karro die. Eric wanted desperately to close his eyes, to block out the sight of his friend being killed. But they stayed wide open, fixed on Karro lying helplessly on the ground.

Words, an inner voice mocked him. *Watch each other's back.* The alliance was just words unless he acted. *If I just watch—or worse, if I leave now, Charles is right: I'm not royalty. I'm not a von Battenburg; I'm a coward.*

A chill passed over Eric's body. *She's my friend; I won't leave her.* The fear he'd felt passed and turned to anger. With every strike the Cherokee inflicted upon Karro, his anger increased. He breathed evenly as he leapt to his feet and charged. As Ebru brought across the war club for the killing blow, Eric hit the warrior's hip with his shoulder, sending him sprawling to the ground.

Before Eric could help Karro, Ebru jumped up with astonishing speed, legs moving fast, and weapon pulled back to crush Eric. The Cherokee brought the war club around hard.

Twisting at the last second, Eric barely dodged the blow. He wasn't so fortunate in the return swing. A sharp buffalo horn embedded at the top of the war club cut into Eric's side.

As he moved, he caught sight of Karro's knife, in a clump of dry grass. He dived under the next blow, and then, coming around, he crouched down, ready for the attack with Karro's long blade in his right hand.

A broad smile appeared on Ebru Subutai's face. "I will make you suffer for the insult of attacking me." The smile vanished as he looked at Eric's hard, cold, gray-blue eyes.

The warrior rushed forward and Eric stepped forward to meet him. Striking hard, the Cherokee was ferocious in his attack, relying heavily on his superior size and strength.

The hours of drills and practicing hand-to-hand combat with Omar helped Eric fight back, at least for a while. But Eric soon felt his strength waning. Ebru was too quick and strong, and Eric couldn't find an opening to strike with Karro's knife. He felt his side wet from his own blood. His breathing came hard and labored, and both legs started to shake.

Across from him, the warrior seemed to glide. Like a deadly snake, he darted in and out, striking before Eric could use his knife.

Ebru swung the club out and around, knocking the knife from Eric's hand. Defenseless, Eric moved warily from side to side.

Suddenly, the warrior tottered, taking a sideways step. Eric looked to see Karro with a thick branch in her hand.

Eric attacked, whipping his leg around in a savage kick. Ebru fell back, and Eric picked up and swung the knife viciously, aiming for the heart. The Cherokee warrior backed away with his hands up and tripped on a rock.

Karro leapt forward to attack, but Eric held her back. "He's not moving."

Cautiously, Eric stepped forward, Karro's knife extended in front of him.

Ebru Subutai lay on his back, eyes opened, staring up at the stars. There was blood on the rock beside his head.

"He's dead," Eric said.

Karro moved beside him and looked down. They stood for several long seconds. The cry of a coyote brought Eric back to the present. "We have to go." He grabbed Karro's arm and pulled her in the direction of the Shoshone village.

"Wait."

"Why?"

Karro ignored Eric. She gathered all of Ebru's weapons. She even took his pouch.

The elder's words filled Eric's mind: *Hide your tracks*. Eric handed Karro her knife and picked up a thin branch with lots of leaves. He started to sweep the ground. "Let's go," he said, continuing to sweep as they left.

fifty-five

Where'd you get these?" Sami asked. His eyes were fixed on the Cherokee items lying in front of him.

"Last night— This morning," Karro corrected herself. She sat beside Eric and across from Sami on some rocks. "We found them by the river, several miles upstream."

"Can you trade them for something?" Eric asked.

"Sure," Sami said confidently.

"I want a Shoshone war club," Karro said. Eric stared at her hard but said nothing.

"I can get you one," Sami said. He looked at Eric. "What do you want?"

"Arrows," Eric said.

"How many?"

"I want to know how to make arrows. And a bow," Eric said.

"Make them? Why? That's work," Sami said.

"Calm Cougar makes the best arrows, has the best bow," Eric said.

Sami shrugged his shoulders. "I'll try. What about the rest?"

"Ask Omar, Abbas, or Isabeli if they need anything," Eric said.

Sami nodded his head and gathered up the items.

Eric got up but winced.

"What's wrong?" Karro asked.

"Nothing," Eric said, holding his right side.

"Let me take a look," Karro said.

"It's nothing," Eric said, tight-jawed. Without warning, Karro's hand pushed on his side. Eric's eyes opened wide and he jerked away.

Karro moved closer to Eric. "Open up your vest."

Sami recoiled from the sight. Eric's right side was black and blue. There was a line across the ribs where Ebru's war club had cut the skin. Around the area, the skin was red.

Turning to Sami, Karro said, "Go quickly and bring the medicine man."

"No. I'm fine." Eric pulled his vest closed.

Karro looked hard at Sami. "Go."

Sami looked at Eric.

Karro turned back to Eric. "Should I push on it again to see if it hurts?"

Eric responded by moving his right side away from Karro.

"The wound is infected," she said. "It must be washed thoroughly, and then buffalo salve applied to work against the infection and protect the wound." Reaching up, Karro felt his head. "You have a slight fever, but it will grow until the infection is brought under control." She turned to Sami and, seeing that he had not left, threatened, "Amazons *never* ask a male twice."

Sami left running.

"To the river to clean the wound."

Eric hesitated. "Will it hurt?"

"You fought a Cherokee warrior," Karro said. "But you're worried over a little cleaning?" She pushed him in the direction of the river. "Yes, it will hurt. Gentleness is not in my nature."

Eric reluctantly started toward the river.

"If you tell anyone I, an Amazon, played nurse to you, I promise you'll regret the day."

fifty-six

It was three days later Eric moved slowly out of his tent. His hand shot up quickly to shade his eyes against the bright sun. It was the first time he'd been out of his teepee in days. Karro had been right: the high fever had come. It boiled his blood and bathed him in a constant sweat as he'd lain restless on his buffalo skin. He felt drained as if he'd been running all day.

Since Kamani was gone, for the past few days Karro had been at his side. She'd worked hard tending the wound and his fever, constantly wiping sweat off his body and putting a cool cloth upon his forehead. When he became too weak, she fed him.

Sami, Omar, Isabeli, and Abbas were constant visitors. As best he could, Sami avoided Karro, as she would put him to work. Omar and Abbas told Eric of the preparations to leave for the buffalos. Isabeli kept Eric up-to-date on the social events and tribe gossip. When the fever finally broke, Sami brought him soup with deer meat and herbs to help him regain his strength.

Today, a call had come for a general meeting of the village. It didn't matter Eric was recovering; he was required to go. It took all his strength to dress. He walked like an old man, slow and hunched over. Every step he took was a great effort.

Everyone gathered in the center of the camp; the meeting was about to start. Karro and Sami spotted Eric and pushed through the crowd to stand by his side.

"How do you feel?" Karro touched Eric's head.

"The fever hasn't returned. But I'm still weak," Eric said. "Thank you both for helping me."

"I'll send you my bill later," Sami joked.

Eric looked around. Front and center before the tribe were the elders and Stemann. "What's the meeting about?" he asked.

Before Karro or Sami could answer, Angry Bear stepped forward and raised his hands high. Everyone stopped talking and gathered closer.

"My people," Angry Bear started. "Yesterday a warrior came upon a dead body. It was the body of a Cherokee warrior."

A gasp of horror rose from the tribe. Eric heard the murmured concerns. Were the Cherokee close by? Would they be attacking soon?

Angry Bear again held up his hands to quiet the crowd. "Our warriors have searched the area and have found no Cherokee warriors close by. They did find a small hunting party's camp that had been used several days back. We are safe." Raising his voice, the chief continued, "When the area around the dead Cherokee warrior was searched, a Shoshone moccasin print was found."

Eric's body stiffened at Angry Bear's comment. He turned back to Karro, but her attention was focused on the object in the chief's hand.

Angry Bear raised his hand high over his head. In it was the Cherokee war club Karro had brought back.

"There is a young warrior among us who knew of the Cherokee. He knew of the danger, but his strong spirit drove him to act. What I hold above my head is the war club of the dead Cherokee warrior. It was in the possession of one who has proven himself to be a great warrior."

Angry Bear moved aside and Bolek stepped forward. But it was not Bolek who Eric focused on—it was Stemann. On his face was an expression he had seen many times before. It was the look his father wore when Charles won a card game or a foot race—a look Eric's father never had for him. The look of great pride.

Bolek stepped beside the chief. He stood tall, straight, and with a superior expression on his face. He stabbed both his arms high toward the sky.

The crowd cheered, shouting Bolek's name.

Part of Eric was mildly amused at how easily the tribe had been duped into believing Bolek had defeated the Cherokee warrior. He wanted to laugh. But another part of him wanted to stop the cheering, to let everyone know he'd been the one who fought Ebru Subutai. *Keep quiet. Be satisfied with the fact you and Karro returned alive.* Shinichi's words returned to him. *Stay out of trouble.* He must not do anything.

Turning, Bolek received a nod of approval from Stemann.

A sudden push to Eric's lower back propelled him forward, causing him to collide with the Shoshone in front of him. There was a domino effect, as everyone in front of him was sent to the ground. Eric looked down at the angry faces glaring up at him.

He turned to see Karro standing behind him with her arms crossed. He opened his mouth, but before he could say anything, an angry voice boomed from the front.

"Who disturbs the celebration?" Angry Bear demanded.

Eric froze as everyone looked in his direction. A warrior grabbed his arm and pulled him forward to Angry Bear.

"You don't learn, Slithering Skunk!" Angry Bear said to Eric as he twirled his horse whip. "For your actions, you will be punished."

Bolek's eyes danced at Eric's grim future.

Eric looked at Karro then quickly down. *Why Karro? You helped me recover. I don't understand.* Eric looked away, trying not to lock eyes with anyone else, knowing the worst was yet to come.

"I will deal with you later," Angry Bear promised. The chief turned back to Bolek, and the smile reappeared. "Tell us how you overcame one of the greatest enemies of the Shoshone people."

Eric didn't listen to Bolek as he lied about defeating the Cherokee warrior. He was trying to come to terms with his upcoming punishment. *Is this because she took care of me? Because I'm a male? I didn't tell anyone. I wouldn't do that.* Despite himself, Eric sneaked a look at Karro, wanting to know.

Karro was busy speaking with Sami, who kept shaking his head. He then looked up wide-eyed at Eric and shook his head even more vigorously. Eric felt his head shaking, too. He somehow knew he wouldn't like what Karro was saying to Sami.

Unexpectedly, a hand knocked him on the side of the head. Angry Bear looked heatedly at him, as did Stemann. "Continue," Angry Bear said to Bolek.

"He attacked. The Cherokee warrior came at me quickly," Bolek said. "He was taller and tried to use his superior height against me. Several times his war club almost killed me in a down stroke."

Angry Bear held up a hand to pause the story. "Down stroke?" he asked.

"Everything happened very quickly, Bolek," Stemann said. "Take your time and think."

Bolek's eyes moved from Stemann to Angry Bear. He hesitated and seemed to be searching for words.

"How did he attack you?" Angry Bear asked Bolek.

"From above like a bear."

Stemann's eyes narrowed as he stepped toward Bolek.

"Ooowww!" Eric suddenly screamed out, rubbing his shoulder. He looked down to see a sizable rock down on the ground in front of him. It hadn't been there before. He looked in Karro's direction. Karro didn't hide—instead, reaching down for another rock.

Angry Bear turned upon Eric, his horsewhip pulled back.

"Tell what really happened, Slithering Skunk," Eric heard Sami shout from far off. "Tell the truth."

"What truth?" Angry Bear demanded, looking around. "Who spoke?"

"The attack was not from above. But side to side," Eric said.

"That is the Cherokee way of fighting." Angry Bear lowered his horse whip and looked at Eric, confused by the boy's apparent knowledge.

"Many people know the fighting ways of the Cherokees, including Shinichi, Slithering Skunk's instructor," Stemann cut in, trying to justify the statement.

Angry Bear nodded his agreement. Suddenly, the chief turned, grabbing Eric by his neck, and yanked him inches from his face. "The truth."

Eric's eyes nearly closed from the pain in his side.

"Hold, Angry Bear. Slithering Skunk is hurt," the medicine man said walking forward from the crowd.

"How?" Angry Bear asked.

"A deep cut on his right side," the medicine man replied.

Angry Bear released Eric. "There's dried blood on the war club." He released Eric and stepped back, looking first at Eric then at Bolek. "I will have the truth," Angry Bear swore. "How did the Cherokee die?"

"A blow to the head," Bolek said quickly.

"Yes," Eric agreed.

Angry Bear growled in frustration. He raised his horsewhip to Bolek and Eric. "One of you will know honor. The other will feel pain and humiliation. This I promise."

Stomping Horse, one of the tribe's leading warriors, stepped forward. "Angry Bear, I found a moccasin footprint under the dead Cherokee."

Eric's eyes widened. *I missed a footprint. If it's Karro's, she'll be severely punished. I can't allow it—I'll say I lied.* "Angry Bear, I—"

"Silence. Stomping Horse, you know the moccasin?" Angry Bear asked.

"Yes. A Shoshone moccasin. A deep ridge on the heel of the right foot."

"Slithering Skunk has that moccasin," an elder said. "I have seen it."

"Take off your right moccasin and show me the bottom," Angry Bear directed Eric and Bolek.

When Eric and Bolek presented their moccasins, Angry Bear waved over Stomping Horse to look.

"It is Slithering Skunk who defeated the Cherokee," Stomping Horse said, pointing to the heel of Eric's right moccasin.

So fast was the horsewhip lashed, it whistled. Across Bolek's left cheek was a slash that stretched from cheekbone to ear. Blood dripped from it, but Bolek didn't flinch.

Angry Bear looked at Stemann standing beside him. With eyes narrowed, he said, "Is this how you teach your young warriors? To claim the honor of another?"

Isauro touched his knife hilt as Angry Bear whirled his horsewhip. Slowly Stemann eased his hand back.

"They are young and do not always listen," Shinichi said, stepping between the two men. "What's done is done."

Angry Bear push Stemann away and clapped Shinichi on the shoulder. "You have taught Fighting Wolf well. Let us all sing his praise."

fifty-seven

Shinichi sighed heavily. "Eric, do you listen to me? Do you want to survive the event?"

"Yes." Eric sat crossed-legged across from Shinichi in the teepee. Kamani had returned safely from her distant search for medicinal herbs and they were eating the evening meal together.

"With the power of the wolf, the young Shoshone attacked the mighty Cherokee. Swift as the wind, striking like thunder, and with the cleverness of his brother wolves," Shinichi recited. "This will be added to the history of the Shoshone. Your second entry."

"Why? Why did you do it?" Kamani signed.

"I had to," was all Eric would say.

"I've never seen Stemann so angry. He has killed men for less. The elders have taken away his position on the council." Shinichi said.

Eric shrugged his shoulders.

"Stemann will regain his position, I'm sure of it," Shinichi said. "Bolek is a threat. He hated you before; now, seeing you will be intolerable. The lash across his left cheek from Angry Bear will be with him for the rest of his life—a mark of shame and humiliation."

"It's Bolek's own fault."

"It's easier to blame others than it is to blame yourself," Kamani signed.

"What's wrong?" Eric asked Shinichi. *He's been anxious since the meeting.* "I'm not afraid of Bolek."

"That night you fought the Cherokee, were there others from his tribe?" Shinichi asked solemnly. He stared deeply into Eric's eyes.

"Six others," Eric said cautiously. *Why does Shinichi want to know? Does he know about Karro too?*

"How did they die?" Shinichi asked.

"Die?" Eric shrugged his shoulders.

"Yes. They were following you. They must have heard you and were after you."

Suddenly the hairs on the back on Eric's neck stood on end. *They could have gotten me and Karro.* His mouth was dry and he swallowed hard. "Why didn't Angry Bear say anything at the meeting?"

"Angry Bear didn't want to scare the tribe. The warriors couldn't identify the creature that killed the six Cherokees." Shinichi drew a picture in the dirt.

Kamani gasped and signed quickly. "A ghost. An evil spirit." She buried her face in her hands.

It's a boot print. Eric's eyes bulged when he looked into Shinichi's face.

Shinichi nodded. "You can't blame Stemann for this one. He was with other warriors that night."

"But...how?" *It's impossible. No white man will come here for more than a hundred years.*

"I don't know. Our first thought was a student snuck a pair of boots to this event. Isauro and I went to investigate." Shinichi pointed to the picture he'd drawn. "The boot prints were a size 14 and very deep. Isauro estimates the man's weight to be more than 250 pounds."

"Who?"

Shinichi jaw tightened in frustration. "We don't know. Nothing like this has ever happened during an event." Eric saw the frustration on Shinichi's face turn to concern. "Eric, please. Be careful."

"Beware the ghost. Its evil spirit will fill you and make you do crazy things," Kamani signed emphatically to Eric.

"Too late," Shinichi said with a chuckle.

"I'll try to be more careful," Eric promised.

"Well said." Shinichi pulled out the two pouches of thin round rocks. "Regardless, only time will tell what consequences your actions will have." Shinichi turned and looked around the teepee. "It was nice while it lasted."

"What?" Eric asked.

"In three days, the tribe will start to move to the buffalo. Since you have no horse to pull your teepee, you cannot take it. Perhaps Sami can get you a good price for it."

"No," Eric said firmly.

"You have no choice."

"Kamani will be forced out again."

Kamani made several signs to Eric.

"Yes, you do matter."

"It's simple. No horse, no teepee," Shinichi said as he started to draw lines in the dirt for a 'Go' game.

fifty-eight

Early the next day, after the morning meal, Eric approached Omar, Abbas, and Sami to see about using one of their horses.

"I can't," Omar said.

Abbas nodded his head in agreement. "It would break the horse's spirit," he said.

"Our horses are trained for battle, not as beasts of burden," Omar added.

Later that morning, Eric concluded, *I won't leave my teepee.* He looked at Kamani walking beside him across the open field. *I can't.*

Kamani drifted off to the right and Eric followed her. They were alone collecting berries, roots, and vegetables needed for the trip. The march to the buffalos left no time to stop along the way.

The basket Eric carried was almost full of berries, and Kamani's pouch had begun to bulge with all the roots and vegetables within.

Kamani pointed to a tree with a clearing under it. She made several signs.

"Yes, let's rest."

They sat under the shade of the tree. Kamani brought out some dry deer meat and handed a piece to Eric.

Eric saw Kamani jerk her head around.

"What's wrong?"

She made a sign.

"Horses?"

She pointed off into the distance.

A few seconds later, Eric heard the thunder of hoofs. Far off on the horizon was the great herd—a familiar black stallion running far ahead in the lead.

It was a depressing sight to Eric. *So many. All I need is one.*

The horses slowed, bunched up, and walked into a ravine. Eric turned his head and looked away. He felt as though he was being taunted—like food being held out of reach of a starving man.

Kamani pulled hard on Eric's shirt. He looked at her as she pointed to the ravine's entrance. She was excited and signed too quickly for Eric to follow.

"Don't sign so fast." Eric watched Kamani take a deep breath and sign to him slower. "You've seen the herd before?"

Kamani nodded and made a few more signs.

"Every day the horses go into the ravine."

She nodded again.

"There's probably food and water in the ravine."

She pointed emphatically and anxiously at the ravine and began signing fast again.

Eric shook his head. "I don't understand."

Pulling Eric closer, she knelt beside him. Quickly, she began to draw in the dirt. Eric watched as she made a drawing of stick-figure animals.

"Horses." Eric nodded in understanding.

Kamani began to draw again.

Eric didn't recognize the curvy lines and straight lines going in different directions, but they were all connected. Puzzled, he looked at Kamani and shook his head.

She first pointed to her stick drawing of the horse. Then the connected curved and straight lines, and finally, to the far-off horses running into the ravine.

"The horses and ravine."

"Yes," she signed excitedly.

"What about them?"

Kamani drew a line representing a horse going between two lines.

"Horses running through the ravine," Eric said.

Kamani then drew the lines narrowing like a funnel. She drew a single row of horses.

Eric stared at the drawings. "I don't get it."

She pointed to his head.

Think. Eric leaned back on his heels. *The horses going into the ravine. The ravine narrows down. The horses have to slow down and go in single file.* Eric's eyes lit up. "I understand."

A smile appeared on Kamani's lovely face.

Eric jumped up. "I have to get a rope." He started running toward the Shoshone camp.

fifty-nine

With a coiled rope slung over his shoulder, Eric climbed to the top of the ravine. He thought back to Kamani's drawing. With the straight line across the end of the curvy lines, Eric understood the ravine did not have an exit. The wild horses would have to come out through this entrance.

I won't have to give up my teepee. The thought brought a happy feeling. *It's easy. I'll catch one of the older horses.* He'd seen a brown mare with white legs that was the last to enter the ravine. *I'll jump on the old brown one when it leaves.*

He took the rope from his shoulder and looked over the edge of the ravine. It was ten feet down. High enough for him to jump on the back of the old horse.

I'd better practice. For the next twenty minutes, Eric walked twenty paces back from the edge. Then, he practiced running to get the momentum he would need to go out over the ravine's edge and land on the horse's back. Eric adjusted the running path several times to make sure he jumped at the narrow opening of the ravine. *Once I'm on the old horse, I'll force it to obey.*

Eric looked up as he heard the sound of hooves pounding against hard dirt. *Only one chance; I have to time it right.*

The sound increased until all other noise was shut out. The first horses were returning to the ravine's opening. He got down and crawled to the edge, staring down at the multitude of colored horses slowing and straining to get through the narrow opening.

At the sight of the powerful animals, Eric's throat became dry and his body was covered with sweat. *It's only an old horse,* he kept telling himself as his courage faded. *Do I really need a teepee? Maybe Shinichi is right, and Sami could get a good price for it. If I have a horse, I'll have to take care of it.* And finally, *I don't need a horse.* Eric relaxed, moving away from the edge, away from the horses. *It's too dangerous.*

But then Kamani's smiling face filled his mind. *Kamani reminds me of mother. I swore to protect her and I will.* He crawled back to the edge to look down at the horse three feet below. *I have to.*

For twenty minutes, Eric watched the wild horses slow down to a walk to get through the narrow opening. Once out, the horses would burst into a full run onto the flat plain toward the rolling hills in the distance, each one seeming to run faster than the ones before it, trying to catch up.

Eric moved fifty feet further down the ravine, and looked at the horses bunched up, waiting to get through the ravine's opening. There were so many horses, it was an hour before he spotted the last horse coming up. The old brown horse with white legs was at the end. Eric shot up onto his feet and grabbed the rope, throwing it over his shoulder. He backed away from the edge and followed the old horse's progression through cracks in the ravine's edge.

It's now or never. His ears filled with hard pounding. *Is it the fierce pounding of the horses' hooves or my heart?* Eric scurried back to his starting spot. He turned, crouching down, ready for the race. He saw the old horse pass a large crevice. Taking one final breath, he launched himself forward and started running as fast as he could. With each step, he grunted with the effort to speed up. The edge of the ravine was before him and suddenly, he was at the edge. With a final grunt, he pushed off as hard as he could and leaped up into the air.

Then, his mind froze as terror overtook him. He continued to fly toward a horse until he felt the two bodies collide.

"Ahhh!" Eric cried out, hitting the horse's back. One leg made it partially over; the other was hanging down. With adrenaline surging through his veins, he yanked himself up. His eyes bulged. The horse's coat under him was not brown—it was totally black.

The black stallion leaped up, its front hooves beating the air.

"Help!" Eric screamed, leaning forward, hands tight like vises on the stallion's mane. "Stop!" Eric screamed. Then over and over again, "Help!" There was no one around to help. His mind screamed, *I'm going to die!*

With all the horses gone, the black stallion bolted forward as if fired from a cannon. Eric held on for his life. He leaned as low as possible, holding on with legs and hands.

"Please. Stop," he begged the charging stallion. He was being thrown about like a small boat on a raging sea.

Eric looked forward. Suddenly, the horse was running fast, its hooves hammering the dirt and its body stretched out long. They ran through the speeding herd on the open plain as if the other horses were standing still.

The wind blowing against Eric's face was cool and refreshing. Eric leaned back, his senses acute. All the tension left him and jubilation took its place. "Run," he screamed at the black stallion. "Run faster."

As if the stallion understood him, Eric felt the strong muscles under him pull hard, sending them forward faster. He'd never felt so excited in his life.

The horse raced at breakneck speed over the plain, the hill coming on rapidly. Under him, the mighty stallion was burning up the miles. But it wasn't fast enough. Eric urged the horse on. "Run!" Eric screamed, leaning closer to the mighty steed's body.

His mind drifted back to a similar time when he'd felt the same freedom on the solar sailing ship. The joy overtook him and he raised his arms into the sky and shouted, "Run. Run like the wind."

The sun dropped and Eric and the black stallion were in the hills within a sparse pine forest. Both were breathing hard. Among several pine trees, the stallion finally stopped, and Eric slid down from the horse's back.

The stallion, hanging its head, didn't move, and Eric leaned against the horse. He looked at the black coat and saw it was full of sweat.

He can't stand still or he'll get sick. He remembered seeing Shoshone riders after a hard ride immediately brush the sweat off their horses with dried grass. Eric threw a noose around the black stallion's head and tied the other end of the rope to a tree. Then, he pulled up dry grass and started to brush the sweat off the black coat. "You're a mighty horse, but I need to take care of you so you don't get sick," he told him gently. Within a few minutes, Eric had removed all the sweat he could.

Next, he untied the rope and pulled. The black stallion didn't move.

"You have to walk or your muscle will cramp up." Eric pulled harder until the tired horse finally began to move.

He walked the horse for thirty minutes and as the stallion continued to walk, he started to breathe normally. All the time Eric talked to him. "You are strong, and when you run your hooves hitting the dirt sounds like thunder." He looked at the black horse and patted his long neck. "I will call you, Thunder."

He picked a few berries and ate them. Thunder nibbled a few. Eric picked another handful and Thunder ate them from his palm. Next, he dug up some roots and fed them to Thunder. Satisfied the stallion was sufficiently cooled down, Eric tied up Thunder and brought him water to drink. While Thunder drank, Eric stroked his cheek. "Thank you for the ride." He looked up. The stars were coming out. "It's too dark to go back. You might step in a hole and hurt your leg." He tied Thunder by a clump of grass and started to gather leaves for a bed.

The sky was bright with moonlight, and Eric talked to Thunder about his home at the Moon castle. He felt good. It was the first time he had talked about his family in a long time.

"I think Father would be proud I rode you. Charles would be jealous." Eric gazed up at Thunder. "I would give George a ride. He'd love it. My mother—" Eric thought for a while. "Mother would be worried I rode you, thinking I'd get hurt." He sat up. "You must have a mother, Thunder. She must be wonderful like my mother." Eric smiled as Thunder nodded with long waves of his head.

He lay back down and stared at the Moon. "I miss my mother fussing over me. I didn't like it before. But now I'd do anything to please her."

Eric drifted off into a peaceful sleep.

sixty

He had awakened early to Thunder's nudges, and Eric had collected more berries and roots to feed the black stallion. Then he led him to the stream and they both drank.

Stroking Thunder's long neck and speaking gently to him, Eric cautiously got up on his back. Although Eric felt the muscles tense under him, Thunder didn't bolt.

They left the hills. Once they were on the plain Eric shouted, "Run, Thunder, run as fast as you can." As if they were of one mind, Thunder leapt forward, soon running at full speed.

When they found the herd, Eric captured the old brown mare and headed her back to the village.

Eric rode the brown mare with white legs to the edge of the Shoshone village. He dismounted, walking to the herd of Shoshone horses, and put the mare in among them. He had missed breakfast, but he didn't care. He was happy—happier than he'd been in a long time.

Standing in front of his tent was Shinichi, arms crossed against his chest and a sour expression on his face. Eric ran toward him and threw his arms around Shinichi, hugging him tight.

Eric felt Shinichi's arms envelop him and grunted gently. "You make it hard to be mad at you."

Eric released him and they stood looking into each other's faces. Both wore wide grins.

"I feel like a father," Shinichi said wearily. "I tell my son he's in danger; I'm ignored." He waved his hands out to the distance. "My words, like a light breeze. There, but not thought of."

"I'm sorry," Eric said. "I didn't mean to, but I was with Thunder."

"Thunder?" Shinichi questioned, squinting at the clear sky. "There was no thunder last night."

Eric beamed. "Thunder the horse. The black stallion."

"I don't understand."

Excitedly, Eric told Shinichi of his adventures the night before.

"Eric, that stallion is wild, fierce, and dangerous. How could you have rode such a beast?" Shinichi shook his head, but said firmly, "And yet, I believe you."

Eric grinned. *Shinichi believes me, just like Mother would.*

"No one else will believe you."

Eric's back stiffened at Shinichi's words, "My friends will."

sixty-one

Three hours later, in the warm afternoon sun, Eric and his friends rode back to the Shoshone camp in silence. Omar, Abbas, and Sami stared at the back of their horses' heads. Isabeli rode behind Sami on his horse with her arms crossed. Karro sat behind Eric on his brown mare.

"I saw it, but I still can't believe it," Omar said.

"Me too," Sami added. "When Thunder came forward I was thinking of who I could sell your brown mare to."

"I—" Abbas stuttered. "I didn't believe the stories about you. Getting the buffalos, taking down a Cherokee warrior...but now."

Eric felt Karro lean against his back. *Did Karro believe me? She was with me getting the buffalos and fighting the Cherokee.* Eric didn't know why, but it was important Karro believe in him.

Eric looked at each of his friends in turn. "We must have trust among us, and always tell each other the truth. It's the only way we can succeed together."

"The truth is, Eric, we all underestimated you," Abbas said. "Now I'm glad to be part of the alliance."

"Together we're strong," Eric said.

"I'm all in, Eric," Omar said. "I got your back."

"Eric, I have your back," Karro said faintly.

Eric felt her rest her cheek on his shoulder.

"Are you tired, Karro?" Isabeli said snootily. "You seem to be leaning against Eric pretty hard."

Eric felt Karro jerk away.

"I was leaning forward to hear better," Karro said quickly.

"Your cheeks are pink too," Isabeli gave Karro a hard wink.

"Are you getting sick, Karro?" Eric asked concerned.

"No!" Karro said abruptly. "Go on with what you were saying, Eric."

"We need to keep an eye on each other," Eric said.

"There'll be times we can't watch you, Eric. Like when we have our lessons," Omar said.

"What was Santos' lesson for today?" Eric asked.

"How to track your enemy," Omar said.

Eric shrugged his shoulders. "Is it important for warlords to be good trackers?"

"It's not the tracking skill. We study the motions of men or women," Omar said.

"The steps may be long strides, short and quick, or deep. If read right, tracks will tell you about the person's nature," Karro added.

"Even group dynamics can be studied," Omar added. "Do they keep together, or do they move apart? Is there a leader, or a cautious group that sends out scouts? It's important for a warlord to understand who he's fighting," Omar said.

Why hasn't Shinichi taught me about tracking? "Can you teach me after?" Eric asked.

"Like you said, Eric, we help each other," Abbas said.

"What are you going to do while we're with Santos?" Karro asked.

"Sami arranged for me to get lessons on bow-and-arrow-making from Calm Cougar."

"No one is going to touch you when you're with Calm Cougar," Omar said. "We'll come see you after."

sixty-two

Eric liked Calm Cougar.

At over six feet tall, the Shoshone warrior had a lean and muscular body, which towered over Eric. His long hair was tied back with a deer leather strap and Eric saw numerous scars from fighting enemy warriors.

Together, they wandered the woods. Calm Cougar explained the characteristics of the wood needed for a good bow. After a long search, they finally found a long oak sampling that met with Calm Cougar's approval.

Although he had a reputation as a fierce warrior, Eric liked how Calm Cougar didn't talk down to him. Everything was a discussion, trading thoughts. Calm Cougar patiently watched him search the rocks for arrowheads. Eric felt right at home in this task after searching for 'Go' stones. When Eric had more than twenty they stopped by a stream and discussed why he'd selected them.

For the feathers needed to guide the arrow's shaft, Calm Cougar favored owl feathers, because they were strong, straight, and carried the owl's wisdom.

They left the woods in the late afternoon with all the items needed to make a bow and twenty arrows. Tomorrow morning, the village would pack up and leave for the buffalos. Along the way, Calm Cougar promised to work with Eric on making the bow and arrows.

The next day, it took Kamani and Eric most of the morning to take down Eric's teepee and gather their belongings. They strapped the teepee to Eric's brown mare and were ready when the tribe moved out.

After the second day of travel, and the tribe had stopped for the night. Eric looked up from setting up his tent to see Calm Cougar approaching. "I have brought you some arrowheads I found," Calm Cougar said, nodding to Shinichi, who was putting the 'Go' stones away.

"Let me see the arrows you've made," Calm Cougar said to Eric.

Eric went to his quiver and brought back the arrows.

Calm Cougar examined each arrow. He noted some improvements Eric could make, but overall, he was happy with his work.

"Please, join us for some tea," Shinichi said.

Shinichi, Calm Cougar, and Eric sat around the fire while Kamani served them tea. Although Calm Cougar talked to Shinichi and Eric, most of the time he watched Kamani.

After Clam Cougar left, and Kamani went to fetch more wood, Eric noted this to Shinichi.

"I noticed it too," Shinichi said. "I believe Calm Cougar is infatuated with our Kamani."

"They'd make a good couple."

Shinichi shook his head. "It will never happen."

"Why?"

"Their social status is very different."

"It doesn't matter if he likes her."

"Perhaps," Shinichi said, giving him a sideways glance. "They can never marry because she has no dowry."

"I'll get her one," Eric said confidently.

"Eric, it would be difficult. Don't get your hopes up."

Kamani came in and both Eric and Shinichi stared at her.

"What?" she signed.

"Do you like Calm Cougar a lot?" Eric asked abruptly.

Kamani's eyes flew open as she blushed.

"Please Eric, a little tact," Shinichi said. He turned toward Kamani and signed. "We believe Calm Cougar has feelings for you."

"But he's a mighty Shoshone warrior," She signed back.

"You are a beautiful woman. The two of you would make a handsome couple," Shinichi signed.

Shinichi and Eric saw her eyes sparkle and watch a dazzling smile appear.

Eric looked at Kamani's radiant face. Once again, he thought, *Kamani is like my mother—with a simple smile, she could brighten a room.*

The smile dropped from Kamani as she shook her head in resignation.

"Don't worry, I'll get you a big dowry," Eric said boldly. *I'll get her one that Calm Cougar can't refuse.* Eric swore.

The next day after the morning meal, Shinichi came forward leading his horse. "In another day, we will be with the buffalo. I'm leaving with some of the hunters to study the buffalo and start the hunt."

Eric looked around and saw all the men and students beside their horses. "Can I go?"

"Your horse is needed to pull your teepee. You'll have to stay with the women." Shinichi started to walk away but then turned back. "I know it won't do any good. But I'm going to say it anyway. *Stay out of trouble.*"

sixty-three

There was no sign language lesson from Kamani the next day. Only the slow mournful chants of sorrowful women.

It started before lunch when a dozen Shoshone hunters returned from the study of the buffalo herd. Eric was by the river with Isabeli. She wanted to know every detail of Calm Cougar and Kamani's recent meeting and was very disappointed when Eric had no more than what he had initially told her.

"Males are blind," Isabeli said. "Didn't you see the bright smile on Kamani's face this morning? If she could speak, she would be singing like a nightingale."

"Outside the tent, after the visit, Calm Cougar asked me to give him sign lessons."

"Perfect!" Isabeli shrieked in delight. "Soon they'll be together all the time. A wedding, then a bunch of Shoshone children."

"Isabeli, they only ate some sweets together."

"Blind."

Eric watched Isabeli ponder for a few seconds, her eyes sparkling. "I'll make it the social event of the year."

"What social event?"

"I'll be in charge. Do all the planning. You and the others will do the work." Eric still didn't understand. *I don't know if I want to.*

It was the pounding of a dozen running horses' hooves that jerked their attention away from Isabeli's matchmaking plans.

"The hunters have returned. Let's go hear about the hunt," Eric said, relieved by the interruption. He jumped up and began walking toward them before Isabeli could respond.

When Isabeli caught up with Eric, they both saw Kamani running frantically toward them. Her face wet with the tears streaming down her face, Kamani started signing before she reached them. "Find out if he's among the dead!"

"Dead?" Eric looked at the village for a brief moment before Kamani started to sign again.

"She says the buffalos stampeded. Many dead," Eric translated.

"How many?" Isabeli asked, but then froze. "What about Omar? Abbas—Sami?"

"Shinichi?" Kamani shook her head violently.

"Stay with Kamani," Eric ordered Isabeli anxiety overcoming him. "I'll find out." Without waiting for a reply, Eric started running as fast as he could toward the village. He couldn't help believing the worst. *They're all dead. Omar, Abbas, and Sami. How can I go on without Shinichi?*

When Eric reached the village, he heard a scream of agony. He ran faster. More screams of pain filled the air.

In the center of the village were a dozen riders. Both horses and riders were breathing hard. Several women screamed while others tried to comfort them, and some of the older women started a mournful chant.

Karro stood beside the riders, offering water. Eric ran to her. "How many dead?"

Before Karro could answer an exhausted rider spoke up, "Eight. Fifteen hurt."

"Shinichi?"

The rider shook his head. "No."

"Calm Cougar?"

"Hurt but can ride."

"Omar, Abbas, Sami?"

The rider's head dropped. "Abbas."

Abbas dead. Eric suddenly wanted to scream with the others.

"Abbas is very brave. His leg was broken trying to save Strong Bear," the rider said.

Eric gave a sigh of relief. *Hurt but not dead.*

The sun was sinking when the Shoshone hunters appeared in the distance. Everyone gathered at the edge of the village, and by the time the warriors arrived, there were two jagged lines of mourners. The women's voices rose in chants of sorrow as Angry Bear led the injured, dispirited hunters through.

The mournful chants grew louder when a hunter rode past with a body wrapped in a blanket across his horse.

Then, Omar came, with Abbas riding behind him. Abbas' left leg was bound with a tree branch on both sides and leather thongs securing them in place. There was a bandage wrapped around his arm. Sami followed directly behind, leading Abbas' horse.

Most of the riders rode through the line of mourners, but the ones with bodies stopped in the village center and the bodies were taken from them.

When Omar stopped, Eric went over and helped Abbas down. With the help of Karro and Sami, Eric took Abbas and laid him on a buffalo skin. Abbas gritted his teeth in pain as he set his leg down.

While Isabeli made Abbas comfortable, Eric and Karro went back to watching the riders ride in. Calm Cougar road in, hunched over his spotted horse. Leather thongs were wrapped around his ribs as if holding them together.

Eric searched for Kamani. He saw her at the edge of the crowd, her eyes fixed upon Calm Cougar. Relief was clearly written across her face.

When all the riders passed, Eric looked around for Shinichi, but he wasn't to be found. He and Karro returned to Abbas and discovered Omar had arrived. He looked shaken, distraught. Eric noticed Sami had several bruises on his arms and legs.

"What happened?" Eric asked Abbas, but it was Omar who answered.

"Ten buffalos were selected and cut out of the large herd. A dozen Shoshone riders drove them out. We all gathered around to form a rough barrier with our horses." Omar looked down at Abbas. "A loud *crack* was heard. Like a large tree snapped in half. A second later, the air filled with the sound of pounding hooves."

"It happened so fast," Sami said. "I never thought such a big beast could move so quickly."

"They're very fast." Eric remembered how he'd only escaped death by inches when the buffalo had attacked him.

Abbas nodded, his teeth clenched to fight the pain. "I saw a buffalo ram Strong Bear's horse and he fell. I charged in on my horse. But when I reached down to help him the buffalo rammed him into me and my horse. It crushed Strong Bear and snapped my leg." Abbas took a strained breath. "If it wasn't for Sami riding in and saving me, I'd be wrapped in a blanket, too."

Karro extended her finger toward Sami. "This Sami? Are you sure?"

"Yes, I saw it," Omar said. "Sami was amazing."

"Thank you, Sami," Abbas said.

Sami stared back, dazed.

Abbas suddenly gave a loud grunt as his face tightened in pain. He shifted his bandaged arm.

"Karro, while Isabeli takes care of Abbas, let's get some medicine for his pain," Eric said.

Before they walked away, Karro looked once more at Sami. "Impossible!"

After Abbas was given the medicine, they took him to his teepee and left him to rest. Karro, Omar, Sami, Isabeli, and Eric walked to the outskirts of the village, listening to the constant chanting by the elderly Shoshone women gathered around the dead in the center of the village.

"Two of the dead were experienced hunters, Strong Bear and Swift Fox," Omar said. "The rest were young. Four were students."

"Who?" Eric asked.

"Masa, Guad, Tony, and Dado," Sami said.

"Guad use to bring me flowers," Isabeli said solemnly.

"Isn't it strange that they're all students of Santos?" Karro said warily.

"That's right," Omar agreed.

"It could be a coincidence," Eric said.

There wasn't much else to say. Eric nodded, then went toward the center of the village.

Death, Eric suddenly realized, was new to him. He thought back to a distant uncle's funeral he'd attended, but it'd had no effect on him. Eric didn't know the man. He'd watched as his father talked in somber, hushed tones with other family members. The feeling he most remembered was boredom.

His distant uncle's death didn't affect Eric. But he'd had several conversations with Dado. He and Masa had spent time together gathering wood for the cook fires. They weren't strangers. When he fought the buffalo and the Cherokee warrior, the possibility of truly dying had never entered his mind. Only now did he feel a chill to his bones, a feeling of vulnerability.

The death chant and songs were loud and clear. Walking past the circle of women singing and chanting around the bodies, he stopped and stared. *Boys my age who've only experienced a short part of their lives—gone.*

Eric looked at the two adult hunters. Both were in their mid twenties. Strong Bear had just married, and Swift Fox had become a father two months ago. *How could this have happened?*

His attention returned to the dead students. Had Guad, Tony, Masa, or Dado selected this event to use their pass? He wouldn't know until the next event.

Now, five of Santos' students will not finish the event. Eric continued on, back to his teepee. *Would it really bother anyone if I were killed?* He knew Stemann and Bolek would be happy. Deep in thought, Eric pulled back the teepee's flap and went in, nearly jumping backward in shock.

Shinichi sat inside, eating a piece of deer jerky and concentrating hard.

He looks tired, his face drawn and his hair is caked with dust. "Why didn't you come with the others?" Eric asked.

Shinichi stretched out his legs and said warily, "Angry Bear asked me to stay behind with several others to see if we could find out what happened."

"What did you find?"

"Not conclusive. But I don't think the stampede was a chance happening."

"Someone started the stampede?"

"I believe so."

"Who?"

"It's a mystery I don't believe we'll ever solve," Shinichi said before taking another bite of his jerky.

Eric sat down across from Shinichi, leaned forward and said, "*only* Santos' students were injured or killed."

"Perhaps it means something—perhaps not." Shinichi squinted at Eric. "But I don't think that what's bothering you."

Eric looked away, "I stood for a while looking at the students lying motionless on the ground. It's given me an uneasy feeling I can't forget."

"Perhaps your senses are trying to tell your brain something important."

"What?"

"Eric, one of the hardest lessons for us instructors to teach students is the reality of the events. Often, the students understand too late the reality and consequences of the situation. Like all youths, they feel they're invincible. But death is a big part of an event—and a big part of a warlord's life."

"I know."

"Do you truly?" Shinichi said sternly, staring deep into Eric's eyes. "A great warlord does not take life lightly. Death is one of the great forces in war. When one embraces the grim reaper with all the destruction, pestilence, and horror he brings, one tries to avoid war at all costs."

"But war is the business of a warlord. Why would he avoid something that will bring profit?"

"Profit is something on an accountant's ledger sheet. A single life is worth so much more." Reaching behind him, Shinichi brought out the pouches of 'Go' stones. "But you are a child of Earth, part of the human race. Humans like a positive ledger sheet."

sixty-four

The next day, the bodies of the dead were burned. Eric watched Bolek, Malek, and Kirill to see their reactions. They showed none. Neither did Fia or Raica.

"We need every able warrior," Angry Bear had said. "We must all work hard to get the buffalo meat we need to survive the winter."

Even though Eric's horse was old, he was required to join the hunt.

The village camped a few miles from a herd of buffalo. Even from this distance, Eric could see the massive mound of animals moving around slowly. Tomorrow, they would start the hunt again.

Eric took twenty new arrows to Calm Cougar's teepee for him to inspect.

"Well done," he said to Eric. "They'll serve you well on the hunt."

After Eric put away his arrows, Calm Cougar said, "I want my first sign lesson."

"But you're hurt, bruised ribs," Eric said. "It can wait."

"No. Now," Calm Cougar insisted. There was an intensity in his look Eric couldn't deny.

So Eric started the signing lesson. The Shoshone warrior bit hard on a leather strap, his eyes watering with the pain as his arms and hands copied Eric's motions. But he would not allow Eric to stop until the midday meal.

"We will continue tomorrow after the buffalo hunt," Calm Cougar said.

"Okay." Then, Eric reluctantly added, "Kamani wanted to know how you're feeling."

Calm Cougar's eyes brightened. "Tell her I am a Shoshone warrior. We do not feel pain. Tell her I'm fine." To show Eric, Calm Cougar sat up, but his face tightened as it turned deep red. "See," he gasped out. "I'm fine."

"I'll tell her," Eric said, then bent down to leave the teepee.

"Sly Fox." Calm Cougar had to say it twice before Eric remembered his latest Indian name.

"Yes."

"Careful," the Shoshone warrior said. "Make sure the old women are not singing your death song tomorrow."

"I will," was all Eric could say.

sixty-five

Eric mounted his old horse and Sami rode up beside him. "Keep close to me," Sami said.

"Thanks," Eric said. "I could use some help."

"No. I want you to protect me."

Eric glanced at him. "But you saved Abbas."

Sami looked around, then lowered his voice. "I didn't mean to. It just happened."

"What?!"

"When the buffalos stampeded, I was scared. My horse was more scared. It bolted, running away. Suddenly, a gigantic buffalo with big horns and huge fangs cut into our path."

"Fangs?"

"Yes. Long and sharp. My horse darted left and we ran straight into Abbas' horse." Sami took a deep breath. "It was madness, and in my confusion, I grabbed on to Abbas, so he could help me. He pulled himself onto my horse. The path cleared, and my horse raced out."

Eric clapped Sami on the shoulder. "I still think you're a hero. And I'll stay close, so we can help each other."

Omar rode up and they started out. The rest of the warriors walked their horses in the direction of the herd.

Twenty yards away from the herd, Eric and all the Shoshone warriors gathered around Angry Bear.

"We lost many good hunters. Be watchful; all must return," Angry Bear said.

Eric looked around and caught sight of Bolek staring at him. Then Malek and Kirill moved in beside Bolek and added their weight to the stare. In return, Eric mock-smiled and waved.

Leaning into Omar and Sami, Eric said, "We need to watch Bolek and his group whenever we can." Both nodded in agreement.

The hunt for the day was small. The hunters shot only five buffalos. The women and girls came out to gather the buffalo meat and skins.

"Where's Isabeli?" Eric asked Karro.

"She's back at the village. She complained of pain in her stomach this morning," Karro said. Then, in response to Eric's concerned look, she rolled her eyes. "She's not sick. Isabeli just wanted to get out of the work."

Eric looked at Karro's basket full of red buffalo meat. "You're a hard worker."

"You sound surprised," Karro said. "I'm not like Isabeli."

"You like being an Amazon?" Eric asked.

Karro stopped and looked at Eric. "It's a great honor to be an Amazon."

"They kicked you out."

"I cannot. I will not leave the Amazons." Eric shrugged his shoulders, and she added, "In truth, every woman is an Amazon."

Eric raised his eyebrows. "Isabeli?"

Karro's face bunched up as if she'd bitten into a lemon. "Yes, even Isabeli. We are strong and can take pain."

"Not more than a man."

"A man?" Karro laughed.

"Calm Cougar's in pain. But being a man he doesn't show it."

Karro looked off at the distant mountains then returning her eyes to Eric she said evenly. "When a woman is pregnant, she's in pain for nine months as her body is pulled and stretched. When she gives birth, the pain increases and intensifies as the baby struggles into the world. The incredible and constant pain would drive a man mad, but is all forgotten when the woman holds her newborn baby."

"You're wrong. Every society has heroes—men who have fought in battles, gravely wounded, but will not leave."

"Eric, there are traits highly praised by all. Loyalty, protecting the weak and sick, and the ability to endure great pain. Men who have these traits form highly regarded societies like the Knights Templar or Samurai. Men try to achieve what women already have. It comes naturally to a woman."

"Isabeli isn't an Amazon," Eric said firmly.

"She is. She makes slaves of men not with a sword, but with a smile."

"Fine. Be an Amazon," Eric said, pulling on his horse's reins and storming off.

With fresh buffalo meat in the cooking pots, the mood of the village improved. The chants were happy. Eric drifted through the camp with Isabeli, Karro, and Sami, each holding a full wooden bowl.

After they feasted on the buffalo meat, they went and sat out in the meadow and listen to the chanting and drums. Through the teepees, they watched people of the village starting to dance in celebration of the hunt.

Suddenly, Isabeli stood up. "Let's dance."

"What?" Karro said.

"Get up and dance." She was already starting to sway her hips.

"Why?" Sami asked.

Neither Karro nor Sami got up.

"Let's dance," Isabeli said to Eric.

Eric shook his head. "I only know one dance."

"I know it, too." She gave a dazzling smile.

Eric stood up. He moved in front of Isabeli and then bowed as he was taught. "May I have this dance?"

Isabeli curtsied. "Yes, I would love to waltz with you."

Eric took a step toward her, extending his right hand. In response, Isabeli closed the distance between them and took Eric's hand. Then his arm went around Isabeli's waist and pulled her in closer.

Around and around they went, the Shoshone drums matching their steps. Karro and Sami watched as Eric and Isabeli moved as one around the meadow.

"They dance very badly together," Karro said to Sami.

"I think they're very good." Sami noted Karro's tightened features and continued. "Actually, they're awesome together. Don't you think they make a handsome couple?"

"No!" Karro said.

"Are they supposed to hold each other so tight?" When Karro didn't answer, Sami added, "You would never hold Eric tight like that."

"No," Karro said solemnly.

The chanting stopped and Eric returned, laughing, happily holding Isabeli's hand.

"That was so much fun," Isabeli said.

"You're a good dancer," Eric said.

"It was *amazing* watching you two together," Sami said enthusiastically. "Right, Karro?"

"Yeah," Karro said, crossing her arms. "Amazing."

From the village, another chant started.

"Let's dance again!" Isabeli said.

"Again?" Eric wavered.

Isabeli extended her hand and smiled. "For me."

Eric was reaching out his hand when Karro leaned over. "A woman and her smile," she breathed into his ear.

"No," Eric said abruptly, pulling back his hand. "I don't want to dance."

"But—" Isabeli started.

"Sami, let's go," Eric said, marching toward the village. Sami followed, jogging to catch up with him.

"What happened?" Isabeli asked Karro, confused.

Karro shrugged, turning back to the dancers with a small smile. "I forgot to tell Eric that women are clever, too."

sixty-six

"**How can** I stop the attacks from Bolek?" Eric asked as he paced in front of his tent.

Shinichi stood off to the side. "Only one way. One of you must leave the event."

Eric stopped in front of Shinichi his face resolute. "One of us must die?"

"It's the only way," Shinichi repeated. "He is a determined and forceful boy. Odds are in his favor."

During the hunt, Eric had been assigned to be with Bolek, Malek, Krill, and several other of Stemann's students. During the hunt, Bolek and the others had driven buffalos with their spears to surround Eric and his horse, attempting to crush him.

Eric still remembered the fear he felt when his horse was knocked down and trampled by the huge buffalos. He only escaped by climbing on the back of the majestic beast and jumping from back to back. Shinichi had ridden up and rescued him at the last minute.

"Will you at least prepare me to better defend myself?"

A look of surprise came to Shinichi's face. "I'm teaching you 'Go'."

"I need more than a game."

"Since I'm your instructing warlord," Shinichi said lazily. "I suppose I should do a little more."

Eric was about to explode with frustration. Shinichi hadn't taught him anything except the names of flowers and bushes in their walk through the woods. They stopped in front of a deep-blue flower with golden veins running through its petals.

Shinichi opened his mouth, but Eric cut him off. "I don't want to know its name or in what time of year it blooms."

"Forgive me." Shinichi over exaggerated taking in a deep breath and letting it out slowly as he pulled on his right ear. "I forgot that you're a rash youth unwilling to take time to view the beauty of his surroundings."

"What about Bolek?" Eric asked annoyed.

"He is strong, quick, and highly trained. And like you, he probably doesn't have an appreciation for nature's bouquet of radiant flowers," Shinichi said.

Eric rolled his eyes. "Later, I promise. Bolek?"

"Understand his strengths. I have trained students who would tell me how *lucky* their opponent had been, or it was a fluke they lost a fight. They were more worried about their pride and shame than preparing for the next time. Go over there," Shinichi said, pointing to a grove of trees.

Eric moved to the grove of many young trees, tall and thin.

"Eric, in your training with Omar, he must have given you fighting routes to practice."

"Yes."

"Show me one."

Eric looked around. There were several small patches of open area, but none bigger than six feet by six feet. "There isn't enough room."

"There's more than enough room," Shinichi said. "Start!"

Eric stepped to the center of the small opening and stood straight with his arms stiffly at his side. He lifted his head and stared forward.

Suddenly, Eric was a whirl of motion. Jabbing, blocking, kicking, as if he were in combat with an invisible enemy. Then he swung around and his arm hit a tree.

"Again," the warlord commanded.

Eric returned to the center of the opening. He came to attention quickly and started again, his body whirling in fighting action until he kicked out and his foot struck a tree, hard. Eric gave a loud exhale of exasperation. "I told you. It's impossible. Not enough room," he roared at Shinichi.

"Is it?"

The warlord moved to the center of the small open area and, like Eric, he came to attention. Shinichi burst into action; he was everywhere—jabbing, kicking, and spinning.

Time and time again, Eric was sure the warlord would hit or kick a tree. But each time, the attack missed the tree and Shinichi continued on. He was like the wind, dodging around all the obstacles with ease. After ten long minutes, he returned perfectly to the center of the open area, standing at attention, as if he'd never left.

Eric moved to Shinichi's side. "That was amazing."

"I've slowed a great deal," Shinichi said as a shallow smile appeared. "When I was younger I could have done all those moves in half the time."

"You didn't hit any trees."

"I adapt. Change the stroke and kick as needed to avoid the obstacle," Shinichi said. "To do this, you must be light on your feet, ever ready to change and establish your balance to strike."

"Show me."

"No, this is something you must learn on your own. Develop your own fighting style."

Eric went back to the center of the open area. He stood at attention, thought for a second, and then took a deep breath. The fighting style was different when he went through jabs, punches, and kicks. Then he was done.

Eric pumped his fist into the air. "Yeah!" He looked at Shinichi. To his surprise, Shinichi's face was covered in disapproval.

"I did it! I finished."

"Too slow," Shinichi said. "Do you believe Bolek will slow up? Allow you to adapt?"

"Sometimes you need to walk before running," Eric said.

"Perhaps in business, but in war, the speed is always on full. You must be the fastest sprinter or you will lose."

Eric nodded. *If I practice at half speed, during a real fight I will go half speed. I must practice at full speed and defeat my enemy.* "It's hard to adapt at full speed."

Seeing the frustration on Eric's face, Shinichi stepped forward. "I jabbed my fist forward. When I saw a tree in front of my fist, I stopped the advancement of my thrust, but I continued attacking using my forearm and elbow. Every part of my body is a weapon."

Eric returned to the center of the open area. As soon as he came to attention, he started. He moved at battle speed with jabs, strikes, and blows until he hit a young tree and stopped. He put the scraped hand into his mouth as it started to bleed. Although he'd failed, the look on Shinichi's face was approval.

sixty-seven

Eric now had a daily route. In the early morning, he would go off and ride Thunder. After the ride, he practiced his fighting technique. Following lunch, he and the other in the alliance took bow shooting lessons from Karro. Then, in the late afternoon, he and Shinichi would play a game of 'Go'.

In each area, he was making good progress.

Although their nightly game he had improved, Shinichi still decisively won every match. No matter if Eric was tired or didn't want to play, Shinichi always drew the lines on the ground and made Eric play a game.

Following Calm Cougar's instructions, his arrows were straight and flew true. His new bow was better than his first. Eric quickly became a better archer but was still far behind Karro.

In the area of developing his own fighting technique, his hands, legs, and arms were always cut and bruised. The sweat poured over Eric, making small rivers as it went down his body. Eric would have said it was impossible if he hadn't seen Shinichi do it.

Today was a bad day. He couldn't move fast enough to miss the trees. He looked down at his bruised hands and every part of him wanted to stop. *I'm a prince. I shouldn't have to do this. I should be enjoying life. Going to celebrations and parties, like my father.*

Then the map on the commandant's wall filled his thoughts. *Because my grandfather and great-grandfather gave more attention to drinking and partying than ruling, the empire is crumbling.*

241

The portrait of Victor the Destroyer replaced the map. *Did Victor ever want to quit? To go back to the easy life? To let others worry about family problems? If Victor hadn't fought on, there would be no Moon castle. If I give up and don't fight, it will all end.*

Even though his body argued, Eric took a deep breath and went back to the center of the opening. He stood at attention and prepared for his fist thrust.

He closed his eyes to calm himself. As he stood still, a sweet smell overcame his senses. The mixture of wild fruits filled his mind. *Isabeli must be close by.*

The powerful aroma took control of all his senses. Eric suddenly realized he was taking deeper breaths to get more. The sweet smell was enticing. Eric took another deep breath.

Opening his eyes, he looked around to find Isabeli. Sniffing like a squirrel, Eric moved off in the direction of the sweet scent. There was movement and Eric was about to call out Isabeli's name when he saw thick blond hair. *It's Fia.*

She leaned against an old redwood tree, seemingly deep in thought, absentmindedly stroking the trunk.

Like a bobcat hunting a wild rabbit, Eric moved cautiously and quietly to get a better look at Fia. He traveled silently in an arc around the tree, always keeping his eyes on her.

Eric found a thick bush and slowly parted the branches to stare at Fia.

She's very pretty—like Isabeli. Mentally, he started to compare the two girls. They were both tall and slender, but while Isabeli had creamy white skin, Fia's was a light olive color. Though different colors, they both had thick and shiny hair that flowed below their shoulders. Isabeli had dark, doe-like, almond-shaped eyes. Fia's were bright-blue with veins of lavender.

"Eric, come over and talk," Fia said.

How'd she see me? Eric wondered as he stepped out from behind the bush. "Hi Fia, I didn't see you there."

"I'm glad I met you," Fia's said musically, her tone enticing. "I'm all alone and wanted someone to talk to."

Eric's face reddened at the thought of Fia discovering him staring at her. He shifted his gaze to look at the treetops above. "The trees are amazing."

"More amazing than me."

"What?" Eric's attention returned to Fia.

"Eric," Fia purred as she extended her bare leg to brush some leaves away with her toes. "Do you like me?"

For a moment, Eric was hypnotized by the soft, resonating sound of her voice, in a dazed stupor he walked to her. "Like you?"

She stood in front of Eric. The sweet aroma was overpowering. Fia leaned forward, brushing her cheek against his as she whispered softly, "Do you like me?"

When she leaned back, Eric noticed a dazzling smile on her face. Deep-red lips surrounding perfectly straight white teeth. The smile encouraged a smile on Eric's face. Her blond hair, oval face, and stunning smile held Eric spellbound as she looked deep into his eyes.

Eric was struck dumb, hypnotized. *Fia's eyes are like bright sapphires, flawless in every way. I could look into them forever.* Eric felt a lightness and a magnetism drawing him toward her.

"Everyone knows how brave and fearless you are. But there's more. Your handsome looks."

"You think I'm handsome?" Eric said hopefully.

"Oh yes." Fia took two steps back and extended one leg as she swept her long hair from side to side. "What do you think of me?"

"You? I think—" Eric felt a hard pull on his left shirtsleeve. He turned his head, surprised by Isabeli's angry look. "Isabeli—"

The slap across Eric's cheek echoed through the woods. His hand flew up to his red cheek that screamed in pain.

Eric wanted to ask Isabeli about the hard slap, but she was gone. Fia and Isabeli were circling each other like Japanese fighting fish.

"Eric thinks you look like a thin hag," Isabeli said to Fia, her lip curling in a sneer.

Fia, still turning in a circle gave a mocking laugh. "If he hangs around with you he knows what one looks like."

Eric forgot all about his hurting cheek when he saw both girls cup their hands, extending their long nails. He jumped between them. "Wait a second. I can speak for myself."

Isabeli's eyes flared at him. "Before you say anything about this witch, know we spotted Bolek behind a tree not far off watching you two."

"Bolek?"

"It was a trap. Omar and Karro drove him away," Isabeli said.

"Is that true, Fia?"

Fia shrugged her shoulders. "Many boys follow me. I promise, Eric, one day you will, too."

"Then I'll take care of you now," Isabeli said, stepping forward.

Eric's arms circled Isabeli.

"Let me go," Isabeli shrieked, fighting to get at Fia. "Let me scratch her eyes out."

"Fia, leave," Eric said, trying to hold the thrashing Isabeli.

"We'll talk again, Eric," Fia said over her shoulder, walking off into the woods.

sixty-eight

In two days, the Shoshones would be leaving for the winter camping grounds. It would take at least three weeks of hard marching. With Thunder's help, Eric had brought a young horse with black patches against white back to camp. He would be able to move his teepee to the winter hunting grounds.

Putting his new horse away. He and Karro gathered their bow and arrows and went into the forest.

"How was that?" Eric asked Karro.

Today he was consistently within eight inches of all Karro's shots. He had expected some praise from Karro, but instead, she picked up her quiver of arrows and started walking deeper into the forest. Eric grabbed his quiver and followed.

"It's easy to hit a target that doesn't move," Karro said when Eric caught up.

"Easy? I've been practicing hard for weeks."

"Hunting trees isn't going to improve your shooting," Karro said.

"What then?"

"What animals have you hunted?"

"None."

"Exactly," Karro said. "The bow was made for more than just shooting objects that don't move. Start hunting."

Eric looked around. He didn't see any animals. He received a disagreeable look from Karro in exchange for his shoulder shrug.

"Look and you will see."

Eric looked right, then left. Finally, he spun all around.

Karro rolled her eyes. "Have you forgotten already the lesson Omar taught you? Track."

"Right…track."

"We've passed several deer, raccoon, and squirrel tracks," Karro said crossing her arms against her chest.

Eric looked at the ground. *I don't see anything.*

When a minute passed, Karro pointed to a broken branch, then to some hoof prints several feet away. "There are three of them. One buck and two does passed here less than an hour ago."

"How do—"

"There was fresh droppings back on the trail. Surely you must have seen it."

"Yes. Of course," Eric lied.

"Eric, you must examine everything. There's a story of events all around you." Karro took his arm and pointed to more deer tracks. "The deer passed here. They were walking slowly. See how the distance between the front and back hooves are close."

Eric spotted the tracks and nodded.

"They have no fear; the tracks of the three deer are far apart. If scared, the doe would be closer to the buck. Let's follow the tracks," Karro said.

Thirty minutes of tracking later, Eric felt a hand block his way. Karro brought a finger to her lips, then pointed off to his right.

Eric didn't see anything at first. Then, he noticed a slight movement. Looking harder, he noticed blending into the woods were the three deer. They stood still; only their mouths moved as they ate from a bush.

Karro motioned for him to shoot his bow.

Eric shook his head. "Too far," he mouthed. He started to move forward, but Karro stopped him. She tapped the side of her nose, then pointed to the right.

Eric nodded his understanding. *The deer will smell us if we go to the right.*

Eric moved slowly to his left. Stepping over a fallen branch, he barely heard the life of the forest around him—the chirping of birds or the squirrels stirring. All Eric could hear was the pounding of his heart.

He looked at Karro moving toward the deer on a parallel path. Her movements were fluid and smooth like a panther.

In contrast, Eric felt every step of his was abrupt and unsure.

Karro stopped and signed for him to shoot.

Moving in front of her for a clear shot, Eric reached around and pulled out an arrow. When it was halfway out of the quiver, the buck stopped and looked up.

Eric stopped breathing and stood motionless. The buck stationary, looked around, and peered in his direction. The large brown eyes stared right at Eric.

Don't look at me. Start eating. Finally, the buck turned and started to eat again.

Slowly, Eric pulled the arrow from his quiver. Gradually, he brought it up and notched it. *Don't move.* Pulling back the bowstring, he calmed himself and aimed. Then, the arrow was away.

A thump echoed throughout the woods and the three deer jumped and ran.

"Eric, the mighty tree hunter," Karro said as they both stared at Eric's arrow embedded in a tree.

"What happened? I was aiming for the buck."

"You were thinking too much," Karro said. She looked off after the deer. "They won't go far. Let's go." She moved in the direction of the deer and Eric followed.

It was more than three hours of following deer tracks before Karro sighted the deer again eating. Slowly, cautiously, she took Eric within forty yards of the deer, and then Karro signaled for him to shoot.

This time he didn't think, just acted like he had a hundred times before—selecting an arrow, pulling back the bowstring, and taking aim at the buck. *This time I won't miss.*

As he released the arrow, the three deer leapt up and dashed away, the arrow flying harmlessly behind them.

Eric whipped his head toward Karro. "I didn't—"

Karro's face tightened as her eyes widened. A deafening growl echoed through the forest. Running straight at them with surprising speed was a gigantic creature. "Bear! It's a bear!" Eric shouted at Karro standing beside him.

In response, Karro pulled Eric's vest in the direction away from the approaching grizzly bear.

Eric ran, dodging around trees and through bushes. He ran as fast as he could, but the growls and snarls were getting closer.

Karro stopped, turned to shoot, but Eric pushed her forward. "No. Run." Looking back, Eric could see the huge bear charging toward them. The grizzly growled, and Eric stared at the rows of long, white teeth with curled fangs on each side.

It's too fast. We're not going to make it. We only have one chance. Grabbing Karro, he brought her to a halt.

"Up!" Eric pointed to a tree in front of them.

Karro grabbed the low branch and pulled herself up.

Eric looked back at the rampaging grizzly bear. Its large head was up, it powerful legs propelling it fast forward toward him. He turning back to Karro. "Hurry…hurry…hurry…"

Bracing herself against the tree, Karro reached down for Eric. He grabbed her hand like a drowning man grabbing a life preserver. Jumping up, he caught the lower branches. "Go," Eric urged. "Higher."

Seconds later, Eric felt a tremendous crash and he lost his grip. He began to fall.

"Eric!" Karro screamed.

He latched onto a branch. A deafening roar filled his ears. Eric's blood froze as he smelled the bear's rancid breath inches away below him. Panic and fear pushed Eric to yank himself up and climb to Karro.

He almost lost his balance as he felt the tree shake. He looked down. "No!" he shouted. It was impossible. The mad bear was climbing up the tree. "Up!" Eric urged. Karro was already scaling to higher branches.

Eric scrambled up and almost climbed past her. He looked back to see the bear thrust its head to clamp down on his exposed leg. He jerked his foot up, and was only scratched by the grizzly's sharp teeth.

"Stop!" Karro screamed at Eric.

"No! Higher!" Eric said, knowing the bear was right behind him. Then, he grabbed the trunk as the tree began to sway. Eric took an arrow from his quiver, stretched out, and drove it hard into the back of the bear's paw.

The bear's intense anger was vivid in its black eyes, which looked at Eric with determination, adding to Eric's fear. The great beast howled with rage. It swung a sharp claw and the arrow flew from Eric's hand.

Suddenly, there was a great crash as the bear lost its balance and fell. It hit the ground hard, but rolled over quickly, voicing its rage in a challenging roar.

To Eric's great relief, the monster didn't climb again. Instead, it circled the tree as it swung its head from side to side, howling its anger. "Stop!" Eric shouted as the bear looked up and began to attack the tree. Clawing, pushing, and biting, it looked as though it was trying anything it could to knock down the tree and bring the two humans before its waiting claws.

"The tree is strong," Eric said, reassuring Karro. But the next moment, he doubted his own words as the grizzly bear bit a chunk out of the tree's trunk. "Someone from the tribe will arrive soon," Eric said.

"No," Karro said. Eric was surprised she didn't seem frightened, only annoyed. "We're too far away."

"But the Shoshones are good trackers."

"It's too late, getting dark."

Eric looked around. The sun was already behind the ridge and falling fast. Soon it would be dark. *We're doomed.*

Karro looked down at the bear and said, "It isn't going to leave soon." She looked around the tree. "We have to position ourselves better."

"What are you doing?" Eric asked angrily when Karro started to move around the tree.

"The branches over there are stronger." She started toward a thicker branch and suddenly slipped on some wet moss.

Eric grabbed her arm to steady her. "Stay still," Eric pleaded.

Karro ignored Eric and moved to the stronger branch she'd been looking at. "Climb over here." Karro pointed to a strong branch beside hers. When Eric didn't move, Karro said, "Do I need to come and get you?"

"No," Eric said anxiously. He looked down at the bear continuing its attack on the tree. Slowly, he began to move over to Karro.

"Give me your vest," Karro said.

"Why?"

"We must secure ourselves."

Eric took off his vest and handed it to Karro. Leaning back against the branch, he felt the hard bark bite into his back.

Karro took her knife and began to cut up the vest into strips.

While Karro was working on his vest, Eric stared down at the angry bear. It didn't seem to be tiring. Then, Eric looked around. He noticed the branches from the neighboring tree were entwined with the one they were currently perched on. Looking at the branches between the trees, he could tell they were strong enough to crawl across. Eric pointed this out to Karro.

"Then what?" Karro asked. "The bear will just move over to that tree."

Eric sighed loudly. *There's no escape.*

"Done," Karro said. She held up the remains of Eric's vest, which she'd cut into strips and weaved into a rope. "Come here."

Eric looked down at the bear, who happened to be staring up at him. Its mouth was fully open as if waiting for Eric to fall into it. "Why do I need to come over?"

"I'm going to tie us to the tree; if we nod off, we won't fall." Karro moved over a little, indicating for Eric to sit in front her.

Eric moved slowly over to Karro, and as he did so, the bear roared its protest.

She directed Eric to sit with his back to her and lean against her. Karro placed her new rope around the extended trunk, then around her, and tied it in front of Eric. She tied it tight, forcing Eric further back into her. "This should make sure we don't fall."

"There is no chance of me falling. Because I'm not sleeping."

Karro's arm was resting beside Eric. He wondered if he could count all the freckles on her arm. It might help him forget about the savage bear below.

The blue under Karro's wristband caught Eric's attention. He moved the wristband.

"What are you doing?"

"You have a tattoo?" Eric studied the tattoo. "What is it?"

"An arrow."

"Yes, it looks like an arrow I made. Why an arrow?"

There was a notable silence before Karro answered, "It was either an arrow or a black stallion."

"Both would be good. A cougar or wolf would be awesome too. I guess it really doesn't matter."

Eric felt Karro's head rest on his shoulder and whispered. "It does matter."

He was about to ask why when a growl reminded him death was so close. Eric stretched, and then his senses went crazy as he began to fall. A tightness against his chest stopped his downward trajectory.

"Careful," Karro said, helping Eric back to a sitting position in front of her and taking the pressure off the rope.

Eric looked around. The night was receding and the tip of the sun could be seen in the east.

Eric was dumbfounded as to why he was up in a tree, tied to Karro. Then it all came rushing back: the sharp pointed claws, powerful body, and sharp teeth. Eric looked down but couldn't see the bear.

"Where'd it go?" Eric asked.

Karro fidgeted behind him, starting to untie the rope. "I fell asleep, too. The bear must have left in the middle of the night." As the rope loosened and Karro inched her body away from him, a bitter wind struck him. Reluctantly, he moved further away to get a better look. In any direction he peered, there was no sign of the bear.

"Wait here. I'm going down to take a look," Eric said. Cautiously, he made his way down the tree. Once on the ground, he looked around but the bear still didn't appear. He glanced at the deep gouges cut into the tree, and patted the tree. "Thank you."

"Come on down," Eric called up to Karro. Within seconds, Karro was standing beside him. "We're lucky."

"We were stupid," Karro countered.

"Stupid?"

"A warrior always knows her surroundings."

Another of Sun Tzu's rules of war. Eric started to walk back, too tired to argue.

sixty-nine

Out of the forest, close to the Shoshone camp, Eric raised his hand to block out the morning sun. To Eric, the camp looked like a green oasis in the middle of the blistering hot desert, promising salvation.

As they approached the edge of the camp, a group of angry-looking men strode toward them. All three of the warlords were with Angry Bear and the elders.

"What's wrong?" Eric wondered.

The two stopped as the men reached them.

Santos stepped away from the group and pointed to the camp. "Go!" he ordered Karro.

Karro looked at Eric confused before she turned and walked away.

Eric looked from face to face to try to read the anger. When he came to Stemann, the look was not of anger, but amusement.

Angry Bear was the first to step forward. "The laws of the Shoshone people are known," Angry Bear said to Eric. "It has always been. Will always be." The men behind him nodded in agreement, except Shinichi, who simply stared hard at Eric.

Not knowing what else to do, Eric nodded his agreement.

"We can't do it now, but when we get to the winter camp, it shall be done," Angry Bear continued. Again, the stern men and Eric nodded in agreement.

Angry Bear and the elders turned and walked back to the village. Only Eric, Stemann, Santos, and Shinichi remained standing together. A smile appeared on Stemann's face.

"May I be the first to congratulate you?" Shinichi said solemnly.

Eric took the offered hand and shook it firmly. *I must have done something great, but what?*

Having released Eric's hand, Shinichi backed away not looking at Eric. Then it was Stemann's turn to extend his hand. "I want also to congratulate you." He said fighting back laughter.

Eric took Stemann's hand and shook it. "Congratulate me?"

"On your upcoming marriage," Stemann said as he threw back his head and roar with laughter.

Kanami paced angrily back and forth in the teepee, signing emphatically to Shinichi and Eric seated in front of a fire. Then she stabbed her finger at Eric and signed, "Eric's too young to get married!"

"Yes," Eric quickly agreed. "It impossible,"

"It's the law. You agreed with Angry Bear," Shinichi said.

Eric threw up his hands. "I didn't know what he was talking about."

"As your instructor, I would strongly suggest from now on you know what you are agreeing to."

Eric dropped his head into his hands and sighed. "This can't happen."

Shinichi corrected Eric. "When we are in an event we are subject to its rules and constraints."

"I'm only ten years old. I can't get married." Eric's mind wandered back to a wedding at the Moon castle—his mother's cousin's. The bride had been in a long, white flowing gown and the groom, in a crisp uniform. Hundreds of people were in attendance to wish them the best and a long marriage. "It's for old people," Eric whined to Shinichi.

"In Shoshone law, a female and male must not be out alone together after they turn ten years old. You just stated you're ten. This law is meant to protect each of you and make sure youthful mistakes are not made."

"Why didn't you tell me?"

"This has never happened to any other student. You are breaking new ground. You will be the first." Shinichi looked up and pondered—Eric was shocked to see a twinkle in his eye. "I wonder what I should get you and Karro for a wedding present."

"It's not funny," Eric said through clenched teeth. "We were in a tree to escape a grizzly bear. I swear it." When Eric saw this had no effect on Shinichi he said, "I won't do it."

"The law is binding to all."

"I'll go with Karro and explain to Angry Bear and the elders what happen. Surely they will understand reason."

"You're not allowed to see Karro until the wedding day."

Eric folded his arms and said firmly, "No. I won't marry Karro."

"Then Karro will die. They will stone her or smother her under several thick buffalo blankets. It is she who will bear the burden with her life."

Eric collapsed in defeat as Kamani began to sign to Shinichi.

"Kamani says she will be honored to make the wedding feast."

Eric groaned.

seventy

Eric stared out into the meadow, his body ridged. There was a chill in the crisp morning air but he didn't feel it.

"I understand," Sami said, trying to catch his breath. "But what can we do?"

Red-faced, Eric clenched his fists whipped around to face the others. "Stop laughing."

This set off another round of laugher. Abbas was on the ground, laughing like a hyena. Omar was bent over, holding his stomach and laughing so loud Eric couldn't hear himself. Seeing Eric's angry look stopped Sami from joining the others.

"Stop laughing," Eric demanded.

It took ten minutes, several more fits of laughter, and a lot of 'Eric the groom' 'Eric the lover' or 'Eric the cursed' before the meadow finally quieted.

Shoulder drooping, and palms opened Eric pleaded. "Help me. I can't marry Karro."

"Eric, you broke the law—you and Karro spent the night alone," Omar said.

"We were up a tree," Eric argued. *How many more times and in how many ways do I have to say it before I'm believed?* He wondered.

"I hear tied together real tight," Abbas said, the hint of a smile creeping back into the corners of his mouth.

"Now he's going to be tied by a ring in his nose," Omar chimed in.

"There was a bear!" Eric shouted.

Omar winked at Abbas. "I hear *bear* wrestling is a sport. Eric, who was the bear—you or Karro?"

"Karro, the Amazon of course," Abbas said, looking at Omar. "Did Karro let you win… sometimes?"

"We didn't wrestle," Eric snapped. "If we did, who says Karro would win?"

"My money's on her," Omar said. Then, apparently unable to help himself, he began to shake with silent laughter. "We have a question. Really. Who is the bride and who is the groom?"

"I hear Isabeli is making Eric a skirt for the wedding." Abbas started laughing.

"Eric the bride." Sami joined in the laughter.

Eric tightened his hands into fists again. "You'd better stop."

"Is Karro going to carry you into the honeymoon teepee?"

"Shut up!" Eric yelled as he went after Omar, who dodged away.

"Amazons like their men soft. You'd better start using honey oil," Abbas said before darting away from Eric, too.

Eric turned on Sami, ready to attack.

Sami threw up his hands. "I wasn't going to say anything."

Eric dropped his hands and let out a sigh of relief. "Thanks."

"I think you're lucky," Sami said, taking a step backward. "Being an Amazon she-man might be fun."

The howls of laughter from Omar, Abbas, and Sami were unbearable. Eric turned and stomped away.

Later in the day, out on the plain, beside a creek Thunder was rolling on the ground, his head moving up and down like Omar's and Abbas'.

"You too?" Eric said, looking down at the horse and collapsed onto the ground. "What am I going to do?"

Thunder waved his head in the direction of the horizon.

"Run away?" Eric looked off to the horizon. "I...I can't. The Shoshone will kill Karro."

The black stallion looked at him and shook his head vigorously. Eric patted his long neck. "You wouldn't force a young boy and girl horse to marry just because they spent the night together, would you?"

Eric watched the horses shake his head and said, "Why can't Angry Bear be more like you?"

He had ridden Thunder longer than usual, wanting to get as far away from the Shoshone camp—and the madness that was consuming his life—as possible.

No matter what, I can't see Karro hurt in any way. Shinichi had warned him about seeing Karro. "The tribe usually favors the male," Shinichi had said. "But because this is so sensitive, both of you will be disciplined."

In frustration, Eric kicked the dirt hard, sending up a small dust cloud. "I don't want to be married," he screamed out at the clear sky.

You have no choice, Eric heard his mind reply.

The following day, after a long march the Shoshone set up camp by an angry river. The swift current whipped up white foam on the river's surface. After crossing the river, it would take less than a week to reach the winter camp.

Eric's eyes fixed on a large leaf riding the rapids. The leaf had no control and had to follow the currents around it. Eric understood he was the leaf. Only seven days remained until he would have to marry Karro. He shifted his eyes to the sky. To Eric, the sun raced across the sky to let the night come and, not to be outdone, the nights ended quickly as well. The days were speeding past.

That evening, Kamani and Isabeli entered the teepee. They greeted Eric with broad smiles, collected a few things, and were gone again. This had become the regular routine with Kamani and Isabeli. Both were constantly together, moving quickly, as if there wasn't enough time in the day.

Their operations room was the teepee. It was the one place Karro couldn't follow. According to Isabeli, Karro had made it very clear she didn't want a big wedding.

"She doesn't understand," Isabeli exclaimed when they returned. "A wedding is a special day; fast and quick just won't do. All her threats won't deter Kamani and me."

Eric got up. All the talk and planning was giving him a headache.

"Where are you going?" Kamani signed.

"Out. For some fresh air."

"Eric," Isabeli said meekly.

He turned back to Isabeli. "Yes."

"I need two more horses."

"What? You said three. Now you need five?"

She shrugged sweetly. "The best doesn't come cheap."

Eric bit back a response and left the teepee without another word. He found Sami by the campfire, eating.

"She now wants five horses," Eric said. A woman offered him a bowl of deer meat, but Eric waved it away.

"Isabeli doesn't negotiate," Sami said. He put down his bowl, licked his fingers, then continued. "I was with her when she spoke to Crazy Beaver about wedding moccasins. Crazy Beaver showed her a normal pair of moccasins. Isabeli shook her head, disgusted, then asked if Crazy Beaver could make special moccasins, one-of-a-kind. Crazy Beaver said she had some rare white deerskin, sansee beads, and dyes."

Eric saw Sami cringe. "I nearly had a heart attack when Crazy Beaver said the price. Before I could open my mouth, Isabeli agreed and moved on to Slender Deer for the wedding clothes."

"Why didn't you stop to her?"

"I tried. But suddenly she had the same deadly look Karro has when she's about to fight. I realized I'm not the one paying for it and kept my mouth shut."

"Thanks," Eric said sarcastically. "What happened to the part about watching my back?"

"I always watch mine first."

Eric laughed.

"Eric, if I were you, I'd bring a couple more horses. The special wedding song with accompanying drums Isabeli ordered won't come cheap."

Eric stopped laughing.

Do I have to bring in the whole herd? How come I don't have any say? I want fast and quick—the less pain the better. His marriage to Karro seemed like a great boulder rumbling down a steep mountain. Every minute it moved faster; now, nothing could stop it.

seventy-one

Three days from the winter camp, Eric had been gone most of the day. He'd ridden Thunder hard until he was sore. Eric still marveled at the black stallion's strength. Thunder never seemed to tire.

Eric was riding his black and white horse and leading six more. Three to fulfill the ones Isabeli had promised for the wedding song and one for Karro's wedding dress. Two more for the continuing spiraling wedding costs.

He hoped this was the last trip to fetch horses, but the voice in his head laughed.

Eric and the horses were coming over a ridge and through the trees when he pulled hard on his reins, forcing his horse to fall back. The six horses behind him whinnied and snorted in protest and shuffled their hooves.

The village—it's like a nest of angry hornets. Warriors were running all around, weapons in hand. The women were trying to corral their screaming children. *The bodies.* Eric saw the line of bodies lying motionless on the ground.

We've been attacked. Eric began to scan the surrounding areas of the village. *By whom?* He didn't see anyone. Cautiously he slid off his black and white horse and tied it to a tree with the others.

Eric took his bow, quiver of arrows, and his war tomahawk tied to his horse. As he'd been trained, his eyes roamed the area for the safest path down to the chaotic village. Moving with stealth, it took Eric more than twenty minutes to reach the village. There was smoke from several smoldering teepees, women chanting in sorrow, and the numerous dead made Eric's blood boil.

He ran to his teepee, fearing he'd see Shinichi among the dead along the way. Eric stopped briefly and gazed at the blackened side, where fire had tried to consume his teepee. He opened the flap and found Shinichi talking with Calm Cougar inside.

"Eric, you're safe." Shinichi let out a sigh of relief.

"What happened?" Eric asked.

"An Ute war party attacked us," Calm Cougar said. His eyes full of anger. "They were brazen, attacking during the day to catch us off-guard. They took most of the Shoshones' horses and scattered the rest."

Eric let it sink in. *With all horses gone, the village is almost defenseless.* "We need to get the scattered horses," Eric said.

"Angry Bear has sent out as many warriors as he can spare," Shinichi said. "But he cannot leave the village defenseless."

Calm Cougar was one of the bravest warriors and Shinichi was his equal. "Why are you here?" Eric questioned Shinichi. "Why aren't you two helping find the horses?"

"I was on my way when Calm Cougar came to tell me the terrible news." Shinichi took in a deep breath and placed his hand gently on Eric's shoulder.

Eric felt his stomach tighten. "Karro, Sami, dead?"

"No," Shinichi lowered his head.

"Omar? Abbas?"

Shinichi shook his head.

Eric swallowed hard. "Isabeli?"

Shinichi nodded and Eric shoulder's sagged. He closed his eyes, feeling a sharp pain in his chest.

"Isabeli was taken by the Ute." Calm Cougar said.

"Taken?" Eric head swung up, relieved. "Not dead?"

"She could be soon," Shinichi said. "Both Isabeli and Kamani were out looking for flowers to make perfume."

Eric turned to Calm Cougar, whose face was tight. "They've taken Kamani, too?"

Calm Cougar nodded slowly.

"What are you doing here?" Eric yelled, his eyes darting back and forth between Calm Cougar and Shinichi. "You have to go after them."

"We have no horses," Shinichi said.

"I have horses."

"You do?" Calm Cougar stepped in front of Eric, towering over him.

"I have seven close by."

Calm Cougar looked at Shinichi. For the first time, Eric saw a bright glint of hope in his eye. "We must tell Angry Bear," Calm Cougar said. "We can gather the scattered horses."

"No. We have to go after Isabeli and Kamani," Eric said.

Calm Cougar shook his head and said calmly. "We must gather the horses."

"No," Eric said firmly.

"Eric," Shinichi raised his voice. "There are many reasons, but you won't agree with any of them. The scattered horses must be collected, the defense must be fortified against further attack, and the loss of two women isn't worth sacrificing dozens more horses or men."

Eric went to the far corner of the teepee and picked up a quiver of arrows.

"You can't go," Calm Cougar said, blocking Eric's way.

There's no way I can take Calm Cougar. Eric dropped the quiver of arrows and sank to the ground. But his mind was racing.

"I must go tell Angry Bear about the horses," Calm Cougar said to Shinichi. He pulled back the flap and raced out.

"Be safe," Shinichi said to Eric.

"What?"

"I know you're going after Isabeli and Kamani no matter what anyone says."

Eric got up quickly. "Yes, I am. With or without the horses."

"I won't stop you. I'll try to delay Angry Bear as long as I can."

Eric picked up the quiver again.

"Goodbye Eric," Shinichi said sadly.

Eric stopped a second, nodded his head, and left his mentor.

Through the chaotic village, Eric ran, looking for the others. Omar was with Abbas, who was wrapping Omar's upper arm.

"Eric—you're alive. We thought you were dead," Omar said. The look of relief on his normally stoic face warmed Eric's heart.

"Where's Sami?" Eric asked.

"We're about to go and search for him," Abbas said. "He ran into the woods during the Ute attack."

"The Ute took Isabeli and Kamani." Eric dropped his voice, "I'm going after them. I need you."

"Okay," Omar said, picking up his weapons. "Abbas and I are ready."

"First, I'm going to find Sami." Eric pointed to the distant ridge. "Meet me there with food, water and weapons." Eric didn't wait for their reply but ran off in the direction of the woods.

Eric and Sami met up with Omar and Abbas on top of the ridge. Abbas held up the food and water.

"Too much," Eric said.

"We'll need all we can carry to follow the Ute," Omar said.

"Wait. Catch up with the Ute?" Sami face turned pale.

"I have horses and we need to move fast," Eric said to Omar and Abbas.

"You have horses?" Abbas asked.

"No," Sami said, shaking his head, and backing away a few steps. "No one said anything about going after the Ute."

"Yes, I have horses." Eric turned to Sami. "You're going to join us rescuing Isabeli and Kamani."

"But Eric—"

"Sami, we can't do it without you," Eric said firmly.

"I'm going, too."

Eric whipped around to see Karro standing resolute, armed with her bow and quiver of arrows. Her eyes were staring at him as if searching for something. Eric couldn't help a smiling appearing at the sight of Karro. Her lips edged up into a matching smile.

"Karro, if you and Eric are together, you'll be in big trouble," Omar said.

"Most likely we'll all be killed anyway going after the Utes. They are one of the most ferocious Indian fighter on the plain," Karro said slinging her quiver of arrows across her back.

"Die? Eric—" Sami started.

"I left the horses over here."

Eric ignored Sami and started sprinting to the horses.

Omar and Abbas were riding fifty feet ahead, east, tracking the Ute. Eric rode beside Karro, with Sami close by.

"Thanks for not leaving me behind," Karro said to Eric. "I could see in Omar's and Abbas' faces they didn't want me to come."

"We're breaking Shoshone law. They were concerned."

"No, they're worried about me as a fighter."

"Omar and Abbas have never seen you under pressure. I have. You're able to stay calm and think clearly. I need you to advise me on what to do." Eric looked at her, chancing a grin. "I think you really wanted to come to make sure I returned to marry you."

Karro shot him an angry look, then matched his grin. "Actually, it's to make sure that if the Ute don't kill you off, I will."

Eric laughed. It felt good to be like this again—friends.

Sami rode up beside them. "Why are you laughing?" he demanded. "We're going to our doom."

"Probably," Eric said. "We have sworn to protect each other. It's more than just words."

Sami snorted, unconvinced. "Karro, if *I* was taken, would you risk your life for me?" he asked.

"The Amazon in me would not allow it," Karro said. "But I would come anyway. You can always rely on me."

Sami looked down, shame written on his face. "I was sure you'd say no," he said. "Okay, I'm not like either one of you, but I'll do my best."

Eric saw Omar and Abbas pull hard on their horses' reins. They waited for the rest to catch up.

"The Utes are not riding hard," Omar said. He pointed to a light dust cloud ahead.

"They know the Shoshones don't have horses to follow," Eric replied.

"We've seen two horses leaving deeper hoof prints," Abbas said.

"They're carrying Isabeli and Kamani," Eric said. "They're both still alive."

"But for how long?" Karro asked. The group looked at the distant dust cloud.

"We should ride parallel to the Ute, then circle in when they get to their village," Karro said.

"Good idea. Right now, the Ute warriors are heavily armed and alert," Eric said. "Abbas, ride ahead and make sure we don't run into any Ute outriders. Omar, make sure we're not surprised from behind."

Abbas spurred his horse quickly off to the left and Omar dropped back. Eric, Karro, and Sami rode after Abbas.

seventy-two

Eric looked to the west; the dropping sun outlined the top of the mountains. Above was a fading sky already showing the first star.

They all crouched behind a large rock on the east side of the Ute village. Like the Shoshones the Utes had set up their village by a water source, a small lake.

An hour earlier, they had watched the Ute warriors arrive at camp. In the center were Isabeli and Kamani, riding in front of two stout Ute fighters. Another pair of Ute warriors took them to a teepee not far from the center of the village.

Eric, Karro, Omar, and Abbas watched the village while Sami stayed forty yards back with the horses.

The drums were loud and the Ute village was in a festive mood.

It doesn't matter if Angry Bear gathers all the scattered horse. Even if the Shoshones had all their horses, we would be outnumbered. Eric looked down on the Ute village that was three times bigger than the Shoshones'.

Karro touched Eric on his shoulder and Eric waved to Omar and Abbas close by.

"There's no choice," Karro said. "One of us has to go in after them."

"If anyone goes into the Ute Village, they're dead," Omar said.

Abbas tugged on his leather vest. "They dress differently."

"Someone has to stay back and create a diversion. And someone must make sure the path out is clear," Eric said.

Before anyone could argue, Eric got up and started to move. "We have a plan; now let's get a closer look."

They saw the Ute boy coming out from behind a tree; he had a broad smile on his face. He stopped in the center of a clearing.

"This is our chance," Omar said.

"It's too wide open. He'll see anyone coming up on him," Abbas said.

Omar, Abbas, and Eric all turned and looked at Karro.

Her eyes widened, clearly not understanding the looks. "What?"

"Distract the boy and we'll jump him," Eric said.

"How?"

"Be like Isabeli," Omar said.

"I'd rather die."

"Karro, you have to," Eric said, trying to make his voice gentler. "Now smile like Isabeli."

After a second's hesitation, Karro's lips twitched, stuttered, and finally parted, showing her teeth.

Eric, Abbas, and Omar stared at Karro. "She looks like she's a wolfhound ready to attack," Omar said.

"Try winking, too," Eric said.

Karro started to wink rapidly.

"Slowly—not like having dust in your eyes," Eric demonstrated, turning his head slightly, smiling, and winking slowly.

"Eric, maybe you should go out instead," Abbas said.

"The Ute's moving." Omar looked concerned.

"You have to go—now." Eric pushed Karro forward.

Karro brushed back her hair and walked toward the bushes separating them from the clearing while Eric, Omar, and Abbas crouched down.

"At least she's walking like Isabeli," Omar said.

Karro parted the bushes and walked forward. The Ute boy's face went through several expressions: shock, uncertainty, and, finally as his eye traveled over Karro, happiness. Then, from behind the boy came a young girl's voice, calling. Uncertainty returned on his face, followed by anxiety. The girl's voice brought a look of desperation to him as he waved Karro away.

Eric watched the boy became agitated as Karro got closer. The Ute boy ran to Karro and pointed a direction for her to go. Karro took one more step forward and slammed her fist hard into his jaw. The Ute crumpled like a broken doll.

Karro stood over him like a victor in a boxing match. Eric looked at Omar and Abbas, shaking his head. "Now she smiles."

They got up to enter the clearing when a large Ute girl came charging out of the bushes and drove into Karro like a battering ram. The two girls were suddenly locked in a fierce battle.

"Tie up the boy," Eric ordered Abbas. "I'll help Karro."

Eric ran and wrapped his arms around the Ute girl. He gritted his teeth as she kicked, twisted, and elbowed. Suddenly, she dropped her head and Eric's ear rang when Karro smashed her right fist into his jaw. He dropped like a rock but didn't let go of the girl.

Karro bent down and hit the Ute girl hard, behind the ear. The fight left the girl and she went limp. Eric released her and got up, shaking his head to clear it.

Omar and Abbas dragged the tied-up boy back into the bushes and Eric followed, removing his vest. In less than a minute, Eric was back dressed like the Ute boy.

"Okay, ready," he said to Omar and Abbas, then looked around. "Where's Karro?"

"She dragged the girl into the bushes," Abbas said.

There was noise behind them and they turned to see Karro come out of the bushes dressed like the Ute girl.

"*What're you doing?*" Eric asked.

"I'm going with you."

"No."

"Why? Because I'm not a boy?"

"Don't start that now." Finally, to Karro's determined look he said, "Okay. Omar, we'll need a distraction. Go to the north. When you see us come out of the teepee with Isabeli and Kamani, give us a few minutes, then shout the Shoshone battle cry as loud as you can. Abbas, we'll be coming this direction, so set Sami here with the horses and make sure the way east is clear from Ute warriors."

"I'll never forget you," Omar said, leaving.

"You were a good friend," Abbas said, clapping Eric on the back.

They don't think I'll make it. Eric watched the two go. "Karro, stay and help Sami with the horses."

seventy-three

"**I'm going!**" Karro said, walking toward the Ute village.

"We have to act normal, like we belong," Eric said, catching up to Karro. "We have to act like the boy and girl."

Karro scrunched up her nose. "Like boyfriend and girlfriend? Why?"

"Just do it. Behave like were a Shoshone boyfriend and girlfriend."

Karro gave a hideous laugh.

Eric cringed. "Stop! What are you doing?"

"When the boys and girls are together, they're always laughing and giggling."

"What else?"

"They're always bumping and nudging each other like it's a game."

"Yes. Good. They also lean into each other like they're sharing a secret."

Eric leaned into Karro, brushing his arm against hers. She stiffened. Getting close to the Ute village, Eric began to giggle, and then gave Karro a playful nudge. She drove her elbow hard into his ribs.

Eric groaned. "Karro, easy."

"I've never done this. Amazons—"

"Did I ever tell you how nice you look?" Eric said, taking Karro's hand and walking toward the village. "When we first met, I thought you didn't like me."

Karro gave a light laugh. "You were fat and clumsy and always seemed disoriented." She laughed again. "You were a baby lost in the woods."

Eric matched her laugh. "I was lost."

"Then you shocked me when you walked up and took Angry Bear's food."

"You thought I was brave?"

"No, I was thinking how stupid boys are."

"I always thought you were special," Eric said, leaning further into Karro. "You're amazing."

"You think so?" Karro leaned closer into Eric. "I don't fit in."

"You're different, have some unusual traits. But that's what makes you special. When I'm with you, I feel time goes by too fast."

"I...I...don't... Amazons don't—it's not right." Karro took a breath and sighed. "But when I'm with you, I...I feel different."

Eric felt Karro squeeze his hand as he watched a Ute woman lead a young child across their path. Eric squeezed Karro's hand back and smiled.

Karro shifted to lean closer. "Eric, I really like—"

"Over there," Eric cut her off.

"What?"

Eric jabbed his finger toward a teepee. "Go. Cut an opening in the back. Get Isabeli and Kamani while I keep watch."

When Karro just stared at him, he pushed her toward the back of the tent. "Hurry."

She looked at him strangely, as if hurt, before turning, taking out her knife and going to the back of the tent.

Eric swung his head from side to side. Through the teepees he spied a few women walking toward the center of the village. Though the night was cool, Eric felt sweat running down his face. Suddenly, he whipped around, hearing a bark. *No. A dog. We're lost.*

A thin, ragged dog came into the opening and raised its nose sniffing the air as Karro went through the hole she'd cut. Eric's attention turned back to the dog as its nose on the ground inched in his direction, then stopped when it was pointed directly at him. Eric stared into its black eyes, then watched the dog's lips pull back, showing its fangs. Muscles taut, the angry beast lowered its head, and a menacing growl escaped as it slowly circled Eric to attack.

Eric backed away, swallowing a scream for help. The dog leapt forward and Eric jumped back.

He heard a loud grunt and received a cuff to the back of his head. Eric looked up into a stout warrior's face scarred with war paint. Eric was thrown down, but his attention shifted from the man back to the dog. The dog growled and charged. Eric threw up his arms for protection against the dog's vicious bite.

Through his raised arms, he saw a moccasin foot speed out and kick the dog back. The dog looked up cautiously at the stout warrior, but then its eyes dropped, finding Eric again. Its gaze fixed on Eric, it sprang up and attacked. Eric heard angry words from the Ute warrior, whose quick hand reached down and grabbed the dog by the scruff of its neck, yanking up. He shouted into the dog's face, then threw him away. The dog cringed down, hunched over; then, tail between its legs, it crawled away.

The Ute warrior walked away and Eric was alone. He sat on the ground, staring after the Ute warrior. In a daze, he got up and moved to the teepee. He watched mechanically as Karro appeared at the tent's entrance, followed by Isabeli and Kamani dressed as Ute women.

Seeing him, Isabeli rushed forward, past Karro. She threw her arms around him and suddenly Eric couldn't breathe. Isabeli's lips were locked on his. Eric pulled back.

"You came for me," Isabeli said, leaning her lips toward Eric again.

Eric stepped back, untangling himself. "Of course."

He smiled at Kamani, and then noticed Karro's scowling face. *What's wrong with her?* There was no time to figure it out— they needed to get out of this camp now. "Come on." Eric waved for them to follow.

He stopped after the next teepee and looked off to the north. *Where's the Shoshone battle cry?* Eric looked around anxiously.

Karro came up beside him, her face tight with anger. "You're like all the other males," she spat before marching off.

"Karro...Karro come back!" Eric said, barely above a whisper.

"My hero," Isabeli said, moving beside Eric and fluttering her eyelids.

Kamani tapped Eric on his shoulder getting his attention and signed aggressively, then pointed.

Eric caught sight of a band of Ute warriors headed toward Karro. He pushed Isabeli in Karro's direction. "Hurry."

He moved quickly and caught up to Karro. Eric grabbed her arm and spun her around. He was surprised to see a tear running down her face. She opened her mouth. "Quiet," Eric demanded. He saw Karro's eyes light up with anger but didn't care. "Ute warriors are coming." Eric anxiously looked to the north. *Now, Omar, now,* he pleaded, but the only sound Eric heard was the approaching men.

He grabbed Karro's hand and dragged her after him, away from the men. The clearing before them, where most of the Ute were celebrating, was filled with cooking fires. Without hesitating, Eric strode into the center of the village. He weaved his way through the cook fires and dodged around Ute men carrying spears and bows and women swaying back and forth in a playful dance. He noted a familiar tree and shifted his direction. *Isabeli, Kamani, please be behind Karro and me.*

Out of the center of the village and within the teepees at the edge of camp, Eric turned. Isabeli's, Kamani's, and even Karro's eyes were wide with anticipation of escape. "It's not too much further," he said reassuringly to Isabeli and Kamani. In a few minutes, they were through the teepees and Eric could see the tree line twenty feet away. "We made it," he said to the others and smiled faintly.

The night air was suddenly filled with a Shoshone battle cry. *Not now!* It was answered by hundreds of Ute warrior battle cries filling the air.

"Run!" Eric shouted, waving the girls in front of him. He looked backward. Through the teepees, he saw warriors sprinting to their horses, and caught sight of several armed Ute warriors running in his direction. Eric turned and ran after the girls as fast as he could.

Karro led the group to the opening. She pulled up and looked around. "Where are the horses?" Eric ran up beside her.

"Sami's run away with the horses," she said.

"No. Over here," came a trembling voice from the shadows.

Sami was wide-eyed and shaking as he stepped from behind a dense bush leading the horses.

"Thank you, Sami," Eric said.

"Almost rode away, Eric," Sami said, his voice quivering with fear.

"But you didn't." Eric quickly took the horses' reins and handed them out. "Fast. On the horses." Eric pulled a horse close and helped Kamani up onto it.

At last, on his black and white, he looked over his shoulder and in the pale moonlight, saw everyone's faces: Karro's glaring look, Isabeli's dazzling smile, Kamani's concern, and Sami's fear. Eric pointed east through the trees. "Come on."

Eric guided his horse quickly through the trees. *Hopefully, the Ute will think the Shoshone are north because of Omar's battle cry, or west where the Shoshone are camped.*

Ahead was Abbas waiting with his horse, already facing east. Abbas had started to trot to come in line with the others. When Eric, Sami, and the girls reached him, he said, "You did it."

"I've done nothing if we don't survive," Eric said.

"Fifty feet ahead the trees stop and then wide, open plain."

Once out of the trees, Eric spurred his horse forward into a run. In the distance, he could see Omar coming up fast at a dead run. Eric veered off toward Omar and everyone followed. A quarter-mile later, he pulled hard on the reins and his horse dug his front hooves deep into the ground. Omar and the rest did the same.

"They're coming," Omar said quickly.

"Are you sure?" Sami asked.

"Yes. The Ute boy and girl you took the clothes from made it back to the village. They steered the warriors in our direction."

"How many?" Karro asked.

"Two to three hundred."

Eric looked back. Though the moonlight shone, Eric could not see the Ute following.

Suddenly, Eric realized this place was familiar. He had ridden Thunder through here before. "Ten miles further there are canyons to hide in," he told the others.

"Hide like cowards? We must stay and fight," Karro said.

Eric dismissed Karro's madness. "We all need to ride hard. Omar, Abbas, take the lead. Make sure we're not surprised."

Both kicked their horses hard and sped away. The rest pushed their horses into a run.

seventy-four

Twenty minutes later, it had become a habit. Every minute, Eric took a look back. For the last five minutes he had seen the Ute charging toward them. He knew they were whipping their horses as if the devil himself was pushing them.

He looked at everyone ahead of him. Omar and Abbas were fifty feet ahead; Karro was ten feet behind them, keeping pace. But the others were slowly falling back. He watched as Kamani bounced around on her horse's back like a small boat in a stormy sea. He could tell her hands were white from holding on so tight. Sami and Isabeli were riding only a little better.

He could see the canyon ahead, like an oasis in the middle of the burning desert. He looked back at the Ute and did the mental calculation. *We won't make it. We need more time.* But there was no more time. When caught, they all would be tortured and killed. *We need just a little more time.*

Eric pulled up on the reins a little, slowing up. *I have to give them the time.* He slowed more, letting the others move further away. He brought his horse to a slow trot and watched the others race away toward the canyons.

I'll never forget you, Omar had said. Abbas had added, *you were a good friend.*

"Goodbye," Eric whispered, already missing them. *At least Karro will be happy she doesn't have to marry me.*

The Moon was passing off to the west. Eric looked up at the large, round ball, its white surface shaded by imperfection.

His past filled his mind. It now seemed like someone else's life or a fairytale he'd read in a book. The Moon castle, with its magnificent halls, ornate ballrooms, and the commanding throne room. Eric grinned with the thought he'd actually slept on a soft, luxurious bed instead of the hard, cold ground. *What would I be doing if I was back there?* A great banquet filled his mind, tables with loads of the most delicious foods, men dressed in uniforms, and women in long gowns. Eric laughed. *Would I be running from Charles? What about George? My father would be in a group of men discussing the politics of the day.* Then, a beautiful face filled his mind. He pictured a tall, slender woman looking around, making sure everyone was having a good time. Eric imagined they locked eyes and the most incredible smile came to his mother's face.

The Ute battle cries filled his ears and returned Eric to the present. He looked after his friends. *They must live. Even if I don't.*

Eric stopped his horse, knowing what he must do. *The Ute must believe I'm more than one rider.* He quickly dismounted and removed the reins from his hard-breathing horse. He pulled off his horse blanket, stretched out the reins, and tied one end of the reins to the blanket and the other end to his horse's tail.

Back on his horse, he looked one more time at his friends speeding away toward the canyons. Then his head shifted to the hundreds of Ute warriors. He could now see the faint line of individual warriors riding hard.

Resigning himself to his fate, Eric slowly remounted. He slapped his horse and it started to run. Eric looked over his shoulder and saw the dust cloud twisting and spiraling behind him. He took in a deep breath and cocked his head in the direction of the oncoming Ute. *I am a Shoshone warrior; hear my challenge.* With every fiber of his being, he belted out the Shoshone battle cry.

seventy-five

A half hour later, the Moon had passed, leaving only residual light, his horse was foaming at the mouth, and the Ute were only a hundred yards back. Eric knew it was time. He pulled out the knife he had taken from the Ute boy. *I won't be taken alive.*

He suddenly heard the hard pounding of hooves coming up fast behind him. *How?* But it didn't matter. He had missed a skilled rider on a swift horse. Eric shifted the knife to his other hand and prepared to fight. He looked over his shoulder to gauge how long he had.

His body jerked about, and he almost fell off his horse.

"Thunder!" Eric screamed. The black stallion was coming up fast. But so were the Ute warriors. His spirit leaped. "Come on, Thunder," Eric shouted. The black stallion slowed to match the tired black and white horse. Without hesitation, Eric threw his hands over to Thunder, clutching his mane. Eric's feet hit the ground and he sprang onto Thunder's back. A second later, Thunder stretched out into a gallop.

Eric howled with joy and his confidence rose. He had a fighting chance.

The Ute won't give up. I must outrun them with Thunder's speed and endurance. A satisfying grin came when he looked over his shoulder and measured how fast the Ute were falling back. The smile faded when he felt Thunder slow. He whipped his head back around. *What's wrong?*

"Faster!" Eric roared. Fast—" Then, his mouth hung open, seeing the canyon's edge.

He leaned back, preparing to slow down, when an arrow sped past him. He chanced a look back and saw the Ute were bearing down on him, trapping their prey. Eric gasped as an arrow sliced his outer leg.

Death surrounded him. The canyon's edge was coming up quickly, and the deadly Utes behind.

Eric leaned forward. He could see the canyon ahead spreading out; there was nowhere to turn. His mind became resolute. Behind was sure death, ahead only a little less. Even though small, a chance was still a chance. *Faster. Run faster.* Eric and Thunder were of one mind; continuing life depended on a single jump. The canyon's edge was upon them. Thunder dashed forward like an arrow shot from a powerful bow.

Eric leaned down close and he and Thunder became one. He could feel the fluid rhythm of the stallion's powerful muscles. His ears filled with the sound of hammering hooves propelling them forward, his eyes fixed on the canyon's edge.

A hard thrust from Thunder's mighty legs rocketed Eric into the open air and space. Time suddenly slowed and Eric's senses were acute. Eyes as big as silver dollars, Eric looked down to the jagged rock basin hundreds of feet below, and his already rapidly beating heart accelerated. His ears turned off sound and his head and eyes jerked around to focus on a small area of sloped land cut between two canyon cliffs. Every part of his body willed Thunder to fly further to make the slope.

Eric felt the hard tug of gravity beginning to slow and pull them down. The canyon was like the mouth of a great white shark opening to the jagged rocks below, its teeth ready to tear his skin and break his bones. In the jaws of the mighty shark, his life would end.

The hard impact jolted Eric and nearly knocked him off of Thunder's back. Eric fought to pull and right himself back when Thunder's left front leg collapsed under him. "Please, Thunder,"

Eric begged. The mighty stallion fought hard, struggling to get his footing, but a misstep sent them sliding down. "Fight!" Eric screamed. Thunder's hind right hoof was at the edge of the canyon wall. A surge of motion sent Thunder fighting to his feet. Shuffling his hooves quickly, he strained his powerful muscles to pull himself up. Every inch was a struggle until, finally, they were on the far side ridge.

Ute was the first thought in Eric's mind. He pulled Thunder around, and at the far ridge, hundreds of Ute warriors rode up watching him.

Forty feet was within an easy bowshot. *I don't care!* Eric thought boldly. He pulled back his head and roared a Shoshone battle cry as Thunder's hooves shot up in challenge.

The Ute all stared at him. It seemed a lifetime until suddenly, as one, the Ute warriors turned and rode away.

seventy-six

Why am I alive? I should be dead left for the coyotes and rats to get me. Eric couldn't understand. Sneaking through the Ute village, riding away with hundreds of furious warriors in hot pursuit, finally leaping across the wide canyon, only to be spared at the last minute. "Why?" he asked Thunder. "I'm meant for something greater. Can I really save my family?" *I have to.*

He watched the figures on horseback grow smaller before turning and riding away. It came upon Eric like a powerful desert storm—total exhaustion. Its sudden appearance sapped every ounce of his strength and he collapsed onto Thunder's back. Thunder, traveling in a slow walk, veered to a patch of trees by a slow-moving river. Under the trees, Eric slid down onto the soft grass. Thunder putting his muzzle into the river was Eric's last memory before falling into a deep sleep.

It was late afternoon when Eric woke up. He got on his hands and knees and crawled to the river. Thrusting his head into the river, he drank until he felt like he was going to burst. Slowly, Eric got up and groaned as every muscle in his body seemed to ache. Slowly, he stripped down and waded into the river, its cool water bringing a sigh of relief. For the next hour as Thunder dozed under a tree, Eric paddled around the river without any care or worry.

Finally, he got out and dried his body in the sun. He looked around and noticed the black stallion far off down the river. Eric whistled and watched Thunder's head jerk upward, then gallop in his direction.

The horse stopped several feet in front of him and Eric beamed. "Thunder." He walked up to the horse and scratched his nose. Then he moved to Thunder's side and began to stroke his long neck. "You saved my life. Thank you."

Eric jumped up on Thunder's back, then leaned down and hugged the mighty stallion. "You are the best horse that ever lived." He pointed them both west, in the direction of the Shoshone village.

Eric found his black and white wandering the low hills. He and Thunder rode up to it, Eric slid off Thunder.

He moved in front of Thunder before he looked down the long valley leading to the Shoshone camp. He brushed Thunder's long hair, and said softly, "I want to take you with me to the Shoshone village so I can always be with you." A few seconds later, Eric shook his head. "You wouldn't be happy." He looked off to the distant plain. "Happiness is running free, leading your herd."

Eric moved to his black and white horse and mounted it. "Goodbye, Thunder," he said sadly. For some reason, Eric felt he would never see the black stallion again.

seventy-seven

The journey back to the Shoshone camp through the valley was long. Eric had selected a trail that would take him along the valley's ridge through the tree line. He wanted to make sure no Utes were following him.

It was very late when he arrived back at the Shoshone village. He tied his black and white horse to a tree and, overcome with weariness, went to his teepee. It was empty; Shinichi was out. He fell onto his buffalo skins and within seconds was asleep.

"Huh, what?" Eric's eyelids sprang open. Strong hands were wrapped around his upper arms and he was forced to his feet. Daring Bobcat was on his right and next to him, on Eric's left, was Swift Deer. Their faces were tight with anger. "What's wrong?" Eric asked.

Both stayed silent but thrust him roughly out of the teepee. The bright morning sunlight attacked Eric's eyes, blinding him and forcing him to blink several times. Then, his vision cleared and before him were twenty Shoshone warriors. He was pushed into them. Several stepped aside, cuffing him as he went by. One tripped him, sending him to the ground, and again strong hands pulled him up. Eric received a hard push from behind, and he was thrown again into the throng of warriors to be cuffed and thumped.

When a hand slapped him across the head, Eric whirled, bringing up his fists, ready to fight.

The warriors moved in as one.

"Stop," a commanding voice barked. Calm Cougar came up beside Eric, making the other warriors pause. "I'll take him to Angry Bear. *Who will stop me?*" None of the warriors moved.

Calm Cougar pulled Eric after him, taking him through the village. As Eric walked through the teepees everyone stared at him. There was a variety of emotion on their faces; surprise, a lot of anger, but mostly fear.

"What's going on?" Eric asked, but like the warriors who'd pulled him from his tent, Calm Cougar remained silent.

Then Eric was overtaken with fear. *Where are Karro, Sami?* He looked around. *Isabeli, Kamani, Omar, Abbas?* None of them were around. *Had the Ute caught them after all?* Eric's shoulders slumped and sadness overwhelmed him. *They're all gone.*

It had all been for nothing. The joy he had felt for beating the Ute was now matched by the sinking feeling for his friends.

In the center of the village, most of the Shoshones had gathered, and they parted when Eric approached. Eric spotted Shinichi standing with the elders several steps behind Angry Bear. Eric couldn't read his face. Shinichi stared at Eric as if he was a stranger.

All of a sudden, Eric beamed. Standing back in the crowd, he glimpsed Omar and Abbas. A few feet away stood Sami. He quickly scanned the faces and found Isabeli with Kamani. Then, he was overjoyed at the sight of Karro among a group of women.

Calm Cougar stopped and stepped aside, letting Angry Bear and Eric come face to face. The look on the Shoshone chief's face matched his name.

Eric knew it was wrong, but with the sighting of his friends, he couldn't force the bright smile from his face.

"You had told him?" Angry Bear said, his question addressed to Calm Cougar, but his angry stare still directed at Eric.

"Yes."

"And still he took the horses?"

"Yes."

"I needed them to go after Isabeli and Kamani," Eric explained.

"Against the needs of the people."

"It doesn't matter," Eric said to Angry Bear. "They're all back now. You can have the horses."

"You have enraged the Ute. By being a boy, not a Shoshone warrior, and attacking them it has insulted their pride. Provoked anger."

"Isabeli and Kamani are safe," Eric said happily.

"All for a painted girl and a worthless mute."

Eric's smile faded.

"They are of little worth," Angry Bear spat at Eric. "Horses are of value. With horses, we hunt and protect the people. With horses, we are able to extend our territories."

Eric's body tightened. "You don't care about the horses, only your fear of the Ute," Eric said, disregarding the gasp caused by his insult.

"When I send the painted girl and the worthless mute back to the Ute, it will not be because of fear."

"No!" Eric stood rigid, eyes defiant. "I won't let you!"

It happened in a flash—quick slashes across Eric's bare chest from Angry Bear's horsewhip. Eric didn't flinch, his gray-blue eyes blazing contempt for the chief.

"I won't allow it," Eric said through gritted teeth.

"I will decide, Screaming Eagle. According to Shoshone law, you must pay the price for taking the needed horses and your actions against the Ute. You will be torn apart by horses. It will be done on the tenth day from now," Angry Bear promised.

The inside of Eric's tent was solemn. Shinichi, Sami, Omar and Abbas sat silently watching Eric. Eric sat cross-legged angrily stared forward as if he was alone.

THE FIRST EVENT: SURVIVAL

"Don't touch them," Eric said coldly, staring straight ahead. Kamani had tried to wipe the drying blood from Eric's chest where the slashes from Angry Bear had cut Eric.

"Please," Kamani signed, her eyes red from crying.

"No," Eric said, tight-jawed. "I want the pain."

"Leave Eric alone," Shinichi signed to Kamani.

Kamani made several signs toward Shinichi.

Shinichi signed back as he spoke, "Eric's blood is boiling. It consumes his mind."

"Talk to him," Kamani signed.

"It will be like talking to a mountain, but I'll try."

Kamani rushed out of the teepee, leaving Shinichi, Sami, Abbas, and Omar with Eric sitting rigidly in the center.

Shinichi looked at Sami. "It's an impossible task convincing Eric. I can explain all the dangers. How one shouldn't continuously slap the grim reaper, inviting death or injury and expect to live."

When Sami shrugged his shoulders, Shinichi looked at Eric. "Will it make a difference?"

There was no reaction from Eric, his back rigid and face stern, eyes like a volcano ready to erupt.

"You know the death sentence gave Angry Bear no pleasure," Shinichi said.

Eric gave a sarcastic laugh, breaking his silence.

"So you are listening?" Shinichi placed his palms on his knees and leaned forward. His voice firm. "Eric, you put your wants in front of the needs of the many. The village was vulnerable to attack. Many could have died."

"I couldn't leave Isabeli and Kamani with the Ute," Eric said, his gaze still fixed on the far wall of the tent.

"We all know that. Even Angry Bear. But he is bound by the law. He would need the support of other chiefs to change your death sentence."

Eric shrugged his shoulders.

"He called you Screaming Eagle. Have you heard the name before?" After several seconds of silence, Shinichi went on. "It's the name of his father, one of the bravest Shoshones who ever lived. He never snuck up on an enemy. He would scream his Shoshone battle cry, giving them time to prepare for a face-to-face fight."

"So, it's an honor in a way," Sami said.

"It's just a name," Eric said coldly.

The tent flap parted and Karro and Isabeli came in.

"My hero," Isabeli said beaming at Eric. "I've come to take care of you." Isabeli cheerfully stepped toward Eric with a wet deerskin and buffalo salve to tend to Eric's wounds.

Karro pulled her back firmly and took the deerskin away. She dismissed Isabeli's angry look and knelt in front of Eric.

"Leave it," Eric told Karro briskly.

Karro ignored Eric and started wiping the dry blood away. Eric grabbed her wrist. "Leave. It."

"Let me go," Karro warned.

"Move away," Eric ordered.

"Don't give me orders," Karro snapped.

"Some Amazon," Eric said sarcastically. *Why is she helping me? I thought Amazon hated males?*

"I won't bother," Karro said, wrestling her wrist free, but then she leaned forward. They stared eye to eye as Karro roughly wiped at the slashes on his chest.

Eric stared back red-faced, teeth clenched, fighting the pain, but kept rigid not flinching.

"Eric, at times you can be so stupid." Karro lightened the pressure as she wiped.

"I'm just a boy, not a mighty Amazon."

"Looking for a *fight*? I'll give you one," Karro said, eyes flashing. "But I'd rather hear what happened to you." She rubbed some of the buffalo salve on his wounds.

Eric relaxed a little as the buffalo salve eased some of the pain.

"What does it matter?" Isabeli stood behind Sami with her arms crossed and staring heatedly at Karro. Her voice softened as she turned her gaze on Eric and smiled broadly. "I was rescued, by my hero, Eric. It's all that matters."

"I want to know," Abbas said.

"I could have sworn you were riding behind us," Omar said. "At the canyon entrance, I turned and saw everyone but you. You were gone and so were the Ute."

Eric looked at Karro. "Are you done?" he said coldly.

"For now," she said, moving away.

"There was no way we were going to make it," Eric said to Omar. "Not without more time. I decided to give you more time."

For the next twenty minutes Eric related what happened after he had left them.

"You speak of riding the black stallion. I've told you no one will believe such a tale," Shinichi said.

"It's not a tale," Sami said.

"We all saw Eric ride the black stallion," Omar said.

"Eric calls him Thunder," Karro said.

"Thunder?" Shinichi asked.

"It doesn't matter. I escaped one death to come to another," Eric said indifferently.

The room fell silent with the truth of Eric's statement.

seventy-eight

Everyone had left the teepee except Karro.

"Food?"

"I'm not hungry," Eric said.

"You have to eat."

"Fine," Eric said abruptly. *Why does Karro care? I'm going to die soon. She should be happy now. She doesn't have to marry me. She'll be rid of me. Just like Charles was rid of me when I left the moon castle with Corcoran.*

"I'll be back," Karro said.

Karro had just left when Eric heard someone else enter. Eric got to his feet when he saw it was Calm Cougar. The Shoshone warrior looked grim and tired.

"Kamani is worried about you. To her," Calm Cougar said briskly. "You are like a son. When you're not happy, she's in pain."

Kamani is special to me too. "Sorry. I'm okay."

Calm Cougar looked away. "I couldn't have gone."

Eric shrugged his shoulders.

"If you had only waited," Calm Cougar said hurriedly. "We could have gotten the scattered Shoshone horses. I would have gone with you—ready to give my life for Kamani."

Eric looked away.

"Why didn't you wait?" Calm Cougar demanded.

"I couldn't." *Why doesn't anyone understand, Kamani and Isabeli mean so much to me. Part of my family. Kamani is like a mother. Just the thought of them being in danger makes me wary.*

"How can I ever truly be with Kamani, look into her beautiful eyes, knowing I failed her?"

"It doesn't matter," Eric said dryly.

"Why should she care for a weak-spirited coward?"

"You're older. You have to think first before acting," Eric said sarcastically. "I'm young. I act."

"You showed great bravery. I will talk to the other Shoshone chiefs when they come."

"What?" Eric looked up. "There's a gathering of the Shoshones?"

"Yes, Angry Bear has called a war council together. Your actions have insulted the Ute. It's better to take the fight to them. Shoshone warriors from other tribes will start arriving tonight."

"How many?"

"The Ute will send out riders to gather more warriors. We want more than a thousand to ride against the Ute."

"A thousand." *So many warriors?*

"Yes, tomorrow night we'll prepare ourselves for battle. The next day we'll ride out to strike the Ute."

"What will happen?"

Calm Cougar took in a deep breath and stared into Eric's eyes. "The Ute are fearless fighters. Many Shoshone warriors will not return. The winds will soon be filled with the saddened chants of women grieving their dead."

"Talk to Angry Bear," Eric begged. "Give me to the Ute."

"A Shoshone would *never* give another Shoshone brave to the enemy. The shame would follow him to the afterlife." Calm Cougar looked solemn. "In battle, I can reclaim my warrior spirit."

Karro returned, carrying a bowl of possum stew.

"I will go," Calm Cougar said. "I must make more arrows." He exited the tent silently, like a light wind.

Eric sank to the ground. "Many will die," he said gloomily to Karro. "But I had to go. I couldn't give up on Kamani and Isabeli."

seventy-nine

The clear sky above was changing to a clear night. The first star appeared, and Eric looked up at it. In the vast sky, it was all alone. That's how he felt—alone. He had gone outside when he heard the shouting—everyone excited at the arrival of Shoshone warriors from another tribe. At the head was a young chief whose sharp features gave him a handsome appearance. But his bare chest and back were a patchwork of battle scars that painted a picture of his ferocity. Behind him were seventy brave warriors. Most were young, in their late teens or early twenties.

The haunting words echoed in Eric's mind. *Many will not return. The winds will soon be filled with the saddened chants of women grieving their dead.*

Though it was a warm evening with only a light breeze, Eric was shaking. *All their deaths will be on my conscience.*

Omar was part of a group of students passing ahead. "Omar," Eric called out.

Omar waved the other students to go on and moved by Eric.

There was another wild shout and a reply that turned Eric's and Omar's attention to the center of the village.

"How many have arrived?" Eric asked.

"Two hundred. More will come tomorrow." Omar stretched his back. "I'm tired."

"What have you been doing?"

"For a thousand warriors, there must be more wood for the fires. Abbas is out looking for materials to make more bows and arrows. Sami was ordered to go hunting for food."

"Sami, hunting?"

"He'll bring something back. Or he'll face Daring Wolf's anger if he comes back empty-handed."

Eric looked up again at the lone star.

"What are you thinking?" Omar asked.

"It would have been better if the Ute had caught me," Eric said.

Omar shoulder sagged from his tiredness, but he shook his head. "Eric, we can't change the past only learn from it."

Eric gave a short laugh. "You sound like Shinichi."

"I'm not wise like Shinichi. I speak from my past. When I wandered the streets of Terenfie I made many mistakes. I learned quickly to survive by not making the same mistake twice."

"Was it a mistake going after Isabeli and Kamani?"

"Don't fall into that trap—questioning your decisions. Life is constantly testing us with hardships and problems. Most people let the tide of events sweep them around, giving them their direction. But there are a few who stand against the tide, who will set a direction and move. They are leaders—not followers. You're a leader."

Eric looked up into the night's sky and stared again at the lone star. "You're wrong. I was only driven by worry for Isabeli and Kamani."

"Many people worried, but you reacted." When Eric shook his head in doubt, Omar clapped him on the shoulder. "Learn so you'll become a better leader."

"It doesn't matter. In ten days I will pay for my decision."

"The future may seem fixed, but no one knows for sure."

A Shoshone battle cry split the air. Then a dozen more followed.

"I'd better get back; I still have a lot of work to do." Omar clapped Eric on the shoulder again before turning and walking away.

When Shinichi returned to the teepee late into the night, he looked as exhausted as Omar. Regardless, he still drew 'Go' lines on the dirt.

"If you're too tired, we don't have to play," Eric said.

"I'm your teacher. I must teach." Shinichi said as he finished the 'Go' lines.

"Soon you will be without a student."

"Who truly knows?"

"Omar said that same thing."

"Many people throughout history have gambled on 'sure' bets, only to lose it all."

"Have you been with Angry Bear?" Eric asked, after putting the first stone on the intersecting lines.

"Yes. Working on a battle plan."

"We can defeat the Ute. We have three warlords with us. Surely you all can devise a strategy to win."

"As I just explained, there are no sure bets. In truth, the odds are heavily against us."

Despite the increased activity outside Eric's teepee, within it was silent as black and white stones were placed, one after the other, on the intersecting line drawn. In a short time, Shinichi was victorious.

"For all you instructors teach about war, I would think you, Stemann, and Santos would welcome this one," Eric said as he put away the 'Go' stones. "It's why we're here. Practice."

Shinichi rubbed his tired eyes. "A ship's captain trains for harsh weather, but it doesn't mean he goes looking for it," Shinichi said. "It is important students experience war, but it would be insanity to go from battle to battle."

"The more wars we're in, the better we will be."

"There have been warlords who have cherished battle, going from one war to another, and history has marked them as insane." Shinichi yawned, reaching for his buffalo skins. "Eric, the loss of lives is tragic. If there is a solution to a conflict without fighting, a warlord from Vulcury will find it. For this reason, we are treasured."

eighty

"**You just** missed Isabeli," Eric said as Karro came into the teepee. She sat down to his right. He had to shift his sitting position to face her.

"I saw her coming out of your teepee this morning, too—doesn't she have any work to do?" Karro asked grumpily. "The rest of us are very busy."

"I guess she's trying to thank me for rescuing her. I'm still her hero," Eric said.

Karro looked away. "Would you have come for me?"

"For you?"

"If I'd been the one taken by the Ute." Karro brought her eyes up to look into Eric's. "Isabeli said no."

"She said no, why?"

"Because you wouldn't have to marry me."

"That's right," Eric laughed, "I wouldn't."

He received an unexpected glare from Karro. "Isabeli was right—you wouldn't rescue me."

"Yes, I would."

"If I was taken by the Cree tribe and Isabeli was taken by the Blackfoot tribe, who would you rescue first?"

Eric waved his hand dismissively. "It wouldn't happen; the Crees never come this far south."

Karro rolled her eyes. "Okay, then. If I was taken by Sioux and Isabeli was taken by the Blackfoot tribe, who would you rescue first?"

"The Blackfoot never take females, only horses."

Karro raised her voice. "If I was taken by Sioux and Isabeli was taken by Apaches, who would you rescue first?"

Eric tapped his chin in thought. "Sioux or Apache? Both are far away. I would need extra horses, supplies and—"

Karro slammed her fist on the ground. "Isabeli? Or me?"

Eric suddenly thrust his nose into the air. "Is that rabbit stew? I love rabbit stew. Quick quail's stew is—"

Karro growled through clenched teeth, got up, and stomped out of the teepee.

A minute later Sami came into the teepee, dusting himself off. "What's wrong with Karro? She just pushed me down."

"She's acting strange—asking about different tribes taking her and Isabeli."

"Why?"

Eric shrugged his shoulders. "It doesn't matter. How many warriors have arrived?"

"Over five hundred."

"Good."

"But the southern Shoshone tribes are not coming," Sami said uneasily.

"Why? We need them," Eric said anxiously. He stood up and began pacing. "Shinichi said the scout reported over nine hundred Ute warriors in their camp."

Sami stepped in front of Eric, halting his pacing. "We need to gather supplies."

"Gather supplies?"

"Save ourselves. Run away before the Ute come."

"I won't give up. The Shoshones are brave fighters."

"There's not enough," Sami said. "They'll get crushed—the Ute will come here and kill us all."

If Shinichi is right, the Ute may win. They will come here after the battle. Eric nodded his head. "We should be ready for anything. Gather the others and come back here."

eighty-one

Sami had told Eric that Karro, Isabeli, Omar, and Abbas would come in the night when everything had settled down. After the sky had darkened Eric returned to his teepee. He now waited for his friends.

Eric sat cross-legged in his teepee, worrying about Shinichi, Calm Cougar, and even Angry Bear. Tomorrow, all would ride out heavily armed to fight the Ute.

"I've found you."

Eric cocked his head toward the back of the teepee to hear better. "What?"

"He will be pleased."

"Who?"

"Lord Sumonja has condemned you. Prince Eric Alexander von Battenburg, enjoy your short time."

Eric's eyes shot wide open. Quickly he got up and leaned toward the voice. "How'd you know my name? Who are you? Who's Lord Sumonja?"

"Cousin, I'm the one who will take your life. Then Zemfira and I will kill all your family. We will end the dynasty of the von Battenburgs. Lord Sumonja will rule."

"No!" Eric shouted.

"George, your little brother, will be next."

Little George killed. He's so young, a good little boy. Eric felt a rage consume him. "I won't let you," he shouted.

Eric sprang up and raced to the teepee's entrance. He pulled back the flap and charged through it, ramming into the others. They all went down in a tangled mess.

"Stop it!" Omar demanded as Eric kicked and thrashed to get free.

Eric ignored him, kneeing Abbas out of his way. Jumping up, he ran to the back of the teepee. The rest quickly followed and found Eric looking frantically in every direction. Then, he ran first one way, then the other. Finally, Eric stopped, breathing hard.

"What's wrong?" Karro asked irritated.

"He said he was going to kill me first!"

"Kill you first?" Sami looked around and moved closer within the group.

"Yes," Eric said, still looking around frantically. "Then George."

"Who's George?" Omar asked.

"My brother. Then the rest of the von—"

"You have a brother?" Isabeli cut in.

"No," Eric said quickly. "A young boy I know."

"There's no George here," Abbas said.

Eric ignored him. "Did you see anyone when you came?"

"No," Sami said. "But just in case, maybe we should go into your teepee."

Eric looked around one final time before followed the others into his teepee. All the time, his mind kept repeating, *Cousin, I'm the one who will take your life. Then Zemfira and I will kill all your family. We will end the dynasty of the von Battenburgs. Lord Sumonja will rule.*

eighty-two

It was late evening when the drums started. First, one large drum gave a mighty boom—then, within seconds, another drum boomed in reply. More drums joined the hard beat until the pounding seemed to invade Eric's body. His heart followed the smaller drums, beating quicker and quicker, pushing his blood faster and faster through his veins.

A blood-curdling scream made Eric jump. The Shoshone war cry. It was answered with deafening screams from hundreds of warriors, like a pack of wolves howling into the night.

Eric remembered how he had screamed the Shoshone battle cry as Thunder thrust his hooves into the air, challenging the Ute. It had started deep in his lungs, the air being pushed out of his chest, and finally culminating in a roar of courage, anger, and madness.

Eric looked at the other students in the teepee. It was affecting them all. They moved restlessly, agitated by the continuous cries and shrieks of the excited warriors outside.

The Shoshone warriors are building themselves into a rage—a vexed frenzy that can only be calmed by the heat of battle. Eric's attention was pulled away by a horse racing through the village.

"Another scout returning?" Omar asked.

"Probably," Abbas said. "Angry Bear sent out many scouts."

A few minutes later, they all heard another horse racing out of the village.

"Do you know the battle strategy?" Eric asked.

"I spoke with Santos. All the warriors will go out together," Abbas said. "When they're close to the Ute's camp, a third of them will break off and attack from the rear. They are hoping the two fronts will confuse the Ute."

"It all depends on precise moves and coordinated attacks," Omar added.

They all jumped back as a face thrust itself through the opening in the tent. It was covered with white and black paint, the eyes hidden. Then, suddenly, the eyes opened. "What do you think?" Shinichi asked eagerly.

"It's a—" Eric looked at Karro for help, then the others. All were as confused as he was. "It's good."

"Good?" Shinichi's disappointment was clear through the paint. "It doesn't frighten you? Drive you into a state of paralyzing fear?"

"Actually, you look funny," Karro said with a wide smile.

Abbas laughed. "You look like a lost ghost."

Soon everyone was laughing, except Shinichi. "I told Quick Quail she was using too much white. Isabeli, you're good with makeup—can you fix it?"

With a smirk, Karro asked, "You want her to make you look pretty for the Ute?"

"Pretty or a clown?" Shinichi smiled. "What a choice."

Calm Cougar entered. There was no laughter in his demeanor—his face was painted red and black with sharp angles. His eyes looked haunting, threatening—as if he was death himself.

"That's the effect I want," Shinichi said, breaking the silence.

eighty-three

It was maddening. The waiting.

It had been a long night. Eric couldn't sleep; his mind was filled with many worries. He forced the upcoming battle from his mind, only to replace it with the threat from the unknown voice to destroy his family. His body wanted to move into a more comfortable position, but he stayed rigid, not wanting to wake Shinichi.

He heard a movement at his right and knew Kamani was not sleeping either.

Like droplets of water from slow-melting ice, the night gradually passed. Kamani got up first. She went to collect food and supplies for Shinichi.

Eric followed her out, not wanting to see Shinichi and think of the upcoming battle.

Kamani signed to Eric, "He shouldn't go."

Eric bowed his head. "I can't stop him," He signed back.

Kamani's eyes were moistening. She turned quickly, walking away.

He watched the cook fires being lit. Among the women, Eric saw Karro bringing more wood for the fires.

Slowly, the village came alive. Within a half hour, the village filled with painted warriors. Food was quickly eaten, weapons checked, and horses gathered. An hour later, all the warriors, women, and children waited outside the village.

The warriors stood somber and bare-chested, horse reins in one hand and weapons in the other. Sharp-featured, long black hair tousled by the cool morning breeze, their black eyes staring forward were windows into the fearless men within.

These are proud, daring, dauntless men. The odds are against then, yet they spit in death's eye, choosing to fight and not run.

Angry Bear stepped forward and looked right, then left, at the long line of men before him. He looked up into the bright morning sky. "Great Spirit," he shouted. "My heart is filled with joy. Before me is the power of the Shoshone; their hearts are pure, they are bold in battle, and they will face death with honor..."

Eric listened as he looked at the men, then the woman, and lastly at the children. Born into hardship, constant struggle, and ever-present death, these were a remarkable people. He now understood the wisdom of Vulcury sending the students here. *Live or die, there is no in between. One day I hope to be worth enough to be called a Shoshone.*

Angry Bear shouted upward, "We will make you and our ancestors look down with pride as we fight bravely, defeat the Ute, and return here the victor."

He thrust the war lance into the air. The warriors joined together in a mighty war cry, and Angry Bear pointed the lance toward the eastern horizon. As one, the warriors mounted their horses and pointed them in the same direction as the war lance. Angry Bear rode forward first, and half a horse length back, the other chiefs started. Ten feet after, the warriors started in unison.

Eric's eyes were fixed on Shinichi riding close to the chiefs. At his side was Calm Cougar. Both held their heads high, shoulders back and straight. *You have survived many battles Shinichi, Calm Cougar. Will this one be your last?*

An hour later, no one had returned to the village. In silence, everyone was still watching the faint dust cloud on the horizon— all bound tightly with hope for the departing warriors. Finally, a rabbit ran by, breaking the stillness as the young children ran to chase it. The spell broken, people drifted back toward the village.

Omar walked up beside Eric, whose eyes were still fixed on the eastern horizon. "Now that the warriors have left, we can eat."

"I'm not hungry," Eric said.

"Me either," Omar said, following Eric's gaze to watch the warriors, who were mere dots. After a short pause, he continued, "I looked behind your teepee this morning and saw moccasin tracks."

Eric broke his gaze, whipping his head around to look at Omar. "Who do they belong to?"

Omar shook his head. "They weren't made from this time."

"Not from this time?" Eric repeated, wondering if Omar had made a mistake.

"They're too perfect. The right and left are identical, the seams are perfectly straight, and they match on both heels. They weren't handmade. Do you think the commandant send someone else to join the event?" Omar asked.

"He wouldn't. Anything else?"

Omar shrugged. "They belong to a tall man. The moccasins prints were large and his tracks were deep. His movements were fluid. So, he's big and athletic."

Like the boot prints Shinichi and Stemann found by the dead Cherokee.

After Omar turned back toward camp, Eric's thoughts were focused. *Cousin, I'm the one who will take your life. Then Zemfira and I will kill all your family. We will end the dynasty of the von Battenburgs. Lord Sumonja will rule.* Still looking out to the horizon, his mind centered on one word. *Cousin?* Eric remembered only four. *They're all younger. A mistake?* No, 'cousin' was emphasized. *I'm being hunted. Then my family. How can I stop it?*

eighty-four

The alliance stared out at the flowing river, watching its lazy current move off into the distance. Although there were things to do, no one felt like working.

"We should leave," Sami said anxiously. "Now."

Omar bent down and picked up several rocks. "I'm not leaving." He threw a rock into the river. Eric and Abbas did the same.

"I'm not going either," Abbas said. "I'll stay no matter what."

Sami faced Eric. "Surely you're coming with me?"

"No, I gave my word to Angry Bear I wouldn't leave."

"If the Shoshones return or the Ute come you're done for," Sami said to Eric.

Eric shrugged his shoulders.

Omar looked at Sami. "I spoke to Santos before he left. The Ute don't kill the young or women. They take them to their village. The ones who settle in are fine; the others get driven off."

"But our instructing warlords will be dead," Sami said. "Who will guide us?"

"If we are meant to be warlords, we'll figure it out," Abbas said.

"Yeah, but what about me?" Sami argued.

There was silence.

"The Ute will recognize you," Sami appealed to Eric. "You're the one who led the rescue and enraged the Ute."

"The Ute highly regard courage. In their society the leaders are the bravest and most courageous," Abbas said.

"That's why they're so fearless," Omar added.

"I'm sure I'll have no problems," Isabeli said. "I will bring beauty to their village. Karro, you may have a problem." Isabeli ignored Karro's threatening look.

Eric threw another rock in the river. "It would be hard being among the Ute, knowing they killed so many Shoshones."

"Soon it will be the past," Omar said. "We must think of the future."

"We won't know for a few days," Abbas said.

They picked up more rocks and continued throwing them into the river.

"I'm sure I could talk the Ute into going ahead with the wedding," Isabeli said casually.

"No!" Eric and Karro screamed at Isabeli, then eyed each other.

Isabeli put her hands on her hips. "I'm saying I spent so much time working on it. It'll all go to waste."

"If the Shoshones come back and Calm Cougar is alive your time won't be wasted," Eric said.

"I saw Kamani pacing back and forth on the other side of the village. She's worried about Calm Cougar," Abbas said.

"I don't want to think about what will happen to her if he doesn't return," Eric said.

"I'm worried about them all returning," Karro said. Everyone turned and looked at her.

"I wonder what Raica would say if she heard you worrying about males?" Eric teased.

Karro turned pale. "You wouldn't."

"No," Eric said with a grin. "None of us would."

"Have you seen them?" Sami asked.

"Bolek and his gang?" Omar asked. "No."

"I haven't seen them either," Eric said.

"Bolek is acting like Angry Bear," Abbas said, "ordering everyone around."

"I saw him on a horse," Karro said.

"He hid a few away," Abbas said. "He sent out Malek and Kirill to scout and keep watch."

Eric picked up some more rocks. "It's smart. The village is very vulnerable right now."

"Especially us," Karro said. "We need to protect ourselves."

"I've collected some bow and arrow materials. I'll make us all bows. Later, I can show you how to make arrows," Eric said.

"At least we'll have weapons to defend ourselves," Omar said.

eighty-five

The late-afternoon sky was dotted with fluffy white clouds slowly drifting east. A gentle wind made the thin tree branches move back and forth like they were waving to each other.

Eric looked up and watched a cloud with tiered appendages sticking from its sides. *The cloud looks like the solar ship that took me to Vulcury.* Eric's thoughts drifted. *It's been almost a year since I stepped off her deck. It has been an adventure.* He looked back at the village, and a feeling deep inside told him the adventure wasn't over.

He walked out of the village, stretching his fingers and hands. They were feeling stiff. For the past four hours, he'd made six bows and helped the others make sixty-three arrows.

Worried about Kamani, he walked the village, looking for her. But deep down, he knew where she'd be. Eric continued walking until he was outside the village. She was standing alone, looking out at the eastern horizon—a lone scout watching for the return of the Shoshones, and one in particular.

She turned when she noticed Eric standing beside her.

He marveled at how beautiful she looked, even weighed down with concern for the man she loved.

"They will come back," Kamani signed.

"Yes. They will," Eric signed back.

Kamani turned back to continue her vigil, and Eric stood to her side.

"I thought I was cursed forever," Kamani started to sign. "Since I was young I've been shunned and mistreated. Life was bleak, and many times I wanted to end it. Most of all I feared the loneliness—of never being with a special man."

"That's all changed now." His hands hesitated. *Is it wrong to say the impossible?* "Calm Cougar will return."

"And Shinichi," Kamani signed.

"Yes," Eric replied. *Am I now lying to myself?* "Shinichi is like a father to me." The words came flowing out to Kamani. "He has always stood by me, since the beginning of my training. When I was down, he gave me encouragement. When I was too confident, he corrected me. And when I felt I couldn't go on, he nudged me forward. I miss him." Eric gave a light laugh. "I even miss playing 'Go' every night and losing."

"They will come back to us," Kamani signed.

It was then Eric noticed a dust cloud approaching fast. It wasn't coming from the east but from the north.

Eric pointed at the quickly approaching rider. "Maybe he brings news." Eric watched the rider push his horse hard, racing through the village. At the center of camp, he pulled up hard, causing the horse to dig its hooves in the dirt.

Suddenly, Bolek appeared and ran up to the rider. It was Kirill, and he leaned down and spoke to Bolek. Bolek looked back toward the north and pointed. Kirill tugged hard on his horse's reins, turned, and raced back out of the village. Eric and Kamani could see Bolek bark orders and wave everyone forward.

"Let's go," Eric said, starting toward the village. Soon, Eric and Kamani were running fast toward the gathering Shoshones.

"**We must** defend ourselves." Bolek stood on a small mound that marked the center of the village. Flanking him were Malek, Fia, and Raica. "They're an hour north."

Eric heard gasps of horror from several of the women; others turned pale.

But the air was suddenly crushed as a woman began screaming hysterically over and over, "We will all die!"

Bolek turned to Raica. Raica went to the screaming woman
and slapped her so hard her head snapped back and she fell backwards to the ground.

Eric stepped beside Karro. "What is it?"

"A war party of Crow warriors. Kirill saw them. They're
coming directly toward us."

*The Crows, they don't take prisoners. Kill and pillage is their
way.*

"We'll set up defense here, make a barrier," Bolek ordered.

"No!" Eric shouted, stepping forward.

"I'm the lead—"

Eric cut in. "Here they'll run us down with their horses. We
must cross the river to go into the dense forest. There are ravines
to hide in a short distance away."

"I don't hide," Bolek said. "I'm a fighter."

"Yes, but you'll be hampered by the women and children,"
Eric said.

Bolek looked down at Eric for a long second, then raised his
voice. "We'll go to the forest on the other side of the river. Get any
knives and weapons you have and meet at the river."

Eric rushed back to Karro. "Get Sami and Isabeli. I'll find
Omar and Abbas. We'll collect the bows and arrows and meet you
at the river."

Karro, Sami, and Isabeli stood together, apart from the others. Eric, Omar, and Abbas joined them with the bows and arrows.

Eric handed a bow to Karro, Isabeli, and Sami. "We'll cross
last. Make sure everyone got across safely."

"Give me the bows and arrows!"

310

Eric shifted to find Bolek marching toward him, leading Stemann's other students and some of the Shoshone boys.

"Give them to me."

We need Bolek as an ally, not an enemy. After a second's hesitation, Eric took Isabeli's bow and handed it over to him. Sami quickly passed over his bow.

A Shoshone boy reached for Karro's bow. She batted his hand away.

"That's all you're going to get," Eric said, handing Bolek two dozen arrows. When he saw Bolek tighten up he added, "We can fight each other or work together against the Crows." He waited a second before adding, "We'll finish our fight later."

Bolek gave a sly grin, causing the scar Angry Bear gave him for lying to stretch.

"Let's go," Eric said to his followers, indicating the river. By the time Eric got out of the river, all of the women and children were already across.

Eric looked back across the river and saw Kirill riding toward Bolek, demanding every ounce of speed from his tired horse. Kirill leaped down and reported something to Bolek, who nodded several times and then waved for the students and Shoshone boys around him to cross the river. He looked around and stopped when he caught sight of Eric. He raised his hand and flashed all his fingers in the air twice.

"Hurry. We've only got twenty minutes," Eric said to the others around him. "Push the women and children to the ravines. They're a mile away."

"We won't make it," Sami said.

"We have to," Eric said. *If we don't make it to the ravines, the Crows will ride us down like sheep and cut our throats.*

311

eighty-six

"The Crows are burning the village," Sami said cowering at the sight.

Eric could see black smoke rising into the blue sky through the trees.

"Why? All the valuables." Sami shook his head in disbelief.

"They're burning everything to make sure they kill anyone who's hiding within," Eric said.

"Your teepee." Sami cringed.

"It doesn't matter," Eric said. "The people are important. The Crows will be here soon. Push everyone hard; we must make it to the ravines to survive."

Several women and a few children stopped. In the distance, they heard it. The Crow battle cry—the sound of a screeching eagle diving on its prey.

Like pack wolves Omar and Abbas pulled back their heads and screamed the Shoshone war cry, answering the challenge.

"Stop!" Sami shouted. "You'll tell them where we are."

"We're leaving enough tracks a child could follow us," Eric said. "Sami, keep on pushing the people ahead."

Sami ran, waving his arms and hands frantically to quicken their pace.

"Omar, Abbas," Eric called out and pointed to their arrows. "Let's stick a few Crows. It should slow them down." He hesitated, looking at Karro, who was a dozen feet ahead. *Can I put her in harm's way? She'll hate me if I don't.* "Karro," Eric shouted. "Come with us."

Looking around, he found Bolek and waved his hands in broad sweeps. When he had Bolek's attention, he acted like he was shooting a bow and arrow. When Bolek nodded, Eric pointed back to the approaching Crows. Bolek nodded again.

"Let's go," Eric said to Karro, Omar and Abbas.

Eric ran two hundred yards and stopped. "We'll attack from here. Get thirty feet apart. We have to get them to believe there are more of us." Eric pointed to a tree split in two by lightning. "When they pass the tree, shoot three arrows as fast as you can. Run back twenty yards and shoot three more. After, run as fast as you can to the ravines. Hopefully, Bolek will have defenses set up." Eric raised a bow and an arrow, ready to shoot. He heard the clear sound of horses coming through the trees and caught sight of a Crow warrior, small and lean with taut muscles stretching his copper skin. His face was painted with black lines. A few seconds later, more painted warriors came into view.

Eric lowered his bow a little and stared. Within the army of Crows was a large horse that towered above the smaller Indian horses. On the giant horse's back sat a tall man with broad shoulders who gave orders to the Crows with quick motions. If they weren't out to kill him, Eric would have laughed. The tall man, twice as big as the rest of the Crow, made the Indians around him look like small children on ponies.

Karro raised her bow and so did Eric. The Crows were a few feet away from the split tree. He sighted the big man, but it was a Crow warrior on the tall man's left who passed the tree first. The next second, an arrow from Karro buried itself in the Crow's chest, sending him to the ground. Eric released his arrow, but another Crow jerked his horse in front of the tall man and Eric's arrow stuck out of his shoulder.

Quickly, Eric shot two more arrows, and two dead Crows fell to the ground. He turned immediately and sprinted the twenty yards, then turned, bow ready to shoot. "Watch out!" he screamed, and leaped behind a thick tree as a barrage of Crow arrows came at him like a dam bursting. He saw Omar hugging the ground; Karro was behind a fallen tree, and Abbas was shooting an arrow. Without looking, Eric shot his arrow in the direction of the Crows and shouted, "Run!"

Eric dodged in and around trees as Crow arrows rained down on him and the others. Karro was only a step behind, running full out.

The ravine entrance was less than fifty feet away when something struck Eric's hip hard, causing him to fall sideways and hit the ground. He looked up. "Karro?" She had knocked him down. Her head spun around and Eric's gaze followed it to see an arrow embedded in a tree. But it had come from the ravine—not the Crow.

Who's shooting at me? Eric didn't have time to think; he still had to get to the ravine. He targeted the other side of the ravine entrance away from where the Shoshone arrow had come.

A step away from the ravine, a Crow arrow sank into Omar's thigh and he collapsed. Abbas threw his bow away and reached down, pulling Omar up.

"Leave me!" Omar shouted.

Abbas didn't answer, only dragging Omar after him. They were through the ravine and turned off to the left. Eric and Karro followed.

"Shoot!" Eric shouted to Karro and Abbas, who had picked up Omar's bow when he fell.

The Crows were less than sixty yards away. Most had dismounted and were running in bunches toward the ravine. Behind them, mounted Crows fired arrows.

Eric hit one above his heart but the falling warrior had no effect on the others, who ran like madmen, swinging their knives and tomahawks, ready to kill.

When they were thirty feet away, a torrent of rocks and arrows from the ridge of the ravine flooded down on them. The Crows pulled up for a second to understand the new threat. Eric looked up to see every Shoshone woman and child throwing rocks or sticks at the Crows.

"Up!" Eric ordered after shooting another arrow into a Crow warrior. Abbas pulled Omar forward and Eric got under his other arm to help Omar up.

At the top of the ravine, Karro whipped around, shooting two arrows at the first two Crow entering the ravine. Both fell down dead as a dozen Crow warriors stormed into the ravine. They all suddenly stopped as rocks rained down.

"Save yourselves!" Omar shouted. Both Eric and Abbas ignored his pleas, taking him out of harm's way and dropping him behind a rock barrier.

"Omar, take out your knife. The Crow don't take prisoners," Eric yelled at him.

"If I go, I'll take a few with me," Omar promised.

Eric got up and returned to the fight. More Crows entered the ravine and shot arrows up at them, driving the Shoshone back.

Eric fired three more arrows; then, when he reached down into his quiver, there were no more. He grabbed the end of the bow to use it as a club. Bolek and the other students were making a stand at the narrow path up the ravine. Eric ran to them.

Ten Crows rushed forward and Bolek was the first to step forward to fight. Eric was about to join in when he saw Crow warriors climbing over the ravine's face. Eric shouted at Karro, "Follow me." Then he saw Sami a dozen yards back, behind a tree. "Come on."

Sami shook his head.

"Come on," Eric demanded. He bent down by the ravine's edge, and when the first Crow raised his head above it, Eric swung his bow as hard as he could at the warrior's head. The Crow dropped like a rock.

Karro kneeled beside Eric, banging the hands of the Crows who were trying to pull themselves up. Eric's head jerked back as a Crow leapt up and launched his tomahawk at Eric's face. In a flash, a rock sped past him, hitting the Crow in the head and causing him to fall backward to the ravine floor below.

Eric turned to see Sami standing ten feet behind him with another rock, ready to throw. He looked around. The Crows had breached the top of the ravine. *We're losing.* Eric gritted his teeth at the sight at the dead Shoshones scattered around him, and caught a glimpse of another Crow warrior rising above the ravine's edge. Maddened with rage, he screamed the Shoshone battle cry. His bow snapped when it slammed into the Crow's head.

He pulled out his knife and grabbed the wrist of the Crow warrior who was thrusting his own knife toward Eric's chest. Instantly, Eric knew this was a battle he was going to lose.

The Crow's tight face and determined look were backed by strong muscles. He threw Eric over onto his back and straddled him to try to drive his crow knife into Eric's heart.

Eric gritted his teeth as he fought the Crow warrior. But inch-by-inch the Crow knife was moving closer and seeking to pierce his chest and let his blood flow out.

The Crow's eyes bulge with disbelief. Eric knew his were doing the same. *How?* Shoshone war cries filled the forest like a pack of angry wolves ready to attack. Both Eric and the Crow warrior turned their heads to see hundreds of Shoshone warriors running through the forest. Leading them was Calm Cougar. He was death himself appearing. Before him, the Crows were leaping up and running away.

But the determined look on the face of the Crow warrior Eric was fighting returned. He felt the Crow's steel muscle bear down on him. He let go of his knife and used both his hands to hold back his enemy's blade. The muscles were too strong and the warrior was on top, leaning on the knife. Eric felt the knife scratch his chest. *This is it, the end!* Then the warrior stiffened, went limp, and then the body fell on him. Eric looked up and saw Karro with a bloody knife in her hand.

He pushed the warrior off him, jumped up, and looked about, ready to fight. That's when he saw the tall man staring directly at him fifty yards away. With hundreds of Shoshone warriors approaching, the tall man pulled up his bow as if he had all the time in the world. He fitted an arrow and aimed at Eric.

Eric turned to leap away, but a hand grabbed his ankle, and then another grabbed his thigh. The tall man aimed and released. Eric dived on top of the Crow warriors, knocking them both back. He felt the arrow go directly over him. Rolling and vaulting himself upward, his hands were already raised, ready to fight.

But the Crows were dashing away, fleeing as the Shoshone warriors stormed the ravine.

"Eric." The sound was between a moan and a hard cough. Eric turned his body and his heart sank. Sami lay on his back with the tall man's arrow sticking out of his chest.

"No!" Eric screamed, running to Sami. Karro was already by his side. Sami's eyes were open, staring up into the clear blue sky.

"I'm sorry," Eric said, all else forgotten. Karro looked away. *He was shooting at me.* "I'm sorry," was all Eric could say again.

"Eric," Sami said as he fought to keep his eyes open.

"Sami, I'm—"

"Listen. To the north, within a tree with red mushrooms at its base, you'll find enough to buy another teepee." Sami said through a gasp for breath.

"I can't," Eric said, his eyes moistening.

"You have to."

Eric nodded. Then, his shoulders slumped as Sami's eyes closed. *Sami's gone.* Eric dropped his head. *It should be me.* He ventured a look at Karro. Her eyes were moist and Eric heard several quick gulps of air.

"Eric."

Eric's head jerked back up. "Yes."

"Don't take the first offer. Pay half." There was a soft groan, and then Eric saw Sami's body relax as his chest sank, releasing his last breath.

eighty-seven

The tree was not far from where Eric now stood. It was to the northwest, beside a grove of young trees.

The five friends had taken Sami's body to the picturesque grove and buried it deep in the ground. When digging the grave, Abbas discovered a rock the size of a fist. Its shiny-yellow surface told everyone of its great value: gold. It was a good omen. They placed the gold rock upon Sami's heart.

Karro, Isabeli, Abbas, and Omar, with a branch for support, left Eric there, alone.

He returned to Sami's grave the next morning staring out, but turned when he heard footsteps.

"Karro told me where to find you," Shinichi said stepping beside Eric in front of the burial mound.

Eric said nothing and turned back to looking at the western horizon.

"Sami was a good boy," Shinichi said.

"He's dead because of me. Sami was safe behind the tree."

"I can tell you a hundred reasons why you're wrong. But you won't listen."

"No."

"But I'm your mentor so I have to try." Shinichi looked down at Sami's grave. "Eric, life is a turbulent river with strong currents. We all think we're great swimmers who can fight the strongest current—able to set our own direction and know the outcome. But there are rocks below the river's surface, side currents, and drops that are unseen. Eric, you are a good swimmer, but you'll never navigate the river perfectly. You want to fight the current when sometimes, you just have to go with the flow."

"I want out of this river," Eric said as his shoulder drooped and tears began to make their way down his cheeks.

"The river is life; escape only takes you to another river."

They stood there in silence for many minutes before Shinichi turned.

"How?" Eric asked wiping the tears away with the back of his hands.

"How?" Shinichi echoed, turning back.

"How did you return, alive?"

"The river's wayward currents can bring unexpected surprises." A small grin appeared on his face as he shook his head. "When we rode out, I personally calculated our chance of survival was less than one in twenty. We needed a miracle."

"Then how'd you survive?"

"You supplied the miracle."

Eric's head swung up, his confusion plain.

"We rode toward the Ute in good formation through low, rolling hills. In a small opening, we came upon several Ute chiefs waiting alone on horses."

"What were they doing?" Eric asked.

"Nothing. But what caught my attention was they were not painted for war. Beside me, Crazy Beaver exclaimed, 'The gods love us. We will capture them and have victory.' Like a herd of angry buffalo, we approached." Eric heard anger enter Shinichi's voice and he looked at him. "We were fools!"

"Why?"

"Like ghosts rising from the grave, hundreds of Utes appeared from the ground. They had buried themselves. Then, from all four sides, surrounding us rode more Ute warriors. We had ridden into a trap; we were cut off, boxed in. 'The gods hate us,' Crazy Beaver then exclaimed." Shinichi shook his head. "We were surrounded by two thousand battle-hardened Ute warriors."

"Two thousand!" Eric's jaw dropped.

"I saw the warriors around me tighten their grip on their weapons. The Shoshone would not surrender." Shinichi released a heavy sigh. "Well, I thought to myself, *I've had a good life and it's over.* Then, the Ute chiefs rode up to Angry Bear and said, 'We will return your horses.'

"There were gasps all around me. It was like saying the sun was going to fall. We all stood dumbfounded. 'We want the young Shoshone brave' the Ute chief said firmly. Angry Bear looked around uneasily. 'What Ute trick is this?' he asked.

"The Ute chief's eyes narrowed, but a second later he was telling the story of your rescue of Isabeli and Kamani."

Eric swallowed uneasily.

"The Ute chief praised the bravery of the Shoshone boys and girl in the daring rescue." Shinichi gave a short laugh. "I'm sure Angry Bear wanted to argue its stupidity instead of its bravery, but he kept quiet. The Ute chief continued and told how hundreds of Ute warriors chased the brave boys and girls with great determination, and then how, suddenly, the escaping Shoshones turned—or so the pursuing Utes thought. After several miles, they realized they had been tricked. The Ute chief said their anger was like a volcano erupting, and they pushed their horses harder. They were like maddened bears on the hunt, ready to tear apart the boy who had led the rescue."

"'The black demon horse appeared,' the Ute chief said, as if it was magic. They all knew the horse. Many brave Utes had tried to catch the black stallion and failed. They had concluded an evil spirit lived within the horse. So when it appeared just after the Shoshone boys and girls disappeared, the Utes were uneasy. And when it sped to the boy, they were shocked. The Ute are great horsemen, and when they saw how the boy jumped on the black stallion at full run, they were astonished. The powerful horse's long strides left the Ute behind. But the Ute knew the horse was sprinting toward a deep canyon. They followed."

Shinichi stopped his narrative, causing Eric to look at him.

"Even I had to lean in when the Ute chief told the next part."

"Why?"

"He said the boy *flew*." Shinichi moved his hand in an arc, then looked at Eric.

The whole forest was silent, waiting for Eric's explanation.

"It wasn't me. It was Thunder. He jumped the canyon."

"When they saw you on the other side they weren't shocked; they knew."

"Knew what?"

"They knew you were Brave Bear, the greatest Ute warrior-chief reborn."

"'No!' Angry Bear screamed. You were Running Horse, the renowned Shoshone warrior feared by all. Angry Bear then told how you had single-handedly defeated a mighty Cherokee brave. And how, with your bare hands, you had thrown three gigantic buffalo down. 'He is Running Horse,' Angry Bear shouted again.

"The Ute chief's jaw tightened. 'Brave Bear,' he demanded. 'Running Horse,' Angry Bear yelled, raising his war lance. 'Brave Bear,' the Ute chief roared, grabbing his tomahawk. The Utes began moving in, and the Shoshones brought up their weapons for battle.

"That's when I stepped forward."

"You?" Eric asked, cocking his head slightly, trying to understand.

"Yes. I held up my hands and shouted you were Running Horse, Brave Bear, and all the great Indian warriors."

"What! They believed you?"

"Yes. Because I told them I was your priest."

"My priest?" Shinichi grinned at Eric's incredulous look.

"Angry Bear confirmed I was always with you. I then told them when you walked the mountains shook and when you screamed, mighty trees fell, and when you waved your hands the clouds blocked out the sun."

"You didn't."

"I put it on very thick. If I didn't there would have been a vicious battle and many deaths."

Eric shook his head. "What happened then?"

"The Ute chief offered fifty young horses for you."

"Fifty! Did Angry Bear accept?" Eric asked.

"No. He shook his head and took it as an insult." Shinichi grin turned into a broad smile.

"But that's a fortune!"

"The offer had nothing to do with it. Indians love to barter. They each think they are crafty, superior negotiators. For the next three hours, we stood in the hot sun. The Shoshones acted like every offer given by the Utes was a great insult, every counter-offer by the Shoshones was an insane price, according to the Utes. We rode back with seventy horses and fifteen buffalo hides."

Eric stood tall, took in a deep breath and stared Shinichi directly into his eyes. "When will I be sent to the Ute?"

"Never. Angry Bear and the Shoshone chiefs feel you are too valuable."

"But the seventy horses and fifteen buffalo hides?" Eric asked confused.

"Are for your son."

"My *son*?"

"Your warrior spirit will be in your sons. The Ute will send over a bride."

Eric gave a little chuckle and grinned. "At least Karro won't have to marry me."

"She will. Shoshone can have many wives. Angry Bear also wants you to have Shoshone sons. He likes Isabeli's idea of a grand wedding. A big event for all the Shoshone chiefs to see. Angry Bear even sent out riders to invite the Ute chief."

Eric grin dropped from his face and he felt fire in his belly. "But I have a choice. It's my life!"

"Eric, you are in the turbulent river. You can swim in any direction. But there are directions carrying heavy consequences for many. Like war with the Ute." Shinichi backed away, giving a nod of respect to Sami's grave. "I'll leave you to make your decision."

eighty-eight

"It's time," Omar said to Eric. Omar looked at Eric and attempted a smile, but it failed. He looked down moving slowly to the center of the clearing. His bandaged left leg causing him to winch after every step.

Eric nodded his head, turned in from the edge of the clearing and walked to the center. Abbas stood close by. *Sami would have been here, too.* He brushed his hand across his wedding clothes made of soft, light-tan deerskin. Hundreds of beads decorated the front and back of his shirt. An hour ago, Isabeli had finished painting his face.

Did I make the right decision? It feels so wrong. The past few days since the Crow attack and Sami's death, Eric had wandered the forest alone. Even now, his troubled mind repeated the same question. *Who am I? A prince of the Moon Empire? A Vulcury student? A Shoshone warrior?*

Yesterday he had found himself miles away. He whistled several times, hoping Thunder would appear, but the mighty black stallion never came.

He felt so alone, so confused; the turbulent river had him and he felt like he was drowning. Then his mind filled with another person who at one time had felt the same.

"Why are you smiling?" Abbas asked.

"Quiet Dove," Eric said.

Eric saw his own happy smile mirrored on Omar's and Abbas's faces. Kamani now had a Shoshone name: Quiet Dove, a beautiful name for a beautiful woman. When he had told Angry

Bear he would go through with the wedding ceremony, there was one condition. Angry Bear's broad smile had disappeared. But it reappeared when Eric said, "Calm Cougar's and Kamani's wedding ceremony must be first."

This morning, when the air was still light and crisp, it happened—in front of six hundred. They made a handsome couple. Shinichi officiated over their ceremony, and his speech to the gathered crowd was heartfelt as, like Eric, Shinichi loved them both. When it was over, Shinichi openly wept with joy.

When Eric went to congratulate the couple, Calm Cougar moved back as Kamani stepped forward and put her arms around Eric. The warmth of her embrace sent Eric back in time to his mother's loving arms. All too soon, it was over.

Calm Cougar clapped him on his shoulder. "You are always welcome in our teepee."

She will never be alone again—Calm Cougar will never leave her side. And she will have loving children.

Eric made sure Kamani did not wed empty-handed. By Shoshone standards, he was now a wealthy man. The seventy horses and fifteen buffalo hides were his. Although she argued vigorously with many hand gestures, Eric gave her half of his wealth for a dowry.

It was difficult for Eric to speak. He nodded his head and left the happy couple to greet the others who wanted to wish them happiness.

Eric nodded for Abbas to start. Omar, with his bandaged leg, set the pace. It was slow and solemn; no one spoke.

Everything is happening so quickly and yet everything is going so slowly. The time until the ceremony rushed forward, but the constant nagging voice within made every second felt.

Abbas was leading them out of the woods when Isabeli caught up to them. She seemed more anxious than when the Crow had attacked. "Do you all remember what you're supposed to do?"

Even though Eric, Omar, and Abbas all nodded their heads, Isabeli went over the plans again. "Abbas, you will walk in first. It's not a race, so don't walk fast. But too slow won't give the right tempo for the ceremony." She moved on. "Omar, don't fall behind. A little pain doesn't matter."

Oblivious to the boys' raised eyebrows, Isabeli squealed with delight. "There's over two thousand attending. Eleven Shoshone chiefs, two Ute, two Arapaho, and a Cheyenne, representing six tribes. This ceremony will go down in Shoshone history with the other heroic deeds," Isabeli promised. "If this isn't perfect, Angry Bear will be so embarrassed. Can you imagine the shame whenever he meets the other chiefs?"

Omar, Abbas, and Eric all kept quiet, somehow knowing it was safer.

"I have to go and make sure Karro is perfect." They all watched Isabeli scurry off.

"Karro will stand her ground," Omar said.

"I'm not so sure," Eric sighed. "Let's get it all over with."

A low hilltop had been chosen for the ceremony site so everyone could see. A single great tree with green leaves formed a wide umbrella over the spot. A few days ago, Eric had seen the place swarmed with an army of women and children as, under Isabeli's orders, they made sure all unsightly shrubs, bushes, and fallen foliage were removed.

Why does it have to be so many? Eric looked out over the thousands who were standing and waiting below the hill. They all looked at him and smiled as he passed. Most were genuinely happy, but Stemann's and Bolek's smiles were closer to smirks.

Beside Bolek was one person who did not smile. She didn't hide her contempt and hatred. *If people weren't around I know,*

Raica, you'd happily shoot an arrow through my heart. For the shame I bring on your Amazon family, perhaps it will be tomorrow.

Abbas, he noticed was walking too fast, but he didn't care. He marched up the hill behind Abbas and Omar, who were only looking ahead.

Eric was amazed—under the tree's umbrella was a mural of white and pink flowers, like gentle raindrops among the leaves.

At the top of the hill were Angry Bear and the fifteen other chiefs. Each was dressed as befitting a chief of his own tribe, with numerous eagle feathers in their hair. Angry Bear gave him a nod as he passed and Eric returned it.

Calm Cougar and Kamani, still glowing from their earlier ceremony, were also on top of the hill. Calm Cougar would stand for Eric and Kamani would stand for Karro.

Eric continued walking until he was standing in front of Shinichi. *Why does he look so jovial? He's acting like a father at his son's wedding, finally seeing him leave to start his own life.*

The murmurs and rustling stopped as the distinct wedding drum started. A hard *boom* was heard every three seconds. The drums didn't change as they announced the arrival of Karro.

She had started her journey at the Shoshone village three miles away. Eric could see the crowd part to let her through, and everyone's eyes followed her as if they were hypnotized by her presence.

Eric turned away. *She agreed to the ceremony. It must be tearing her apart within as she is an Amazon.* He looked past Shinichi, out across the hills to the tree-covered mountains far away. *The turbulent river is controlling me, pushing and pulling me in the wrong direction.*

He heard Shinichi clear his throat, and dropped his eyes to look at him. He seemed to know what Eric was thinking. He gave Eric a nod and wink of encouragement.

Then he watched Shinichi's eyes leave him and travel to his side. He felt Karro's presence, but he still didn't turn. *Will I see hatred if I look?*

Karro would take Kamani's place in the teepee, he reasoned. Everything would return to normal—the nightly game of 'Go' and Karro giving him bow-shooting lessons.

Shinichi raised his voice so everyone could hear. "I have known Karro for a long time. She is a rare young woman who represents the long tradition of Shoshone women: thrifty, enduring, and loyal. But she is so much more. She has the courage, determination, and will of a Shoshone warrior. During the recent battle with the invading Crows she was at the forefront of the battle, risking her life to save as many Shoshone as possible."

Touched, Eric looked at Shinichi. *Thank you. She'll cherish your words.*

Shinichi turned to Eric. "Eric is a brave Shoshone warrior." At this point, Eric tuned Shinichi out and turned his thoughts to the turbulent river. *I'm a bad swimmer. The events marked my life were thrown upon me, pushing me underwater and I just thrash around enough to keep my head above water.*

"Turn and face one another," Shinichi directed.

He heard Karro turn and he followed. Eric was thunderstruck. *Is this really Karro? She's beautiful.*

Karro's face was lightly painted in several colors that highlighted her high cheekbones, bright eyes, and full lips. Her hair was loose and it flowed in waves down her shoulders and back. How Isabeli had gotten it so thick and shiny, Eric had no idea. On her head was a skillfully worked leather headband with intricate designs in a rainbow of colors. Woven around the headband were small white flowers. *It's as if she's a crowned Princess.*

Karro raised her head and looked into Eric's eyes. For a second she searched, but for what, Eric didn't know. The large brown eyes shone like the sun. All too quickly, she looked down again.

Eric watched her lips quiver, then say, "I will." Shinichi shifted toward him. "Eric, will you defend Karro through…"

He looked at Shinichi. *Why is he saying it that way? He knows I can only answer one way.*

But I won't! I will not let the rivers current toss me around. He looked at Karro, gazing deep into her eyes. *How will she feel about me after?*

Shinichi paused and Eric could feel his stare and the stares of the thousands present. Eric took a deep breath, looked at Karro, and said, "I—"

Blackness and numbing cold suddenly surrounded him, pulling him away. He knew the other students and warlords were filling the same thing. The event had ended and they were returning to Vulcruy.

Eric let the bitter cold invade him as he wondered. *Where will the river take me next?*

the end of the first event

I hope you enjoyed 'Prince Eric Alexander – The First Event'. Please visit **www.vecesena.com** or **www.rrwaters.com** for more books and short stories by V.E. Cesena. Sign up for the newsletter to keep up to date on new releases.

Links to purchase books **www.vecesena.com/links** or **www.rrwaters.com/links**

If you enjoyed this book please leave 5-star rating at Amazon and comment what you liked. But I welcome all comments

Prince Eric Alexander
The Second Event: Tragedy

By

V.E. CESENA

Book II - Prince Eric Alexander Series

One

The area is extensive with a red Torii, a Japanese gate at the entrance. It leads to a pristine rock garden with pink, yellow and salmon azaleas, white camellias and lavender hydrangeas outlining the borders. In the center is a pool of koi fish swimming lazily under red and gold lotus flowers. On a large stone base, in the center of the pool, is a lifelike statue of a ninja in a fighting stance.

Moving to the edge of the pond, Gnechko, the Commandant of Vulcury the Warlord Academy, stops and stares at the statue. He let his eyes drift from the statue to the long bamboo shoots beyond the pond.

The warlord Corcoran, a few steps behind, looked around Shinichi's pristine compound. He stopped at the Commandant's side.

"Shinichi added a statue to his garden," Gnechko indicated the ninja statue.

"His ancestry is from Japan," Corcoran said as they inspect the statue.

"What?!" Corcoran shouted suddenly, jumping back behind the Commandant.

Gnechko shifted his body into a battle stance, ready to fight. The statue's flailing arms missed him by inches, before splashing into the pond. A few seconds later, the Commandant's body relaxed as he looks at a boy sitting in the pond.

Shinichi stepped forward from behind a large azalea bush. Shoved his kimono's long sleeves up and claps his hands together hard in anger. "Eric, you're not listening!" he said in exasperation.

"I'm trying," Eric slapped the water in front of him in frustration before wiping the water from his eyes.

Gnechko stood at the pond's edge gazing down at Eric. "Your mimicking of a warrior statue was very good."

Seeing Gnechko, Eric gets up, removes his ninja mask, and steps out of the pond. "Thank you, Commandant." Eric gave a wary side-glance at Shinichi and said sarcastically, "But I've only held the statue position for a *fraction* of the time required."

"Correct. A small fraction." Shinichi joined the group. He turned to Gnechko. "Eric fights me at every turn."

Gnechko studied Eric as he rubs his chin in thought. "Eric, how old are you?"

"Just turned sixteen," Eric said as he pushed his fingers through his wet hair.

"A teenager," Corcoran chuckled.

"I'm old enough to know what's good for me." Eric folded his arms across his chest. "I don't want to learn, Aikido."

"Eric, this isn't a democracy. Shinichi, your instructor Warlord, sets your training. But—" Gnechko looked at Shinichi. "I agree with Eric. Jiu-jitsu is what I have always taught when I was an instructor."

"Jiu-jitsu has its merits," Shinichi nodded. He interweaved his fingers into a tight clasp, forming a powerful bond. "However, for body control, meditation, and discipline, Aikido is hard to match. Eric must unify his life's energy to harmonize his spirit. If Eric can master Aikido, he'll know more than how to strike his enemy, but conquer his internal demons too."

"Karate is what Eric should learn." Corcoran straightens his hand and makes a chopping motion. "I'm an expert."

"A demonstration of Karate against Aikido is an excellent idea," Shinichi said.

"It's not fair. Me against the boy." The edge of Corcoran's lips pulled back into a smile.

336

"A true demonstration is, expert fighting expert," Shinichi pushed up his long sleeves, tying them back. He bowed then slides into a fighting stance. "I will be your opponent."

Corcoran's face soured, "I would Shinichi. . . for Eric's sake. But my back." He winced as he stretched. "I wouldn't be much of an opponent."

The Commandant's eyebrows furrow together as he glares at Corcoran irritated. He grunts his displeasure and dismisses Corcoran. The sound of small pebbles crunching under his shoes is heard as he squares himself to Shinichi. "This isn't a social call." The Commandant looked at Shinichi and then at Eric. "During the last Event, did anything seem unusual to you?"

"Other than almost being trampled by buffalo, shot at by Ute warriors or—" Eric winced. "The marriage ceremony."

"Marriage?! You must always be watchful for *any* danger." Corcoran's smile faded under Gnechko's hard stare.

"No, Commandant," Shinichi said.

The Commandant noticed Eric's face tighten. "Eric?"

"Before the Shoshone went to fight the Ute, I heard someone call my name."

"So what?" Corcoran said.

"Prince Eric Alexander von Battenburg?" Eric said.

"Are you sure?" Shinichi asked.

"'Cousins, it is I, Madhu, the one who will take your life. After, Zemfira and I will kill all your family. We will end the dynasty of the von Battenburg's. Lord Darko Sumonja will rule,' were the exact words," Eric said to Shinichi and the Commandant.

Suddenly all the warlords were bearing down on him with hard stares. *Do they think I'm lying? Why is Shinichi's face so animated?* "I would be the first he would kill. Then my little brother, Prince George."

"Did anyone else hear?" Shinichi demanded.

"No, but Omar saw tracks. 'He swore the moccasins were too perfect to be handmade by Indians."

Shinichi's eyes narrowed. "Impossible."

"Impossible?" Eric said angrily, his cheeks reddening. "At the last battle with the Crow, a man shot an arrow at me. He wasn't an Indian; white, tall, and powerfully built." Teeth clenched, Eric remembers the arrow sticking out of Sami's chest. Taking the life of his dear friend.

"In the heat of battle, fear rises and one sees many imaginary things," Gnechko said evenly.

Why has Shinichi gone so pale? Eric shook his head at Gnechko. "He was real and wanted to kill me."

"Impossible," Shinichi said faintly.

Eric noticed his instructor saying it to himself. "There's more." Eric shifted his body uneasily, water dripping from his soaked clothes and took in a deep breath. "He looked familiar."

"You've seen him before?" Corcoran asked.

"No, but there's something familiar about him," Eric said, shrugging his shoulders.

"Could someone outside of Vulcury have gotten into Eric's first event?" Corcoran asked.

"It's never happened before," Gnechko said, rubbing his chin. He glanced at Eric. "Anything else?"

"I believe him. I will be the first to die."

Two

Shinichi led them through the rock garden, past lavender hydrangeas, to a low table under a covered patio. He gestured for them to sit on the pillows that surround the low table. On the table Shinichi placed small porcelain cup in front of each and pours in tea.

Corcoran took a sip of the bitter green tea and set it down quickly.

Making sure Shinichi wasn't watching, Eric nudged his tea cup away.

Gnechko took a generous sip, places the cup down in front of him, and stares into the tea for a few seconds before looking into Eric's eyes. "Eric, the von Battenburgs have many enemies. Presently, the Moon Empire is at war with Quidem. It's an old conflict, but your family is losing."

A smile appeared on Eric's face. "When I'm a warlord, I will lead the empire's armies. Victory will be ours!"

"Brash, arrogant, and overconfident, you are a young student who still has four dangerous events to pass," Gnechko said warily.

"I will be a warlord. I will return to the Moon Castle. I will be glorious like my grand uncle, Prince Victor the Destroyer."

The Commandant gave a deep sigh and shook his head. "There isn't time. In addition, there is a new enemy. This enemy is much more aggressive. They've won every battle so far."

Eric crossed his arms angrily. "Who are they?"

"I don't know," the Commandant said.

"Work harder!" Eric demanded as his features tightened.

The Commandant gave a mocking bow. "Yes, my lord prince."

"I will not apologize for my position in life."

"Time is running out," the Commandant said, his face stern. "Your Father, the Emperor, is a poor leader."

Eric's gray-blue eyes stared hard at the Commandant, but he stifled a fierce reply.

The Commandant stood up and marched directly at Eric to stand in front of him. "Your father gives control of his armies to men and women who haven't earned it. Leadership positions are given because of their social status. He fills the top ranks of the moon armies with Duchesses, Barons and Lords. None of them know, understand, or care about the art of war. The Empire needs real generals."

"Go to my Father. Offer him the service of Vulcury. Train his generals," Eric pleaded.

"Like you, the Emperor's too arrogant."

"Vulcury started because of the lack of military training," Eric said.

"Yes. Vulcury was started by two warlords," the Commandant said. "No longer were leaders using strategy and tactic as the bases of battle plans. War had become barbaric, killing and slaughtering were the driving force for victory."

"Wars must be won," Shinichi looked at Eric. "But should be at the minimal loss of lives and destruction."

"Vulcury is a military school, a war college. We teach the Graduates under actual conditions. The events are real-life experiences. So real, ninety-nine percent of the Student perish during the five events." The Commandant's features softened. "There are twenty-two Students who will not join you on your second event. The odds are against you surviving to help your family."

"I'll beat the odds," Eric said confidently.

The Commandant stared at Eric. Then locked eyes with Shinichi. They both shook their head, resigning to Eric's unearned confidence and knowing the deadly hardships to come.

"The next event starts tomorrow," Corcoran said, bringing everyone's attention to him.

"Where will it be?" Eric asked.

"You'll find out when you arrive." Shinichi pointed to the large stone base out in the middle of the koi pond. "Eric, work on perfecting your stance. Commandant, I would like a private word with you."

Three

Eric and Corcoran watched the two warlords leave into Shinichi's Japanese style home.

"You've changed," Corcoran said, studying Eric as they left the covered patio.

Eric walked to the koi pond and stares at his reflection in the still water. He had grown. Physically, his features were sharper. His raven-black hair and gray-blue eyes are more dominant. He lifted his arms, and they are muscular. Gone is the fat little boy going into the last Event. "I'm older."

"It's more than that," Corcoran said. A second later, he adds, "You've never thanked me."

"Thanked you?"

"For bringing you here, to Vulcury."

"I'm a Prince of the Moon Empire. I had all the luxuries of my position at the Moon Castle before you took me away."

"You were fluffy," Corcoran shook his head. "You don't want to be fluffy."

"I spent the last event on Earth in the eighteenth century as a young Shoshone brave. When I was not fighting buffalos and bears, I battled Ute and Cherokees for my life. Life was a constant battle to survive."

"I miss the events," Corcoran said languidly.

"Did you hear what I said? Several times I almost died," Eric said evenly.

"You didn't. You toughened up. Got a chance now."

Eric regarded a koi fish in the pond. "A chance?"

"Yes. To survive."

Eric rolled his eyes, shaking his head and hacks out a mocking laugh.

Corcoran continued. "Before being brought to Vulcury, I was an orphan like the other students. As an orphan on the streets, you learn quickly to be tough and self-sufficient. If you don't, you don't survive. You've never been an orphan."

Eric dismissed Corcoran's words with a wave of his hands.

"Would you go back to your old life?" Corcoran crossed his arms against his chest. "Being fluffy?"

Eric opened his mouth, but the words didn't come out. He thought of his life being waited on. Always told what to do. Finally, he said, "I miss my family." His lips came back, forming a smile. "I even miss Charles, my older brother who constantly tormented me." He couldn't help his sudden sadness. *I miss my Mother. She was always there when I felt any pain. To turn a dark day bright.*

"Would you go back?" Corcoran repeated.

"No." Eric looked directly at Corcoran. "I'm like a boy who's outgrown his sandbox."

"With each event, if you survive, you will change." A broad smile came to Corcoran's face. "You will become a warlord."

"What's the next event?"

"Don't know Eric, but it will be harder than the first."

Eric remembered running over the backs of stampeding buffalo, trying desperately not to be crushed. "Nothing could be harder."

"The next event will be. Trust no one."

Eric shook his head. "I have to. I've formed an alliance with other students."

"They've forgotten it," Corcoran said coolly. "If not, break it yourself."

"No, we will help each other through all the events," Eric said confidently.

Corcoran let out a heavy sigh. "The alliance will fail. You will die because of foolish faith in others."

The image of Karro the amazon filled Eric's mind, causing a grin to appear and stay for several long seconds. He remembered Isabeli, Omar and Abbas. It was four years since the last event and seeing his friends. *Have they changed their minds?*

And what of Bolek, Krill, Malek, Fia and Raica. *Will the fight between us continue?* Eric wondered.

What new and unexpected dangers will the second event bring?

Made in the USA
Las Vegas, NV
26 August 2024

94467554R00193